FEAR IS THE SAME

Carter Dickson

Fear
is
the
Same

William Morrow & Company

New York · 1 9 5 6

for
Dwye and Daphne Evans

Contents

FEAR IS THE SAME

i

"Out of the Cradle,
Endlessly Rocking . . ."

Though it was scarcely six o'clock, Lady Oldham and her companion, Miss Crumpet, had already dressed for dinner. Lady Oldham was reading aloud in the drawing-room. In order to heighten the novel's horrific effect, they had drawn close to the fire a round table covered in green baize, with only one candle burning on it.

Tales of wonder and terror were now all the rage. But this newest one, called *Ambrosio, or The Monk*, was whispered to have other lures besides the usual haunted castles and rattling chains. It was said to be shocking and indecent as well.

Lady Oldham cleared her throat.

"'As the pale rays of the moon glittered through a tall lancet window . . .'" she intoned, and bent closer to the candle flame.

"Hem!" said Miss Crumpet.

Lady Oldham was very fat and had a loud, throaty voice. In her excitement, some hair-powder dusted down from under the ostrich plumes to an expansive bosom in a yellow silk gown. Miss Crumpet, thin and bony, sat bolt upright with her hands clasped together.

Neither of them paid the least attention to Jennifer, which was just as well. Jennifer, head down, was half-sick from fear of a very different kind.

11

" 'As the pale rays of the moon glittered through a tall lan-cet window, and shone on her fair breast exposed as she lay senseless, Ambrosio uttered a scream which rang through the lofty, vaulted hall. Immediately . . .' Hup!" said Lady Oldham, with a kind of ladylike hiccup.

Jennifer rose abruptly from the table.

Both Lady Oldham and Miss Crumpet, their mouths open, looked slightly annoyed. But propriety triumphed.

"Quite right, m'gel, quite right!" boomed Lady Oldham, that old sinner. "This is Literature, no doubt; but it's not fit for the ears of a well-brought up gel like you."

Miss Crumpet gave Jennifer a look at once approving and slightly arch. Miss Crumpet had once been engaged to an officer of the Royal Navy. Though their romance had dis-solved in tears and hysterics at Bath, she was supposed to have gained mysterious knowledge which made her more than spinster if less than wife.

"Indeed, yes!" she agreed briskly.

"It's not that," Jennifer blurted out with truth. "But I— I must dress for dinner."

Lady Oldham frowned.

"La, m'gel!" she said. " 'Tis easy to see *you* were brought up in the country."

"Is it so, madam?"

"No lady, m'dear, is ever dressed." Here, becoming sud-denly conscious of the kind of double-meaning she always sought in others' talk, Lady Oldham grew forbidding and drew herself up. "That's to say, she don't dress because she is dressed by her maid. Now run along, m'dear, because we must read—hem! Because you must look your best to be re-ceived by His Royal Highness."

Both ladies nodded so vigorously that more hair-powder drifted down. Jennifer turned and ran.

She ran because fright in loneliness was preferable even to fright in others' presence. She ran because the big, green-hung drawing-room, with its one candle and its meagre fire, was darker and more terrifying than the readers of such novels could ever have imagined.

Hurrying out into the foyer, she was relieved to see they had lighted all the candles there. The black-and-white marble foyer looked bleak, like the glass prisms of its candelier, and it smelt as musty as the drawing-room. But they had lighted a large fire.

Being physically as well as mentally cold, Jennifer spread out her hands to it. Then, rising, she saw her face reflected in the mirror over the Adam mantelpiece.

Her face was the same. Beauty, of a sort at least, she had always been told she possessed. But the features seemed wildly unfamiliar, framed in shining brown curls which fell down over her shoulders from the forehead-fillet. Both Lady Oldham and Miss Crumpet, of course, would have been too well-bred to take notice of her lack of hair-powder and ostrich plumes.

"That means—" she whispered to her image.

As any dazed mind will become obsessed with trifles, Jennifer concentrated on hair-powder and on the thinness of the clothes she wore.

"In this year 1795," she whispered to the mirror, and felt a faint shock.

Tentatively she repeated, "Seventeen ninety-five." Between the shining brown curls her own face, rather broad and high of cheek-bone, had lost its pink-and-white complexion. It was pale. In her eyes, grey with thick black lashes, the black pupils were dilated against the iris. Even the passionate mouth and rounded chin seemed unreal.

"This is the year," she whispered eagerly, "of Mr. Pitt's tax on powder. It is killing a fashion already half-dead. Fervent Whigs still wear powder, in protest."

It was as though she were mumbling some dim, half-forgotten lesson.

"Yes!" she said. "And, because of the French War, we must wear mostly thin-spun English cottons or muslins. We must—"

French War? What have you learned, little fool, of any French War?

And, whatever voice had spoken in her own brain, those words were true.

She did not know who she was. She was not even certain of her own surname. Since yesterday afternoon she had been lost, completely lost, in a world whose half-lights and rattling wheels only bewildered her.

Well, what memories have you retained of another life, perhaps a hundred and fifty years in the future?

There were so few memories. Pitifully few, except some last odd glimpses. Of a street, and rain falling. Of heartbreak, because Phil was in danger. In deadly danger, of prison or even of the gallows. And she had cried out some words.

If only she could find Phil in this world! If only that grave-faced young house guest they had introduced her to as Lord Glenarvon could have been Phil himself!

Such a mad notion made Jennifer want to laugh. Phil, with his infectious enthusiasms and sometimes his black depressions! Phil, whom she loved so very much! And this last thought did not make her want to laugh at all.

Thus Jennifer, in her loneliness, almost broke down. She closed her eyes; fiercely she fought back the sobs which *would* close her throat and choke her; she sat down, huddled, on a footstool by the heartening fire, praying and praying that nobody would come in and see her in that condition.

Presently her eyes did clear, after a fashion. But it was still of no help. The eighteenth-century panels of Oldham House, in Hill Street off Berkeley Square, again closed round her like a dungeon.

She must go upstairs, now, to what they said was her

room. She must find the woman they expected her to call
Nanny, who was a combination of maid and duenna. Nanny,
otherwise Mrs. Poppett, firmly believed in ghosts and all
marvels. If she confided the truth to Mrs. Poppett, she
could at least learn about her present life.

Jennifer rose up.

She smoothed out the skirts of her white muslin frock.
With an effort she marched across the foyer. She was halfway up a wide wooden staircase, at the back, when for some
reason she stopped and glanced up. At the head of the stairs,
looking down at her steadily, stood Lord Glenarvon.

A light April rain was pattering across the chimneys of
Oldham House. Despite the light of more than twenty candles, it remained dim to Jennifer's eyesight. Lord Glenarvon
bowed, clearing his throat.

"Good evening, Miss Baird," he said with stately courtesy.

It wasn't possible. It was absurd. And yet—

Dear God, how much like Phil he looked! He seemed
older, yes; Phil could not have been more than thirty-three
or four. This man was, or appeared, nearer forty. Yet out
from each flowed the same force—vitality? intensity? mere
force of intelligence? Phil's same glossy dark brown hair,
unpowdered, was drawn back and tied at the back of his
collar.

How well and carelessly, too, he wore his clothes! She
looked now at a black tight-fitting coat with a rolled collar,
over a red Tory waistcoat, which accentuated his wide
shoulders and narrow hips. She looked at the red-topped
black boots and white doeskin breeches which country
squires, towards the end of the eighteenth century, insisted
on wearing in London as well.

For perhaps ten seconds more these two stood motionless, ghost-troubled in the eerie light. Again Glenarvon
cleared his throat.

"Yesterday, madam," he said in his courteous voice, "when I had the honour of being made known to you—"

Briefly he smiled, so exactly as Phil used to smile that Jennifer felt a stab of near-certainty. But the smile faded.

"Pray forgive my boldness," he added. "But may I have the pleasure of hearing your Christian name?"

"It—it is Jennifer." Her throat tightened. "And may I, sir, have the pleasure of hearing yours?"

"Mine?" he said absently, and then woke up. "Mine? Oh! It is Philip."

His brown eyes narrowed, with the puckers at the outer corners: just as she had seen Phil, baffled, when he had attempted to tell her something and always failed. And Jennifer was now sure. This man either was Phil himself, or some demon-created illusion of the man she had once known. Even at risk of being considered out of her wits, she must burst out and tell him.

She must tell him—what?

What, exactly, could she remember? Out of all her groping she plucked back only vague impressions; he had been at Cambridge, he had served in some war or other; he was again at some kind of study; or was he? But what was his profession? When and where had they met? When fallen in love? Amid all the dizzy clangour of time distorted, she could clearly remember only a street, and rain falling, and the death pursuing him then as it might be pursuing him now.

But it was Phil's own voice she heard.

"I could not have forgot!" said Glenarvon, and struck a clenched fist into the palm of his other hand. "Surely, madam, this is not our first meeting?"

Blind panic swam across Jennifer's wits.

"If it is not, sir," she answered, and curtseyed on the stairs, "then it must be yours, of a certainty, to remember when and where?"

Glenarvon's face went as white as his neckcloth. Jennifer did not see this; she was retreating hurriedly down the stairs.

"And now do excuse me, sir," she faltered. "*I* had forgot. I left behind—a needle-work box, yes. In the drawing-room, I think."

He bowed.

"The fault was mine, madam," he replied, and tried to smile. "I have come near to making a great fool of myself. And I must make haste to dress; my wife awaits me."

Jennifer, at the foot of the stairs, did not look up.

His wife, to be sure! The much-admired and flaunting Chloris, Lady Glenarvon! Jennifer would not have believed that the mere word "wife" could cut and hurt so much, making her heart seem to swell up as they said your arm swelled up if you were bitten by a snake.

Therefore she did not see the look on the face of the man who only yesterday awoke to the fact that he must be Philip Clavering, fourth Earl of Glenarvon. She did not guess that his face looked older only because, in his other life, he had undergone a far worse shock than he knew. It was just as well that he could not remember; he would remember soon enough.

Philip Clavering was more bewildered than Jennifer, because he could recall even less than she. He knew only that he had been flung back into the past, amid a great roaring. And he had awakened, under curious circumstances, at Jackson's in Bond Street.

"Jackson's. *Why?*" he said aloud, and gnawed at his lip on his way to his wife's dressing-room.

Outwardly, at least, he could carry off the deception with some degree of ease. He could not understand this, either; yet it was so.

These odd people, with their posturings and affectations and quizzing-glances, spoke with much the same pronunciation as in his own time. True, there were certain pe-

culiarities of Whig speech: "yaller," and "obleege," and
"cowcumber." On the other hand, if you were believed to
be a Tory, you did not even have to talk through your nose
like a Whig. More difficult was the phraseology, the turns of
speech from the beflowered to the blunt. But these, inexplicably, seemed to float back to him as though he had
learned them somewhere else.

Yes! He would enormously have enjoyed this deception, if
it were not for the confusion and pain and love associated
with—

"Jenny," he said aloud.

Philip, about to knock at his wife's dressing-room door, let
his hand fall. He turned and strode down the passage towards his own dressing-room.

Much information about himself, by dexterous listening
between yesterday afternoon and this evening, he had
gained already. Much more he meant to have. And in his
dressing-room, with painted china ewer poised above
painted china basin, his elderly manservant awaited him.

"Hopwith," heartily cried the present Lord Glenarvon,
"we dine tonight, I believe, at Carlton House. With his
Royal Highness the Prince of Wales?"

Hopwith inclined his head in reverence.

"That is so, my lord."

"Now here's a cursed oddity, Hopwith!" said Philip. "I
mean, you know, that my wife and I should be guests of
Lady Oldham, with our own town-house so close by!"

Hopwith carefully poured hot water into the china basin.

"Scarcely such an oddity, my lord, with your own house
undergoing repairs. If your lordship will be good enough to
remove his outer clothing—?"

"Ah, yes," said Philip, and flung his coat across the room.
"Furthermore," he continued, sending waistcoat flying after
coat, "this dinner tonight is to be a small and intimate one.
His Royal Highness enjoys a holiday from his honeymoon at

Basingstoke, after the distresses of his recent marriage. The dinner should not end much later than midnight, unless—"

"My lord?"

"Unless, I was about to say, it should graciously please His Royal Highness to become more than commonly drunk?"

"Truly, my lord, that is always a consideration."

Philip looked at Hopwith. He considered the man's unshakable composure. And an imp of the devil walked into his heart.

"Tell me, Hopwith. Is it true that Lady Jersey, on His Royal Highness's wedding night, put a large dose of Epsom salts into the bride's food at supper?"

Hopwith looked really sad.

"Such is the common report, my lord."

"But that no harm was done? Since His Royal Highness, being well foxed by too much iced punch, fell with his head in an empty grate and slept there?"

Hopwith, begging to differ, said that much harm might have been done. The question of an heir to the throne was of the deepest importance. Soberly and sincerely he blessed the Prince and Princess of Wales.

Philip, feeling rebuked, could only seethe. He permitted Hopwith to wash him, somewhat meagrely in Philip's opinion; and to clothe him in evening dress—all black, save for diamond buttons and buckles, and white neckcloth—with Hopwith's most careful flourishes.

"After the dinner, I believe, my wife and I must leave by coach for our country-house." Philip's eye slid sideways. "It's a cursed vexatious world, Hopwith! So far as that?"

"Surely not far, my lord?"

"Eh?"

"With Widestairs on the river, my lord, only a little beyond the village of Chelsea? Her ladyship, I trust, will not find the journey too fatiguing?"

"No. No, I daresay not. Still—"

Now Philip rushed at the crucial question. He should approach this, he had decided, after the fashion of the languid men of the world he had met the night before. One of them, whenever the matter of women was mentioned, had leaned over confidentially and fetched up a tolerably hideous leer.

("Egad, Glenarvon! Saw a deuced fetchin' little filly at Almack's. Damme, yes!")

And Philip couldn't do it.

Apart from feeling a damned fool if he talked like this, something in his nature revolted and shied back. When he thought of Jennifer's face, so strangely framed in the shining light-brown curls, and Jennifer's grey eyes wide open—

"Hopwith," he said quietly, "I have met a most attractive young lady here."

"Indeed, my lord?" enquired Hopwith, with a gleam of interest in his faded eyes.

"Yes. Strictly between ourselves, I—I find her most desirable."

"I am honoured by your lordship's confidence," exclaimed Hopwith, showing his first sign of life. "May I venture to ask the young lady's name?"

"Miss Baird, I think. Jennifer Baird."

All the interest drained out of Hopwith's face.

"Indeed, my lord," he murmured. "A touch more to the neckcloth, perhaps?"

"No matter for the neckcloth! Who is she?"

"I believe, my lord, a niece of Lady Oldham. A country relation," Hopwith stressed the damning adjective, "who is being cheered by a visit to town and by other prospects. Now, my lord, as to powder for the hair—"

"*Who is she, curse you? What do you know of her?*"

"The young lady, I fear, should not be honoured by your lordship's attention just yet. Now for the hair-powder, my lord, I am aware that the Tory party no longer favour it. None the less, a proper courtesy must be shown to His Royal

Highness. His Royal Highness, of course, may not too
openly favour the Whigs. Yet I am creditably informed, my
lord, that he pours Marshall's brown-powder most liberally
on his wig. Marshall's brown-powder—"

Philip blew up.

He damned and blasted Marshall's brown-powder, only
just saving himself from adding that it sounded like an in-
secticide of which His Royal Highness no doubt stood in
need. But, as he flung towards the door, some quality in
Hopwith's patient, unangered gaze stopped him.

"If I might suggest it, my lord—"

"Yes, Hopwith? I—I ask your pardon for my bad manners.
What is it?"

Hopwith looked steadily at the Turkey carpet.

"Your lordship is much changed," he said.

"Changed? How?"

"But I do not think," said Hopwith, with his gaze still on
the carpet, "your lordship's true friends will be displeased
by it. *I* am not."

Philip looked at him for a moment, and then ran.

Bewildered, fearing lest he had made some bad blunder,
yet obsessed by the image of a Jennifer Baird who was at
once so close and so far away, he hurried down to his wife's
dressing-room.

The noise of the late April rain slid fanlike above his
head. This passage, though heavily carpeted, felt chilly to
one fashionably dressed in knee-breeches. Once more, in
lifting his hand to knock at the door, he hesitated.

Most men would have considered themselves fortunate to
be married, even in a dream, to such a woman as Chloris.
She was handsome, she was flamboyant, she was very mature
at the age of twenty-five. Her hazel eyes slid sideways and
promised a great deal—though, he suspected, fulfilled nothing—under thin painted eyebrows arched against shiny
painted skin. There was invitation even in her hair, a long

and thick tawny-yellow when not powdered. Or she could be arched and coy, coquetting behind a fan.

And yet, though he presumably had known her for only twenty-four hours, he cordially disliked her.

Why? Why was it?

Perhaps it was impatience at her frills and flutings, as when Chloris postured and imitated Millamant in the play. Perhaps—since, after all, we like those who like us—it was her utter contempt for him, not even veiled in public. A heavy painted lip lifted above a shiny fan; a brief glance; that was all. Perhaps obscurely he felt her to be a fraud, or else it might be a strange sense of intimacy or familiarity. As though Chloris, in some other life, might really have been his wife.

The last thought turned him cold. It increased the unearthliness of a position between the worlds, of a fate predestined in whatever century. But he had come here to learn certain things, and he was damned well going to learn them. He knocked sharply at the door.

"Your husband, my dear," he said.

"Oh! *Do* pray enter," replied an oversweet, drawling, poised-for-trouble voice.

And he went in for a fateful interview.

ii

"Ah, Chloris, That I Now Could Sit as Undisturbed as When . . ."

Chloris, Lady Glenarvon, was in the course of being dressed.

Many candles burned in brackets against silvery wallpaper with a continuous design of red-and-green parrots in golden cages. The floor was invisible under a drift of perfumed gowns, considered and discarded. Chloris's maid, a fresh-faced and pretty girl named Molly, stood helpless in this disarray.

Chloris herself, at ease, lounged in a Louis XV chair amid the finery, and enjoyed it. Her long tawny-yellow curls, glistening and arranged for this evening's powder, had not yet received it. She still wore her day stockings, fastened by the new (and smuggled) garters embroidered with such words as "tendresse" or "sincerité," and she still wore her day shoes of Moroccan leather.

Otherwise she wore nothing at all. Anyone might have seen her for a handsome, much-desirable woman; though perhaps, in Philip's eyes, not overclean. So Chloris lounged there, with one heel up on a padded footstool, and regarded him with her dawning smile of polite, idle contempt.

"You need not leave us, Molly," she said.

Molly, scarlet with embarrassment, made a move towards the door of the bedroom.

"You need not leave us," said Chloris, languidly waving

one arm. "La, now! Does anything pass between his lordship and myself which might not be seen by all the world?
You did desire something, my love?"

"Yes."

"And pray what is it?"

"Information."

"Mercy upon us! And could not you have obtained that
from books?"

"Not this information."

Something in the tone of his voice made her sit up.

"Do you not grow above yourself, sir?"

"Then let us have no more of your scenes, madam. I am
weary of them."

Chloris sat up almost straight. The tawny-yellow curls
trembled on her shoulders with her hard breathing. Rage
glimmered in the hazel eyes; those long eyes, becoming so
vivid, made her face warm and human and appealing. They
troubled him despite himself.

"For two years," she said, "I have been married to the most
spineless, poor-spirited creature who ever walked. If it were
not for your birth and especially your wealth, dearest Philip,
do you imagine you would ever have been tolerated at
White's? Tolerated! They laugh at you! The very linkmen
laugh at you!"

"Is it so?" asked Philip, with his eye on a corner of the
room.

"Yet you wonder that there is so little love between us?"

"I wonder at nothing, madam. Doubtless you have other
interests."

"Now there," murmured Chloris, smiling sweetly with her
head on one side, "there you lie. I have never been unfaith-
ful to you. Not once! In public I have been the devoted
wife of an ailing husband—"

Here she began to act again, this time with all the airs

and flouncings of Lady Teazle; and he could have murdered her.

"But in private too," she added in a soft voice, "I have been a most *devoted* wife. All know it and can tell you so! The doctors, sweetest Philip, give you a year to live. Shall I be such a great zany, then, as to be imprudent and lose your very useful fifty thousand a year?"

Still he stood motionless, looking down at her.

"Surely," cried Chloris, "you must have divined all this?"

"I have learned much, my dear."

Chloris hesitated. She could not, or would not, force herself to speak what was in her mind. Furtively, under thin-arched eyebrows, the hazel eyes appraised him up and down.

"How have you come to change so much, since yesterday?"

"Change? Have I changed?"

"Foh! You might be a different man. Your whole bearing is different. Your voice is different. Your walk, even the manner of carrying your hands."

"My hands?" blurted out a badly puzzled wanderer.

"Ay, and more!" She spoke softly; the tip of her tongue moved round the full, painted lips. "Once or twice I vow it frightened me; and then again—no, perhaps not. That dreadful affair at Jackson's yesterday—"

I wish to God, woman, I could tell you what it was!

"If only," Chloris murmured, without looking at him, "if only, two years ago, you had been what you are now! Even as it is, Philip, I find you—"

"Yes, madam?"

"Not displeasing," said Chloris.

Utterly at ease, utterly sure of herself, Chloris shook her curls, leaned back, and surveyed him beneath lowered eyelids.

"Come, Philip. Admit it. You must own you find *me*—not displeasing?"

"At least, madam," he said politely, "I am given full opportunity to judge."

Dead silence.

Chloris went as glimmering white as a delicate china porcelain seen against a light. Her face, a moment ago warm and human and appealing, acquired a shallow blaze of hatred. If there had ever been any honesty in her, it was gone now.

"Molly! My robe!"

Molly stumbled in hastening to fetch it. It was a very large robe, pink and quilted, sewn with many ribbons. As Chloris lazily stood up, and Molly wrapped her round in the robe, Philip mentally threw up a hand to guard his thoughts.

He should not have said that, curse it! With all his heart and soul concentrated on Jennifer, he had made a bitter enemy of one who, he suspected, had always been his enemy. But he had been groping in a labyrinth to find some association, any association, with Chloris in his other life.

And there was none, or so it seemed. One remark of hers, perhaps— But, if any chord twanged in the dark, it concerned Molly, the maid, rather than Chloris, the wife. Why should it? These two were much the same height, which was not tall; they spoke with the same real or affected gentility; otherwise there was no resemblance between them. Because this was unaccountable, it left an after-twang of fear!

Now again, ever and always, he must be on guard. Chloris was sitting down, composed and gently smiling, as though nothing had happened.

"La, I declare I had almost forgot!" she said. "I would remind you of a change in our arrangements. Tonight, after His Royal Highness's dinner, we go down to Widestairs by coach. The weather is *much* too bad for a carriage."

Philip gritted his teeth.

"So I had understood. Well?"

"Well! You and I were to have travelled in the coach. *And* dear Lady Oldham, as our guest. *And,* of course, my dearest Molly," said Chloris, giving the maid a languishing glance. "I vow I could not travel a *step* without my dearest Molly!"

"Granting Molly, what then?"

"It is Colonel Thornton." Chloris looked sad. "Colonel Thornton is a most decided man. His own house, you recall, is not a quarter mile beyond ours. He expressed most decided views against getting drenched by the rain on horseback, and for travelling in comfort. So, dearest Philip, he must take your place in the coach."

For a long time, or what seemed a long time, he looked down at her.

"And why should he do this, madam?"

"Because I wish it," answered Chloris, lifting her eyebrows. "Surely, in the past, you have not minded so trifling a service as following my carriage on horseback?"

"Or being drenched by rain?" asked Philip.

"*Or* being drenched by rain," agreed Chloris.

"*Or* giving up a place in my own coach?"

"*Or—*" Chloris began, and abruptly stopped. They looked at each other.

"You must be brought to heel, Philip," Chloris added sweetly. "You must learn to know my wishes."

"Indeed, madam? Now what if I were minded to take my place in my own coach?"

"I fear Colonel Thornton would not be pleased. He would simply ignore you. And who would stop him?"

"*I* would stop him."

"You?" murmured Chloris, examining her sleeve with a little, secret, derisive smile round her mouth. "*You?* Really and truly?"

Once more Chloris glanced up, and saw his face. Suddenly she sprang up and stumbled among gowns to a place behind the chair, with all the ribbons aflutter on her dressing robe.

The sense of suffocation in that room was not caused by a too-early spring warmth, or by tightly closed windows, or by the heat of the fire. It was caused by the emotions of these two, staring at each other across the back of the chair. Chloris moistened her lips.

"And what is in your mind *now*, you joke of the town?"

"For a minute or two," Philip confessed agreeably, "I had thought of wringing your pretty neck. However, until I meet the gallant Colonel Thornton—"

Chloris threw back her head and laughed. Her thin, brittle laughter, amid the flaring candles and the painted red-and-green parrots in gold cages, rang out with a touch of hysteria.

"*You!* Against Toby Thornton!" She all but vomited her contempt. "When you have owned yourself too cowardly to—"

Her cry was cut off, sharply, by the very softness and discretion of the knock at the door.

"Beg pardon, my lady," said a voice Philip recognized as that of Smithers, the first footman. "But Colonel Thornton and young Mr. Thornton are downstairs."

Philip saw Chloris's face, and whipped around.

"*Smithers!*"

For a moment, evidently, Smithers did not recognize him; and hesitated.

"My Lord Glenarvon? Yes, my lord?"

"Present my compliments to Colonel Thornton and young Mr. Thornton. Beg them to walk up here as soon as may be convenient."

"*Here*, my lord?"

"Yes. Here. Thank you."

"Very good, my lord."

Behind him, now, rose the agitated wails of both Chloris and Molly. He was glad to face the door, because he had remembered something else out of the past.

"Oh, filthy! Hideous!" said Chloris. "To invite gentlemen, and in the evening too, to a lady's dressing-room!"

"But if you lose no time, my lady," said the equally agitated Molly, "you may still go to the bedroom and be unseen."

"Hold your tongue, slut! Is this the prettiest dressing-robe I own?"

"Indeed yes, my lady! You bade me lay out the prettiest, in case his lordship should be here."

"Did I not tell you to hold your tongue?"

"But his lordship is a proper well-made gentleman, my lady, and I thought—"

There was the sound of a slap, and of Molly bursting into tears. Another knock, a brisk and authoritative kind of knock, made the door tremble.

Chloris flew back to her chair. Carefully winding the robe round her, she arranged her elbow on the arm and the fingers of one hand pensively at her right temple.

"Pray come in!" she begged.

Colonel Tobias Thornton, of the King's Royal Dragoons, entered in the splendour of full-dress uniform. Behind him, rather warily, moved his young son Dick. Philip recognized them both, from last night's dinner.

He had especially noted Colonel Thornton, because of the deep respect and even awe with which the others seemed to regard the man. Nobody even brushed his shoulder without a profuse apology. Like the others, Colonel Thornton could leer bawdily when the port went round. Like the others, in his own circle, he could be friendly and even cordial. But his public face was the frozen and fashionable one; and he wore it now, even while his quick alert little eyes, a pale blue in colour, noted everything in the room.

Philip bowed.

"Your servant, Colonel Thornton," he said.

Colonel Thornton caught that formality. He replied in the high, thin voice which subalterns admired for its rasp of authority.

"Yours to command, Lord Glenarvon. I don't believe I have made you known to my son. Dick, this is my old friend Lord Glenarvon."

Dick, a pimply-faced youth of twenty, wore badly fitting evening clothes but passionately wished to behave as a man of the world. Philip's stately greeting impressed him, but so flustered him that he could only mumble.

"Will you not be seated, gentlemen?" invited their host.

Nobody spoke.

Colonel Thornton glanced at Chloris, and hastily averted his look from motives of delicacy. But the emotional temperature went up and up, because Chloris was at the centre of it, enjoying it; and she spoke for the first time.

"Come, Colonel Thornton!" she chided him. "You need not offend me by looking at me! The position, I own, is somewhat delicate."

The colonel dropped his formality.

"Frankly, Lady Glenarvon," he said in his high, complaining voice, "it's devilish awkward. That's to say, a lady's dressing-room!"

"To be sure, to be sure! On the other hand—"

Chloris gave him the same coquettish glance she gave everybody. Colonel Thornton was much swooned over by the ladies, who considered him very handsome. This was because of his commanding air, his high-bridged aristocratic nose, his long cheeks and his sneering, sour-looking mouth.

But, in full-dress uniform, he seemed larger than the room. Under one arm he carried his great cocked hat, with its tuft of short white feathers. Gold cords gleamed from collar to waist across his short scarlet coat, like the vertical line of gold buttons. A white cross-belt ran from his left shoulder to the pouch at his right hip.

"On the other hand," Chloris continued, "we mustn't be too hard on my poor husband. *He* wished to welcome both you and your son, you know."

"*He* did?" asked the astonished colonel, jerking his head over the high black collar. "*Him?*"

"Upon my soul, he did! Didn't you, dear Philip?"

Colonel Thornton was not in the least annoyed. On the contrary, he uttered a high, neighing laugh. His heavy dress-sabre jingled against white breeches and polished jack-boots as he strolled over towards Philip, and slapped him on the back.

"You know, Glenarvon," he said, with patronizing friendliness, "you're what they call a rum 'un! Devil take me if you're not!"

Philip, standing sideways to him and watching him carefully, inclined his head without speaking.

"But you mustn't do it too often, you know," warned the Colonel, as though speaking to a pet dog. "Might be misunderstood. Well! We'll say no more about it. But—" Suddenly his pale-blue eyes narrowed. "I say! What *did* you want of me?"

Nobody could have said why there was such an intense hush in the dressing-room, except for a faint noise of rain beyond closed curtains.

"I wished," Philip said clearly, "to speak to you about the arrangements for going to Widestairs tonight."

"Oh! That!" the colonel said carelessly.

He brushed it away. Tall, quite unconsciously arrogant, he strolled past Philip, flicked at a curtain, and swung round with his high-bridged nose jutting out.

"Deuced good of you, of course," he added, and just refrained from winking at his son, "to give me your place in the coach. Appreciate it. Yes, quite!" He chuckled. "Still! That's happened before, eh? It's not important."

"It is important to *you*, Colonel Thornton."

"Eh? Why?"

"Because you are not going."

"Now make an end of your foolery, Glenarvon! No time for it. What the devil are you talking about?"

"I will make myself clear," said Philip in a louder voice. "You engage to go home to the country tonight, I take it?"

"Yes!"

"Very well," said the other. "Then you may go on horse-back or by hackney coach. You may go home or to blazes, for all I care. But if you set foot in my coach, sir, I shall take great pleasure in kicking you straight out of it. Is *that* clear?"

Chloris rose to her feet, but sat down again.

In the pause that followed, Colonel Thornton did not seem greatly angry; only more languid. But his hand drifted down towards the pair of white gloves, folded neatly over and under his white-and-gold sword-belt.

"Y'know, Glenarvon," he said thoughtfully.

He strolled towards Philip, who remained in the same position.

"Y'know, Glenarvon," repeated Colonel Thornton, with his upper teeth showing, "if you weren't an invalid, if you hadn't admitted you were too damned cowardly to fire a pistol or use a small-sword—why, Glenarvon, I'd make you pay for that."

Lightly, casually he extended the forefinger of his right hand, and ran it up to the line of Philip's waistcoat buttons. Before the gesture could be completed, Philip's left forefinger whipped up the line of the other's gold buttons and landed grotesquely, but with powerful and painful jar, under the root of the high-bridged nose.

Colonel Thornton's head jerked back. Powder rose from

his head like a ghost of itself. The immense black cocked hat jumped from under his arm and bounced across the carpet.

Philip stood back.

"I invite you," he said pleasantly, "to make me pay."

Carefully Colonel Thornton picked up the hat and straightened up. This brought some blood into his face, but he was only stupefied.

"God damme!" he almost whispered, and then addressed Chloris. "Madam, the fellow's mad! He's ravin' mad, I'll be sworn to't!"

"And am *I*, sir, unaware of that?" cried Chloris.

"Well, what's the matter with him?"

"I can't tell. For a moment I hoped—" Chloris swallowed; then her face hardened. "He has been given to moods and megrims, truly, in especial when he wished to do a favour in secret or give a handsome gift. That is part of his weakness. He has *never* been ill-natured."

Colonel Thornton strode over to her. There he paced up and down, the tops of his jack-boots flapping, in querulous vexation.

"*I* don't want to hurt the fellow," he complained. "I've told you before: they'd laugh at me if I knocked over such a poor pigeon with a pistol or a small-sword. Wouldn't do my reputation any good. Not a bit! Damme, why did the fellow come here tonight? What did he want of you?"

"He said 'information.'"

"Information?" Colonel Thornton wheeled around. "Speak up, Glenarvon! What information?"

Then, at last, Philip saw the hopelessness of the wall at which he was battering.

"Little enough!" he said in a dreary voice. "It concerned Lady Oldham's niece, a Miss Jennifer Baird. I wished to—"

"Hold hard!" exclaimed Colonel Thornton, in a completely different tone. "By Jove, I know now!" He looked at Chloris, and his piercing laugh almost split Philip's nerves. "'Do

a favour in secret, eh?' 'Give a handsome gift, eh?' Glenarvon, my boy, I overlook everything! There, that's fair
enough! Emma Oldham's told you, of course? It's congrat-
ulations, eh?"

"I—"

"The little filly," exclaimed Colonel Thornton, "is going to
marry my son. Between ourselves, Glenarvon, this Jenny
Baird is not much in the way of family or blood; we'll hush
that up. But her father's got the rhino, and that's the thing.
Eh?"

Young Dick, embarrassed and red behind his pimples, at
last stiffened and dared say a word to his father.

"Pa! It's not the money, curse me if it is! It's the gel.
Curse me if—"

"Dick, you young lout," snarled Colonel Thornton, "stand
on your own two feet and shake hands with your friend Lord
Glenarvon. He wants to wish you happiness. And it's a
devilish fine wedding-gift, I'll be bound?"

"As to the wedding-gift—" began Philip.

"Yes, my dear fellow?"

"I would first wish to know," said Philip, looking into Dick
Thornton's eyes, "whether the young lady has consented to
this marriage?"

Dick was so eager and confident that he hardly mumbled.
By some optical illusion he seemed to be dancing round and
round.

"Oh, that's well enough, sir! Pa and Lady Oldham arranged it. Not that *I'd* have cared, rot me, if she'd had only
two or three thousand a year! Make yourself easy, sir. *She's*
consented!"

"Then I do wish you happiness, with all my heart."

"And the wedding-gift?" leered Colonel Thornton. "The
wedding-gift? Eh?"

"The wedding-gift, I hope, shall be not unworthy."

All of a sudden, unexpectedly, room and faces began to

swim round before Philip's eyes. There is a point of exhaustion at which a new life hits back too hard.

"But if you will give me leave," he said, "I shall retire from you. It is a little touch of—oh, no doubt my old malady. Besides, I must fetch my cloak and hat. You will permit me?"

A chorus of Thorntons assured him that they would. It was only Dick who regarded him curiously, as though wondering.

"Oh, yes," Chloris said flatly. "The fit has passed. He is himself again."

Philip opened the door, went out into the passage, and closed the door carefully after him. It was cool in the passage, almost cold after that room. He leaned his back against the door and closed his eyes.

What sort of timorous scarecrow, he wondered, had led a ridiculed life in *his* shape and form? That could be changed. By God, it should be! But, after all, was it worth the effort now?

He opened his eyes. The foyer below was bright with candles, but the passages on each side of the broad staircase-landing were more dim. At the back of the landing, facing the staircase, stood three tall and arched windows, each with a deep embrasure for a window-seat, and each hung with brocade curtains.

Someone was sitting in the embrasure of the middle window, between back-drawn curtains of the faint yellow brocade. Someone seemed to be looking at him, and made a gesture as though she would raise her hand towards him, but hesitated.

He ran towards her, a time which seemed to take minutes instead of a second or two, and looked down at her in the embrasure.

"Jenny," he said.

iii

"Jenny Kissed Me
When We Met . . ."

She had been dressed, evidently by Mrs. Poppett, in a silk gown of plain dark blue with a white waist-cord. It was rather full at the skirt, but very high at the waist. Simplicity was coming into fashion; the gown fell well off the shoulders and had a low neckline fastened by a plain cameo brooch. It showed the fulness of Jennifer's shoulders, as the twisting-together of her elbow-length white gloves showed her state of mind.

Her fan, broken in anger, lay on the padded window-seat beside her. She had been crying; tears still stained her face. As she looked up at him, in searching appeal, again she twisted her hands together.

Then she would have spoken, but he stopped her.

"No!" Philip said, with the fury of all despair.

"No what?"

"First I must tell you something. If I am mistaken, as I may be, why, then you are free to think my wits as addled as the others do."

"What did you want to tell me?"

"I love you," he said. "I think I have loved you for a long time. I know that I shall love you all my life."

Jennifer's eyes overflowed again, and she stretched out her arms to him.

A moment later, when he was sitting beside her, holding

her in his arms and kissing her open mouth as violently as she kissed him in return, the interval cannot be called anything except chaotic. And yet, in its own way, it was a fulfilment; he had found her. For the first time, in all his stumbling amid dead-alive shades, he knew an overwhelming sense of peace.

He felt it so deeply that he tried to laugh instead, as he always did.

"In our present state," he said, "it seems a little ridiculous to ask whether we have met before. No, curse it, in all seriousness! In the past—I mean, the future—that is— Anyway, we *have* met?"

"Yes, yes, yes!"

"And loved?"

"Oh, so very much!"

"Jenny, what can you remember?"

"Very little, except that. What can *you* remember?"

"Nothing at all, except you. And—"

Now he could feel fear in his arms. She drew back from him hastily, sitting up straight; but the fear remained, though she tried to laugh, too.

"It's so s-silly," Jennifer insisted with vehemence, "that I can't stop crying. Mrs. Poppett says the worst of these new-fashioned gowns is that they have no pockets, and ladies must now carry an inelegant thing called a reticule if they want a purse or a handkerchief. And I haven't even a handkerchief!"

He took the handkerchief from his pocket, and smiled as he dried her eyes and face. But she was rigid, even chilly; she looked at him as though he might vanish.

"What is it, Jenny? Stop! Gently! What troubles you so much?"

"Do you remember the last time we met?"

"I—no."

"Think! Please! Think hard!"

Her gesture indicated, behind them, the high-arched window with its many panes outlined in oblongs of white-painted wood. Against it the spring rain pattered insistently.

"There was rain," she whispered, with her eyes searching his face. "And a street, I think, which was at or near some steps. 'They'—or something dreadful—was coming to overtake you and crush you. And you kissed me, just as you did now. And I said—"

Memory, or at least partial memory, transfixed her. The grey eyes, with their long black lashes, stared straight ahead.

"Oh, God," Jenny said. "This is *my* fault."

"Jenny, stop talking nonsense! Come closer to me!"

"But it is *my* fault. I cried out and said, 'Oh, if only we could be out of this! If only we could go back a hundred and fifty years in time, and forget it!' You must listen to me, Phil. This isn't a fit of the horrors; I swear it isn't! For just then a little voice—inside my head; I don't know from where—whispered to me and said, *Would it be any different, if you did go back?*

"Then I think there was a clap of thunder, or a roaring in my ears. The next thing I knew, I was sitting in this house, before a fire, in a room I'd never seen before. It's taken me a long time to understand, but I think I see now.

"Don't *you* understand, darling? I don't know whether it's punishment for some wrong or sin, or only whether a wish is granted to teach you a lesson. But we've been carried back in time, just as I prayed. We've been allowed to retain only small bits and pieces of memory. We've got to enact the same horrible story, just as it was in the other life. Only— we don't know what it is."

There was a long, eerie silence.

A draught fluttered the many candles in the foyer below the broad staircase. There was a soft clack of shoes as a footman, in blue and white livery, crossed the marble floor and for some reason opened the front door, looking left and right.

Both Philip and Jennifer caught a glimpse of a Hill Street they had never known in their other lives: a very rural place, with its trees and cobblestones and hitching-posts, under whirling rain.

The footman closed the door with a hollow slam, and retired. This present Philip Clavering, Earl of Glenarvon, knew in his heart that what Jennifer said was true. But he refused to be intimidated by it.

"The same story?" he repeated, rising to his feet and looking down the stairs.

"Yes! With 'them' following you and finally catching you."

"Who are 'they'?"

"I can't say. I only know we must beware of everything we say or do. And—"

Human nature remains the same. It was Jennifer, the ever-loyal Jennifer, who picked up her broken fan, broke it again, and flung it away. Bitterness showed in the soft eyes and mouth.

"Were you married in the other life, Phil? I can't say. Or were *we* married? I wish I knew! But you are married now. To this woman Chloris, and even I must admit she is very, very pretty. Have—"

Opening her mouth to ask another question, Jennifer stopped out of pride. But he knew it instantly.

"The answer is no," he retorted. "I dislike the woman very thoroughly."

"But you live with her."

"In a sense, I suppose. And, speaking of marriages, I daresay I have no right to resent your own forthcoming marriage to young Dick Thornton. However—"

"And do you think," almost whispered Jennifer, "I knew anything of that until half an hour ago?"

"Half an hour ago?"

"When we met on the stairs. I didn't really forget a work box. I ran to my bedroom, and asked Mrs. Poppett about my past life. She burst into tears of joy, and told me all about my marriage. I was brought to London, it appears, mainly to find me a suitable match. Lady Oldham and somebody named Colonel Thornton arranged it all, with Lady Oldham to have a commission on my dowry."

"Did you consent to this marriage?"

"Phil!"

"Did you?"

"What some ghost or devil or other woman may have done a week ago," Jennifer cried, "I can't tell. But *I* never did, in myself. And I won't! I saw that awful young man last night. It made me shudder when I remembered him." A look of the trapped and the lost came into her face. "Can they—can they force me to?"

"No. Nor shall they."

Now, at long last, Philip emerged from the mist and fumbling of more than twenty-four hours. He retained no memory of his past life, it is true. But he was as confident, as sure and quick-witted, as he had ever been there. It brought not peace, but war; and his heart sang.

Kneeling on the window-seat beside Jennifer, he put his hands on her bare shoulders.

"You honestly love me, Jenny?"

"Phil, can you even *ask* that?"

"Then will you go away with me tonight?"

"Of course! Anywhere."

"It would seem that I'm the owner of a country-house called Widestairs, on the river beyond the village of Chelsea. Will you go there with me?"

Jennifer stiffened. "But your wife—"

"In the scheme I have in mind, Jenny, that small matter will be dealt with." His brain ran feverishly on, planning details. "You will take your duenna, of course. In the meantime, will you back up anything I say? Will you—?" He stopped suddenly.

"Phil! What's the matter?"

"'Back up,'" he said. "That is curious phraseology for this age. We have been speaking for the most part in our own idiom, my dear, and we must be careful not to use it when others are present. Which reminds me that last night, and when we met a while ago on the stairs, you managed eighteenth-century speech all but perfectly. Where did you learn it?"

"I think—from you."

"From *me*?"

"Yes. I—I think it was some part of the work you loved. Then there was another kind of work you needed to support you; you loathed and hated it and were ashamed of it. A dozen times you tried to tell me, but—" Jennifer hesitated, one hand pressed to her eyes. "Or was that beforehand? Oh, I can't think! This—this scheme of yours for tonight; you were saying?"

"Will you agree with anything I tell them?"

"Yes, yes, if only you'll take care!"

"Take care? Of what?"

"I don't know! But you're in danger of death, Phil. I'm not exaggerating; you are! And, for all I can tell, it might be closer than we think."

Yes, it might be.

Somewhere in the labyrinth of his memory burned a little flame of fear. Somewhere in this affair he would make a false move, or take a wrong turning. Then he would be cornered and desperate; conscious of his own innocence, yet unable to prove it; lost and fleeing in the rain. But, as the soft rain splashed against the window now, he closed his mind to memory and again took Jennifer in his arms.

"We'll stave it off, whatever it is," he said. "Don't be afraid."

"I'm not so much afraid, now that you're here. I'm a hopeless sort of person, Phil; I always feel, when you're with me, that you can set everything right and I never need worry. But this is different. There *are* dreadful things that concern a house somewhere, and somebody who's dead. There are things I can't explain."

"Then forget them! Does anything else matter?"

"No," said Jennifer, and held him even more tightly. "Nothing at all matters, now that we're together again."

"La!" struck in a new, cool, poised voice. "That must indeed be a satisfactory arrangement for you both."

Chloris, dressed to the very top of fashion, was standing not three feet away from them with her back to the top of the staircase.

Chloris, in a silvery low-cut gown slashed with red, and a red waist-cord, wore over it a pelisse of wine-coloured velvet. The top of her powdered hair was tightly fitted with a silvery half-turban from which upreared two ostrich plumes. Cosmetics turned her beautiful face into enamel like that of a life-sized doll, and in her right hand she carried a fan of ostrich plumes.

Though her voice remained quite steady, Chloris's hand trembled as she gently waved the fan.

"Did you hear me, my love?" she asked. "I said it must indeed be a satisfactory arrangement for you both?"

Jennifer would have sprung away guiltily from him, but Philip held her fast until he had fitted on his mask of manners and speech. Then he rose to his feet, bringing Jennifer with him.

"So it is, my wife," he agreed politely. Then, to Jennifer, "You had best go and fetch your coat. And bid Mrs. Poppett to be in readiness for tonight."

Jennifer ran.

Chloris's fan waved a little more quickly.

"For tonight?" she asked, in a higher voice.

"Ah, yes," said Philip. "I forgot to inform you that Colonel Thornton may have his place in the coach. I travel to Widestairs with Miss Baird in another coach; and, for propriety's sake, with her duenna."

He glanced quickly to his left, nearer the dressing-room door, where stood Dick Thornton and the colonel. He had not before observed how unpleasant could be young Dick's face, mouth open, breathing heavily through the nose, pimples starting out against pallor.

But Colonel Thornton, like a good campaigner, waited quietly until he could control his rage. Then he slowly drew the white kid gloves from his belt and strode forward.

In the frozen stillness, the passages and the foyer below seemed to be filling with people. Molly peered out of one dressing-room. Hopwith, carrying Philip's cloak and hat, glanced out of another.

Below, in the foyer, the first footman had opened the front door. Torches now flared in link-brackets on either side, showing coaches in the street. Three other footmen, carrying wraps or cloaks, emerged into the foyer. From the drawing-room, at the right, issued the fat figure of Lady Oldham and the thin figure of Miss Crumpet.

But nobody had eyes for anyone except Colonel Thornton.

Slowly swinging his gloves, flinging Chloris aside as though she did not exist, he faced Philip in Chloris's place, his back to the stairs.

Everybody there heard his voice as his upper lip lifted again.

"Even getting down on your knees, Glenarvon, won't save you now."

"Colonel Thornton," said Philip, "I have grown weary of you."

The colonel hardly heard him.

"*You'd* kick me out of your coach, would you? *You'd* kick anybody anywhere? Well! This time, my whining friend, you're going to accept a challenge."

His right arm was already back. Now it swung forward, viciously, to slash the gloves across Philip's face.

What happened then happened so fast that the onlookers hardly saw it.

In Chloris's eyes her husband merely seemed to jerk up his left arm, elbow out, in a gesture she had never seen before. Gloves, hand, and scarlet-clad arm slipped as harmlessly over Philip's arm as though Colonel Thornton were performing some exercise at the ballet.

At the same instant, as the colonel flung himself forward off balance, Philip's powerful right hand gripped the gold cords at the right-hand side of his uniform-tunic, and spun him round completely to face the stairs. More spectacular was the murderous kick in the seat of Colonel Thornton's breeches.

As always, when the mind is paralyzed by shock, a split second's time seemed to take half a minute. Colonel Thornton appeared to hang in the air above the stairs, face down, his jack-boots kicking and his arms flung wide.

Then he landed, about a third of the way down, with a crash which made every candle flame jump. As he rolled the rest of the way, the gold scabbard of his dress-sabre so whacked and banged and clattered that it sounded like soldiers beating at a door. Hair-powder raised a fuming dust; the cocked hat sailed away. He came to rest on the black-and-white marble floor, momentarily stunned.

What Philip remembered best afterwards was the iron composure of the footmen's faces. Not a man of them stirred from his place, not even Smithers, the first footman, holding open the front door and looking over his shoulder with mouth wide open.

Instead it was Lady Oldham who spoke.

"Lord God Almighty!" she boomed, in complete stupefaction.

"My dear Lady Oldham," whispered Miss Crumpet. "Hem!"

Instantly Colonel Thornton was on his feet, unhurt, un-ruffled, completely master of the situation, with his upper lip still lifted.

"A small accident, Lady Oldham," he said.

"Er—yes," said Lady Oldham. "Hem!"

"Indeed yes," agreed Miss Crumpet. "Hem!"

Philip, at the top of the stairs, glanced at Chloris.

"Will you excuse me, my dear?" he asked.

He walked slowly down the stairs, pausing on the way to pick up Colonel Thornton's fallen gloves. These he tossed at the colonel's feet, otherwise ignoring the man, and went up to Lady Oldham. He took her fat, beringed hand and raised it to his lips.

"Madam," he said, "it much distresses me to have been obliged to kick the colonel downstairs. However, since time is short before the carriages leave, may I humbly beg a word aside with you?"

Still in stupefaction, Lady Oldham upreared her bust and her yellow-and-purple ostrich plumes.

"Lord God—" she was beginning again, with one of those long and hair-raising oaths which belonged to her youth and the freer speech of the middle eighteenth century, when Miss Crumpet cut her short.

"*I* shall be in the writing-room, Lady Oldham," she re-marked acidly, and sailed away.

Colonel Thornton's high voice sang out commandingly.

"Lord Glenarvon!"

"You spoke to me, sir?"

"Nothing," said Colonel Thornton at his most formal, "must disturb His Royal Highness at Carlton House. During the dinner, at least, we must all appear to be friendly. Immediately afterwards, however—"

"I shall be at your service, Colonel."

Now it was Philip's turn to give him a look of contempt. It was a near thing; one of the footmen could not quite stifle a guffaw. Colonel Thornton heard it, and went deadly white. Philip should have observed that his sour-looking mouth was also mean and dangerous.

But he did not see it. Handing Lady Oldham into the drawing-room, he closed the door.

"Lady Oldham," he went on, "I believe you stand *in loco parentis* to Miss Jennifer Baird?"

"I dessay that's what they call it," said Lady Oldham doubtfully. "Why?"

"A marriage is being arranged between your niece and young Dick Thornton, the colonel's son. You, as is usual, will of course receive a commission on the dowry."

Lady Oldham stared at him. She bridled up in a haughtiness which would have awed a bench of bishops, but Philip, where Jennifer was concerned, could not be awed by anyone.

"Hear me!" he insisted. "Whatever this commission was to have been, I will double it, triple it, quadruple it tomorrow morning, if you will refuse your consent to the marriage. Will you engage to do this, madam?"

There was a pause.

"Hem!" said Lady Oldham, with her brisk businesslike little eyes fixed on him. And then, "Would you go as high as five thousand?"

"Willingly."

"Done!" said Lady Oldham briskly. Then she burst out. "But damme, lad, what ails you? The most spineless man in London is suddenly become the most outrageous rip since I was a gel and George the Second was alive. What ails ye?"

"Nothing, madam. Do you in truth dislike it?"

Lady Oldham slapped her thigh and swore she didn't. In proof of this, she boomed out an elaborate anatomical oath which might have been composed by John Wilkes in his heyday.

"But five thou—!" said Lady Oldham. "You're devilish determined to lie with the little gel, ain't you?"

"My intentions, madam, are strictly honourable."

"Hey?"

"Strictly honourable, I assure you."

"But, odd's life, man! You've already got a wife!"

"That," Philip said through his teeth, "can also be arranged."

Lady Oldham stared at him, stricken fearful. There was a soft tap at the door.

"The coaches, your ladyship!"

Lady Oldham, waddling badly, hurried out into the foyer. All the guests for the dinner were there, in silence like powder packed into a gun-barrel, between two lines of solemn footmen.

Jennifer, a thick blue shawl around her shoulders and fastened with another cameo brooch, was still innocent of hair-powder or plumes. Beside her stood Dick Thornton, with a sort of uncertain snarl, in a long dark cloak, his evening cocked-hat, or *chapeau de bras,* under his arm.

Chloris, reasonably warm in her wine-coloured pelisse, languidly swung the ostrich-plume fan and did not glance up. The wide-open front door let the rain blow in, and flutter candles wildly, while Colonel Thornton in his scarlet-lined cloak waited for Lady Oldham to be helped into her own pelisse and given her own fan.

Still nobody spoke.

Still in pent-up silence, which could be felt through the very pores of the skin, Colonel Thornton gave his arm to Lady Oldham, and handed her out to the first of the waiting coaches. Springs creaked; a door slammed; then, over the whip-crack and the shuffling clatter of hoofs on cobbles, the coach moved away.

Dick, still with that uncertain glare, extended his arm to Jennifer. She glanced at Philip, then casually took Dick's arm. They moved towards the door as another coach clattered up. But Philip could be quiet no longer.

"Mr. Thornton," he said.

Dick hesitated, but did not turn around.

"I regret this," said Philip, "and there must be fair play in it. Should you care to accompany us to Widestairs, I am happy to invite—"

Dick swung around.

"Go to hell!" he screeched, with tears of rage in his eyes. "I'll be even with you tonight, so help me! This is a job for Moggs, and I'll tell Pa so!"

"If you please, Mr. Thornton!" Jennifer said sharply.

Then Philip, as in a dream, was left alone with Chloris amid the blowing candle flames and the lines of footmen like waxworks.

"If you are quite ready, my dear?" he said to Chloris.

Behind him Hopwith, appearing from nowhere, offered him his long black coat and slid the *chapeau de bras* under his arm. Chloris waited, watching him from behind her fan, until this was done. As he extended his arm, she put her white-gloved finger tips gently on his wrist.

Then, as they went towards the door, Chloris's fingers slipped over his wrist and tightly gripped it.

"Philip," she murmured.

For the first time he felt completely helpless. From under her eyelids she gave him a glance which was not only of languishing admiration, but—what he could not have believed of her—of frank amorousness and sensuality.

"If you are *quite* ready, my dear?" he repeated.

"Darling," said Chloris.

And so, unconscious of the terror that night was to hold for all of them, they went out in the rain to the third coach.

iv

"His Royal Highness, the Prince."

Seated near the foot of the dinner-table at the side of Mr. Richard Brinsley Sheridan, under the dazzle of lights and the flow of chatter, Philip found his disquiet at times verging on a fit of the horrors.

Mr. Sheridan, though a trifle time-dented, retained most of his Irish charm. Still Member of Parliament for Stafford, as well as manager of a newly rebuilt and ruinously expensive Drury Lane Theatre, he had finished his second bottle. Closer and closer were thrust his purple cheeks and his fiery nose.

"—and that's the very truth of it, egad!" yelled Mr. Sheridan, beckoning a footman to refill his goblet.

"I am much your debtor, sir," yelled Philip, "for such good report out of France. What news have you of Napoleon?"

Mr. Sheridan abruptly set down his glass.

"Who the devil's Napoleon?" he asked.

"Hem!" said Philip, scrambling back in desperate haste to rearrange dates in his mind. "Between ourselves, Mr. Sheridan," he added, lowering his voice, "the man's true name is Buonaparte."

"Oh, ay?"

"Yes. He is a French artillery-general, Mr. Sheridan, who —who has just suffered a reverse at Toulon. However! Informed opinion, sir, has determined that he will soon display considerable military talent."

"Buonaparte, hey? An Italian?"

"I believe, sir, he was born in Corsica."

"This is another trick of Billy Pitt's, I'll be sworn! (Saving your politics, Lord Glenarvon, and here's a toast to ye.)" Mr. Sheridan brooded, under the frizz of his upstanding greyish hair. "Napoleon Buonaparte, damn my great eyes!" he said. "Never even heard of the fellow."

"Make yourself easy, sir; you will."

Another roar from the head of the table cut him short.

Jennifer, seated at the right hand of His Royal Highness George Augustus Frederick, Prince of Wales, was blossoming out in a way Philip would never have believed possible. The wine was flowing pretty freely now; Jennifer took many sips to keep up her courage.

Wine heightened the beauty of her face, and of the pink-and-white shoulders rising from the dark-blue gown. Contemporary political questions, of which she could know little or nothing, were being flung at her head from every direction. These Jennifer would parry or evade with a wit which roused Philip's admiration.

Every man at the table was applauding. Lady Jersey, small and bewitching, seated at His Royal Highness's left hand, had turned green with envy and was fanning herself more vigorously. Then Philip caught the hazel eyes of Chloris herself, turned on him with a fixed and speculative stare.

He could not avoid Chloris's eyes. They reminded him too much of what had happened with Chloris, in the dark coach on their way to Carlton House. For, God knows, his "wife" was attractive.

And, despite himself, his mind went back to that scene.

He and Chloris had been alone, except for the coachman on the box and two footmen up behind. A smell of mud was everywhere, even inside the velvet-mustiness of the coach. In the haze of a rainy night, Hill Street and Berkeley Square looked as though they were set in the depths of the countryside.

A thump of iron-shod wheels on cobbles flung Philip against the right-hand window. Past him flowed the lighted spectre of Lansdowne House, and, back to back with it, of Devonshire House facing Piccadilly. Chloris spoke from her seat in the dark corner.

"Well!" she observed casually. "Then you imagine yourself to be in love with this country wench?"

No reply.

"Did you hear me, Philip? I asked whether you imagined—"

"There is no 'imagine' about it, my dear. I *am* in love with her."

Emotion, as always, could be felt flowing from Chloris as palpable as the cream-of-roses perfume she now wore. But she did not announce, in her customary forthright way, that she would like to slit Jennifer's nose. Instead she touched her lips with the long ostrich-plume fan.

"Good lack! You surprise me! And moreover, Philip, is it altogether wise?"

"How—wise?"

"Well! Considering your indifferent health, and that your heart may give way at any moment—"

Ta-ta-ta sang a key-bugle in Piccadilly.

Past them thundered and lunged a dim shape. Doubtless a mail-coach from the White Horse Cellar. As they turned down the long slope of St. James's Street, they found it very softly lighted from nearly every red-curtained window. Sputtering torches wove a maze in the rain where linkmen trotted before sedan-chairs, and illuminated Chloris's face.

"Once and for all time," snapped Philip, "let us make an end of this nonsense about my poor health. There is nothing wrong with my heart, nor ever has been."

"Liar," murmured Chloris behind her fan.

"Liar, madam?" said Philip. He knocked the fan aside and seized her shoulders under the claret-coloured pelisse. "Had

I suffered from poor health, should I have visited Jackson's yesterday? Should I have been so ready to kick your precious colonel downstairs as I am ready to deal with him in any way he may choose?"

"But—!"

Inspiration came to Philip.

"For the past two years, and for good reasons of my own, I have chosen to play the invalid and the popinjay. That time has ended, Chloris. By God's damnation, it ended tonight! Much as the fact may distress you—"

"Distress me, you say?" observed Chloris, without looking at him.

"Yes! You deal with a different man, and you will favour me by recognizing it. In the meantime . . ."

In the meantime, they had bumped left into tree-lined Pall Mall. More sedan-chairs were here; and to Philip occurred the ghostly, grisly thought that in a few more years these chairs would be gone, replaced by the more convenient hackney coach. But he had little time for abstract speculation.

After some fashion he could never understand, Chloris was now sitting very close to him, and his arms were round her.

"In the meantime," heavily whispered Chloris, with a quick-breathing kind of giggle, "we are far too close to Carlton House for—" Again she giggled. "Nevertheless! If you promise not to tumble my gown, I shall not protest at being kissed."

Take care, warned a clear but faint voice in his brain. *Take care, idiot, or you will involve yourself in calamity beyond control!*

He did not take care. He was only human, like the rest of us. He kissed her. And, so dexterous was Chloris at various ramifications of the business, that it was some moments before he drew back his head.

"Oh, how hideous this is!" whispered Chloris. "Pray tumble my gown, do! Pray—"

"*Ho-o-ld!*" rang out a heavy, intoning voice from outside the coach.

Light struck at them through the right-hand window, from many flambeaux set in brackets along the length of a stone-fronted house with rather small windows. The horse-hoofs danced with a hollower clop and ring as they swept under a portico.

Philip, disengaging himself, gave a quick glance left and right out of the coach windows.

Towards his left, beyond the portico pillars and another colonnade of fluted stone pillars, there stretched up the hill only a dismal little *cul-de-sac* called St. Alban's Street. No Regent Street as yet existed, and several ghosts walked over Philip's heart.

Towards his right, where Waterloo Place should have been, a glare-and-shadow of torches trembled along the façade of Carlton House. It appeared low in outline because one of its three floors had been built down behind it into the immense gardens at the rear. The shock to Philip's nerves of dead bones conjured up again was momentary but visible; he stumbled in alighting, and almost fell.

"My sweetest!" breathed Chloris, rearranging her gown as she alighted. "Oh, my love! You are not ill!"

Chloris's words carried clearly to the ears of Jennifer, just as she entered the great doorway past a swarm of flunkeys in Hanoverian livery. Jennifer glanced over her shoulder. Then Chloris, on Philip's arm, was ushered through the doorway and presently into the Chinese drawing-room.

In the Chinese drawing-room, bedecked with yellow-silk wall curtains as well as a profusion of Chinese furniture, were already assembled Lady Oldham, Colonel Thornton, Dick Thornton, and Jennifer, together with two ladies and a

gentleman whom Philip at first failed to recognize, when
the presence of His Royal Highness was announced.

"Be pleased, good friends," said the Prince of Wales, in a
pleasant and throaty bass voice, "to consider that I am not
here at all. But this does not in any sense, I assure you,
lessen the cordiality of my welcome."

Again he bowed. And Philip instantly decided that all
the lampoonists had been wrong about him.

True, His Royal Highness was very fat and somewhat
gross. But his passion for cleanliness was much in evidence.
There was no ostentation in his dress, adorned only with the
blue ribbon and blazing Star of the Garter, nor any ostentation in his bearing.

His large face might be red and bloated, under the curls
of his famous brown wig; but his grey eyes held a lively intelligence when not wine-blurred or tearful. Above all he
had a genuine charm of manner, an ability to put people at
their ease with half a dozen words, which might have made
him the best diplomat in Europe.

This was much in evidence when he sat down on a yellow-
silk sofa, crossed his legs without apparent difficulty, and
beamed on the company as they were presented in strict
order of social precedence.

"Ah, Lord Glenarvon!" he said in his brandy-rich voice,
and produced a snuff-box. "I am, of course, familiar with
your admirable books."

Books? What books?

"Though I confess, Lord Glenarvon, that I find your
lighter historical works more to my taste. May I offer you a
pinch of snuff?"

Philip, despite his fear that he would do something
damned silly, accepted the pinch of snuff and dealt with it.

"Though a word in your ear, my lord," added the Prince,
also taking snuff. "Be advised by me in one respect. Never
allow my friend Mr. Sheridan here into persuading you at

dramatizing one of your works for the stage. He's a sly dog, is Mr. Sheridan; and he'll whistle every guinea out of your pocket if he can. Eh, Sherry?"

Behind the yellow sofa had materialized two figures much at home in the Chinese drawing-room. One was the tiny, enchanting Lady Jersey, with her melting dark eyes, who was His Royal Highness's present most-favoured mistress. It was she who had put Epsom salts into Princess Caroline of Brunswick's supper when Princess Caroline was married to His Royal Highness less than a fortnight ago.

The other person, lounging, was the fiery-nosed Mr. Richard Brinsley Sheridan. But Mr. Sheridan, for some reason, was in such a high good-humor that he would not have replied to the Prince's last gibe, even if the latter had observed him.

"*And* Lady Glenarvon, by Jove!" the Prince exclaimed.

His Royal Highness sat up straight, mouth open, and surveyed Chloris with frank admiration in his bulging grey eyes.

"Egad, madam!" he said, and slapped his thigh. "I'll not say, mark you, that other women grow less beautiful with the years. 'Twere slander and injury, I vow, to a sex I love only too well! But I would know, Lady Glenarvon, why *you* appear more beautiful each day."

"Why, sir, 'tis no riddle of the Sphinx."

"Then do you read it, I humbly beg!"

Chloris, in her low-cut silvery gown with the red waistcord, swept him a deep curtsey.

"Why, sir," she smiled, "you have but to look at my husband. We are, I dare swear, the happiest married pair in all England!"

Each word was meant for Jennifer, who went white with rage. All the same, it was an error. His Royal Highness's expression changed and grew tragic.

"Marriage," he said, and stared gloomily into space.

There was a dead silence.

"Marriage!" intoned His Royal Highness. Suddenly he rolled up his several chins and glared at a footman hovering near.

The footman leaped forward.

"Your Royal Highness?"

"Iced punch," said His Royal Highness. "What the hell's the matter with you? Iced punch!"

The footman scurried. So did other footmen. Turning back after this blast, with all good-humour restored to his red and bloated face, the Prince of Wales smiled on them.

"Ah, my most dear Lady Oldham! *Your* beauty, assuredly, will never fade—"

"Oily young flatterer!" boomed Lady Oldham, shaking powder and highly delighted. She herself was not guiltless of flattery with that word "young," but the Prince merely inclined his wig.

"—since it is preserved, I was about to say, in the salt of wit and anecdote. You must tell me again that anecdote of how my revered great-grandsire, King George the Second, dropped down dead on leaving the water-closet. Would that my own esteemed sire—hem! We must not speak of politics. This gentleman, I take it, is—?"

Major George Hanger, the Prince's Irish aide, presented Colonel Tobias Thornton.

Instantly the Prince of Wales threw out his immense paunch, squared his shoulders, and assumed that bluff military air he loved so well.

"We are well met, sir!" he thundered. "I too am a soldier and a cavalryman, having the honour to command the Tenth Light Dragoons. Your fame is not unknown to me, Colonel Thornton, nor (may I whisper it discreetly?) your reputation as a duellist."

Colonel Thornton bowed gravely.

"That reputation, sir, may be enhanced soon," he said. "Meanwhile, may I have the pleasure to present my son

Richard, whom I venture to think (ha, ha) a chip of the
old block? And also Miss Jennifer Baird, who is shortly to
wed my son?"

Philip strolled forward.

"Now there, I fear," he said, "the good colonel is mistaken."

Colonel Thornton whipped round.

"Despite the worthiness of Mr. Thornton and his good
father," Philip went on, "Lady Oldham, as Miss Baird's
guardian, has forbidden her consent. She feels that the
young lady is too young, too inexperienced, too— Is it not
so, Lady Oldham?"

"It is so," agreed Lady Oldham, sticking out her broad
under-lip. "Damn my soul if it ain't."

It is a matter for speculation what might have been said
or done then, if they had not been overrun by a troop of
lackeys carrying trays of goblets in chased gold. Philip saw,
with alarm, that each goblet must contain well over half a
pint of iced punch. Yet each guest, following the host's example, drained a goblet without pause. Again following his
example, they drained a second goblet.

All this time His Royal Highness's eyes had never strayed
from Jennifer, who stood before him in anger and pride.

Anger tinged with colour her shoulders and cheeks, and
lent sparkle to her eyes. The very simplicity of the blue
gown, the soft unrouged mouth, the sheen of wax-lights on
her light-brown curls, made her stand out vividly in such a
bedizened assembly as she curtseyed.

"Would it please your Royal Highness," she said in a soft
voice, "if I were to have a word in this?"

"The pleasure, madam, would be greater than you know."

"*I* shall never marry!" declared Jennifer in a ringing voice,
and whacked down her second empty goblet on a convenient
tray.

"These are harsh words, madam, from such pretty lips."

"I hate men!" said Jennifer, stamping her foot. "But as for wives—foh! They are even worse!"

"As how, madam?"

"They are foul-mouthed, shrewish, overdressed, and despicable. Though loudly they boast of their refinement, they lose not even an opportunity to cuddle in a coach. Fie!"

" 'Fore gad, madam," said the Prince, rather shocked at Jennifer's words but impressed by her philosophy, "it is well that you are not obliged to marry a woman. However! There is much truth in what you say about wives. Now *I*, madam, have a wife. This lady—"

"Please! Oh, please!" murmured the honeyed voice of Lady Jersey, from behind the sofa.

Leaning forward, she slid her white arms down on either side of his head, leaving marks of rice-powder on the black coat. Then she raised melting dark eyes at the rest of the company. Though Lady Jersey was forty-two and a grandmother, nobody would have guessed it.

"For shame!" she chided them. "This dear man meets with nothing but crosses and vexations! Must you plague him on so sore a matter? And would it not be better, sir, if we went down to dinner?"

"This damned wife of mine— I beg your pardon, madam?"

"Dinner, sir!" whispered Lady Jersey, against his ear. "There is carp, I believe, and roast mutton. Would it not be better—?"

" 'Fore gad," cried His Royal Highness, gobbling at Lady Jersey's hand as he kissed it, "you are in the right of it, as usual! Dinner, by all means. And another glass of iced punch, if you please. Thank you. Er . . . Sheridan, my dear fellow!"

Unobtrusively Mr. Sheridan gave him a shove in the back, so that he surged to his feet without the least awkwardness.

Refreshed and at his best, George Augustus Frederick made a figure truly regal and magnificent.

"Lady Jersey, my arm. Miss Baird, my other arm. No, no, I protest! You shall sit beside me, Miss Baird—see to it, Major Hanger!—and regale me with more of your fascinating conceits. My lords, ladies, and gentlemen! If you will follow us?"

That was how—each man or woman seething from some different cause—they marched out into the scarlet-papered foyer, and down a broad staircase to the lowest floor.

Philip, more disturbed than he would have admitted about Jennifer's rage, walked in silence beside Chloris. Chloris herself was too calculating, too clear-headed, to make any comment about Jenny in public. But his silence goaded her to frenzy.

"Oh yes," she whispered.

"What's amiss?"

"Your country bumpkin *is* pretty, after a fashion. She has good teeth, and at least a moderately good *taille*."

"Oh, for Christ's sake!"

"Philip!"

"If you mean she has a good figure," he whispered back, "why can't you say 'figure' instead of '*taille*'?"

Chloris's astonished glance, as they descended the stairs, partially restored his own sanity. In polite society, of course, no lady of quality had a figure. *Taille* was French and therefore discreet. These extraordinary delicacies of speech, combined with such flat crudities and relish for double-meanings, made him want to roar with laughter.

But it was not funny at all. Better drink so much wine that— No, stop! He couldn't drink!

Some compulsion out of his other life, inexorable, seized him and commanded him. He was in vigorous health, and liked to drink. But he must not touch even wine.

They were at the foot of the stairs. Towards the back of the house, a line of full-length windows opened on the gardens. The rain had cleared. A full moon shed deathly daylight over clipped lawns with trees and statues.

Though Carlton House had not yet the gaudy splendour it afterwards attained with a golden drawing-room, a library, and a Gothic conservatory, the dining-room into which they were led was gaudy enough. Under a ceiling painted to represent a summer sky, at a flower-banked table with its chairs upholstered in scarlet, they sat down to a dinner fast becoming uproarious.

"—and the damned scoundrel Pitt," yelled Mr. Sheridan, "now speaks of a tax on incomes. Taxes, ecod! I can remember when they wanted to put a tax on tombstones. Here's the King howlin' mad; here's the Tories firm in power; here's a French war that'll go on forever just because George the Third don't like the way they govern 'emselves. Damme, what a country!"

Philip agreed that the times were indeed parlous.

"I'd cut me throat, ecod," said Mr. Sheridan, "if—" Here he paused, looking happily sly. "We-el! You'll hear the good news soon. *That's* my consolation, Lord Glenarvon; that, and venerable Madam Drury. D'ye go often to the play, my lord?"

"It is a long time, I fear, since I have visited Drury Lane."

"Then come and see us!" cried Mr. Sheridan, seizing Philip's hand. "Promise you'll come and see us!"

"If the boxes are not already bespoke—"

"Boxes? No! Come and watch a rehearsal. And if you've an odd guinea or two lying about, Lord Glenarvon, you might do much worse than buy shares in venerable Madam Drury. Eh?"

"I have no doubt of it, sir."

"But away with all this!" cried Mr. Sheridan, making so

dramatic a gesture of contempt that he nearly fell off the chair. "Away with such squordid matters of lucre! A gentleman don't talk business. But if you deign to visit us, my lord, I should be vastly obleeged if you could do so within the next two days."

"Within the next two days?"

"Alas! Even so!"

"But why?"

"Ah! That's the secret!"

Mr. Sheridan's expression grew very grave. Lowering his voice, he leaned forward and tapped the table.

"Now Prinny there," he added, nodding towards the head of the table, "is a true good fellow. He is, upon my honour, for all they say about him! And no man on earth ever deserved the wife they gave him!"

Philip coughed.

"This marriage, one hears, is not—altogether fortunate?"

"Oh, bejasus!" said Major Hanger on Philip's right.

"Hark'ee, now!" insisted Mr. Sheridan, pointing a finger like one who wishes to be fair. "He had to marry somebody or other, damme, or they'd never have paid his debts. But must the old King choose, of all people, Madam Caroline of Brunswick? And the true fault, I say, lay with Jimmy Harris in not warning the Prince beforehand."

"Lord Malmesbury did not warn him, then?"

"Not a word, bleed me! My lord, you should have seen Prinny's face when first he clapped eyes on the woman. But he's a gentleman, allow it! All he said was, 'Harris, I am not well; pray get me a glass of brandy.' "

Here Mr. Sheridan pointed his finger with even more intensity.

" 'Tis not that she's hard-favoured. No! But the woman's cracked. God damme! She's as cracked as a chaney plate, very near as cracked as the old King Himself. Have you heard what happened at their first public dinner, before they were wed?"

Philip replied, truthfully, that he had not.

"Well!" said Mr. Sheridan, brooding. "Madam Caroline was wearing her hair piled up on her head, all stuck over with combs. It was no cleaner than the rest of her, but that's by the way. Someone at the table, in all innocence, said that Englishwomen have pretty hair. 'Mein Gott,' shrieks out Madam Caroline, 'und haff I not priddy hair, too?' Out came the combs, every one of 'em. Down tumbled her hair, all over the table and into Jimmy Harris's soup. My lord, you should have seen Prinny's face *then*."

There was a slight pause. Philip struggled hard, and succeeded, in remaining as grave as his companion.

"But what did His Royal Highness say, Mr. Sheridan?"

"Nothing!"

"Nothing at all?"

"Not one word in public, mark you, even after they were wed! And all the accurst woman would do, every night, was stamp up and down the bedroom saying, 'Mein Gott, I am wexed.' "

Mr. Sheridan sprang to his feet, and stood majestically while he drained another bumper.

"Here's to a gallant gentleman, say I," he declared, banging down the goblet on the table. "Amid woe and sorrow, amid public travail and domestic affliction—amid, in short, all those manifold adversities which the honourable gentleman will so readily perceive, he has come here tonight, on an errand which does credit to his kindly impulses and his generous heart. And why, sir, is he here?"

"Frankly, I haven't the slightest idea."

"I repeat, sir, why is he here? Why are we here assembled under this roof? What subject, sir, shall we presently discuss?"

"All right," snapped Philip, who resented being glared at as though from the Opposition Benches. "What *are* we to talk about?"

Mr. Sheridan smote the table a mighty blow with his fist.

"Marriage, by God!" he cried triumphantly. "That's what it is! Marriage!"

$\mathcal{V}$

"Cry, 'Havoc!' and Let Slip . . ."

At the sound of that sinister word, marriage, which seemed to spread alarm and despondency whenever it was uttered, there was a hush at the other end of the table.

Mr. Sheridan, having forgotten the House of Commons, sat down gracefully and turned to beam on Philip.

"Marriage?" exclaimed the latter. "And pray who is to be married?"

"*I* am," said Mr. Sheridan, with modest pride.

He was perhaps not at his best. One knee-buckle had come undone, his neckcloth was disarranged, and there were wine-and-snuff stains down his waistcoat. But he had not grown stout. His charm of manner, his rich tenor voice, more than compensated for the long vinous face and the nose at which they said you could light a fire.

"When my first wife died, Lord Glenarvon, I had thought all love buried in her coffin. I was wrong; I am the first to own it. Three days hence, on the twenty-third of April, I shall be united in holy wedlock with the fairest, the divinest, the most glorious of all her sex!"

Then Mr. Sheridan's enthusiasm overflowed.

"Ah, my incomparable Hecca!" he cried, lyrically addressing the ceiling in the midst of a dead silence. "My green-eyed divinity! My soul's beloved! My little bit of brown Holland!"

Through the overheated dining-room, through the wine-

64

fumes and the sickly-sweet odour of red-and-white roses, clove a throaty bass voice of overpowering dignity.

"Mr. Sheridan!" it said ominously.

Mr. Sheridan rose to his feet, put one hand inside the breast of his long-tailed coat, and gravely confronted his host.

The Prince of Wales also arose, though with a slight stagger. But his gesture was easy and graceful as he focussed his eyesight.

"Mr. Sheridan, sir," he said sternly, "you are not sober."

"Your Royal Highness, sir," answered Mr. Sheridan, throwing his arms wide in heroic frankness, "I allow it."

"Well! In that case," said His Royal Highness, immediately relenting and growing magnanimous, "we'll say no more about it."

"Sir, I am deeply grateful."

"Sir, it was nothing. However—"

Though their host said no word, his royal eye conveyed an obvious and sinister command to sit down. Mr. Sheridan's eloquence, when he was really wound up, had reduced the House of Commons to tears at the impeachment of Warren Hastings. The Prince of Wales wanted nobody stealing his thunder now.

Mr. Sheridan sat down.

During a pause, while their host waited, the Prince's massive body seemed to loom above the table like a balloon, above a forest of tall candles, in gold sconces, now leaning at all angles in the heat. The candles, with a sputtering noise, threw crooked lights over the red walls, the blue ceiling, the footmen who stood rigid behind each chair.

But most of all they weirdly illuminated the face of His Royal Highness, now lobster-red, and his moist sentimental eye.

"Good friends," he began, in a voice choked with emotion, "for a moment, it is true, I was displeased."

A pause, for regal effect.

Each guest looked down solemnly at his or her plate—
except Philip, whose lungs were growing stifled in the flower-
scented moist heat, and Jennifer, who was biting at her
under-lip. He caught her eye; he saw she was regretting her
outburst of anger, and longing for peace-overtures to be
made. Up soared his spirits again.

"But I was displeased," warmly continued the Prince,
"only because Mr. Sheridan's announcement was premature.
I wished to make it."

"And I'm sure you should have!" piped up Lady Jersey,
with alcoholic tears.

"I am here, as you are aware, incognito. Onerous duties,"
and the Prince shuddered slightly, "compel me to return to
Basingstoke tomorrow. Nevertheless, I deemed it only just
that, on the eve of his marriage to Miss Hester Jane Ogle, I
should do some honour to my old and valued friend. He is
distinguished not only as a statesman, upholding staunch
Whig principles, but as the author of those true immortal
comedies, *The Rivals* and *The School for Scandal.*"

First a murmur, then a spatter, then a roar of applause
ran round the table.

Mr. Sheridan did not respond to it. For a brief instant he
seemed to look back over his life—and it was not comedy
at all.

The Prince was much moved.

"To this small dinner," he thundered, swaying a little, "I
have invited only those who, though not perhaps of the
highest social distinction, are noted for the purity of their
private lives. They can't catch me this time, by God! There'll
be no news for the scandal journals tonight!"

"My dear!" whispered Lady Jersey, and tugged at his
sleeve. "My dear! Hem!"

"Ah, yes," said the Prince, instantly and majestically re-
covering his dignity. "As I was saying. As a wedding-gift to

Mr. Sheridan and his bride, I have purchased a bauble, a trifle, a mere nothing," and, by the airy flirt of his fingers they knew that this trifle had cost at least two or three thousand, "which I shall present to Mr. Sheridan, in its proper place, at the end of our happy dinner. Until then, let us say no more! Until then, I can only add—"

His voice grew emotional. His several chins were raised. To Philip's horror, and Jennifer's consternation, tears overflowed his eyes and streamed down the bulging cheeks.

"I can only add," he said, "that I wish Mr. Sheridan more happiness in his second marriage than I have attained in my first."

And he bowed his head.

The applause was deafening. It beat and buffeted round the red walls, against impassive footmen; it swirled the poisoned air in a room where no window was ever raised.

Philip turned to Mr. Sheridan.

"But, hang it," he protested, "this is not his first marriage!"

"Hey?" said the other, very quickly.

"Mr. Sheridan, I am weary of all this play-acting and false emotion. The Prince was married, secretly, nearly ten years ago. In December, 1785, he was married to Maria Fitzherbert at her house in Park Street, according to the dispensation of the Roman Catholic Church."

Mr. Sheridan, stricken sober, turned round a white mottled face.

"Documentary proofs of the marriage to Mrs. Fitzherbert," said Philip, "have been discovered since then. They—"

"For God's sake, hush! D'ye want him excluded from the Throne?"

But it was too late.

Philip's last statement had pierced barbed through the storm of applause, and everyone heard it. The applause stopped. Then, in an instant, it burst out more loudly than

before, as though mere volume of noise could blot out the
memory of what had been said.

Only now did Philip realize the deadliness of his blunder.
For many years all the prowling rumours of this secret marriage had been unproved and unprovable. Such rumours
were flatly denied by Mr. Fox in the House of Commons, on
the pledged word of the Prince himself. They had to be
denied; according to the law, no man who married a Catholic could ever be king.

When Philip said that documentary proofs had been discovered "since then," he had meant discovered in modern
times. But they might all think *he* held evidence which
would—

And, clearly, most of them did think so.

The applause was dying down through sheer tension;
again you could hear the hiss and flutter of the candle flames.
At the head of the table, with a goblet in one hand and his
other hand pressing a napkin to his mouth as though he
were about to vomit, the Prince of Wales still stood motionless. Flickering lights caught the great Star of the Garter
against his coat, and the glare of his moist grey eyes.

"Lord Glenarvon, I believe," said the Prince, "is a Tory."

And, very nearly as sober as Mr. Sheridan, he threw the
napkin on the table.

"Well, sir?" he added. "At my own table," and his child's
eyes grew more moist, "you have impugned my honour and
you have told lies. Have you neither explanation nor apology?"

Philip, with a jerk of nerves twitching in the calf of his leg,
rose to his feet.

"Sir," he said doggedly, "I cannot distort the truth. I have
told no lies, as Your Highness is well aware."

At the shock of this apparent insolence, Major Hanger
half-rose up and Lady Jersey put her face in her hands.
Chloris, her paint raddled with the heat, looked at him in

fury and dismay. Lady Oldham opened and shut her broad
mouth like a fish. Only Jennifer was completely bewildered.

"But this I may add," continued Philip out of a dry throat,
"both as explanation and apology."

"Well, sir?"

"In law, I think, the marriage of a prince royal needs first
the consent of the King. This consent was not obtained.
Therefore Your Royal Highness's marriage to Mrs.—"

"No names!" snapped Mr. Sheridan. "No names!"

"Therefore your first marriage, sir, was not legal. In a moment of foolish irritation, inspired by I can't say what, I
spoke words of which I am heartily ashamed. Accept my
assurance that I hold no documentary proofs; that such evidence will not be discovered in your lifetime; and that I
myself shall never mention this matter again."

Instantly Colonel Thornton, red-coated and jack-booted,
was on his feet. His high, strident, insufferable voice sawed
the air.

"Tomorrow," he said, "Your Royal Highness's friends will
make very sure he does not speak of it again. Tonight, however—"

The colonel, glancing to his left, stopped and smiled.

Lightly, in a stirring of foul air, a footman slipped along
the table with a tray and a sealed letter. His bow and his
eyebrows indicated a request that the letter might be de-
livered to Colonel Thornton.

Colonel Thornton read the letter, and crushed it up in his
hand as though he held someone's neck.

"Here's good news, sir!" he said with pleasure.

"Eh? About what?"

"Have I Your Royal Highness's leave to go for a brief stroll
in the gardens? Accompanied, I hope, by Lord Glenarvon?"

The Prince, furious, stared back at him.

" 'Fore gad, Colonel Thornton," he thundered, "do you

forget, do you all forget, in whose presence you stand? To suggest a duel in the garden of—"

"Duel? Sir! I am all too conscious of Your Royal Highness's presence! And I had no such thought in mind."

"Then what the devil d'ye mean?"

"This letter, sir," said Colonel Thornton, crumpling it again, "comes in reply to a note-of-hand despatched nearly two hours ago. It tells me that a—a person, an acquaintance of mine, has arrived here to wait upon me. I would wish Lord Glenarvon to meet him."

"What person?" demanded the Prince.

"Merely an acquaintance of mine, sir."

"What person, I say?"

"His name, sir, is Moggs."

The name meant nothing whatever to Philip, or to any of the four women at the table. But clearly it was familiar to Mr. Sheridan, to Major Hanger, and to the Prince; Dick Thornton had known it well. Mr. Sheridan sprang up.

"Nay, now, hold hard!" he protested. "Let's have fair play!"

Colonel Thornton looked him up and down without interest.

"You will oblige me, Mr. Sheridan, by remaining silent when I address His Royal Highness. It is not your birth which gives you access to Carlton House. For all your talents, Mr. Sheridan, you must really have an occasional reminder that you are only an Irish lout."

"Now is he, bejasus?" yelled Major Hanger.

Both Mr. Sheridan and Major Hanger, on their feet, took a diving step forward. Philip, between them, locked one arm round each and held them back until they caught the Prince's eye, and stopped. Lady Jersey began to whimper and blubber behind her fan.

"Think, sir!" rasped Colonel Thornton, still unruffled. "This man," he nodded at Philip, "has insulted you to your face. Could he get a better lesson than a lesson from Moggs to keep a civil tongue in his head?"

His Royal Highness glared at the goblet in his hand, glared at the table, and hesitated.

"No, perhaps not." He raised his eyes. "That is, if Lord Glenarvon—?"

Philip swung round to Colonel Thornton and spoke in a loud voice.

"I accept your challenge, whatever it is," he said contemptuously. "I am at your service." Then he turned back to the Prince with courtesy. "And also, sir, though you may not credit me, at yours."

Again the Prince hesitated, and looked down at the table.

"Damme, Glenarvon," he muttered, "but you've got pluck."

Then, as he banged down his empty goblet on the table, his mood changed.

"Very well!" he said with balloon-like dignity. "But I know nothing of this, and I desire to know nothing. If two of my guests ask leave to go for a stroll in the gardens, I am happy to excuse them. That is all; we say no more! The rest of you will kindly be seated."

Colonel Thornton took two long steps back, bowed to Philip, and gestured towards the double doors.

"After you, Glenarvon," he said.

"Not at all!" smiled Philip. "After *you*."

"This won't do, Glenarvon. I insist."

"And *I* insist," said Philip. "Come, sir, precede me! You need fear no repetition of what happened on the stairs to-night."

That heavy stab went home. Colonel Thornton's lips darted back over his teeth, and he half-lifted his hand. Philip laughed in his face.

"Bedad!" muttered Major Hanger, eyeing them over his shoulder. "I've seen people who hated each other. But never like this."

"Hanger!"

"Your Royal Highness?"

"Pray be seated."

Feelings were strung so high that it seemed, for a second, Major Hanger might not obey. But both he and Mr. Sheridan sat down. Lady Oldham, that hearty beldame out of another age, was frankly enjoying this. Chloris, nostrils dilated, seemed to be pondering and speculating; and yet, beneath the surface, savouring it, too. Jennifer had turned her head away.

Colonel Thornton nodded and strolled towards the big double doors, painted black with gold, which a major-domo hastened to open. Philip strolled after him. Nobody spoke, but even the eyes of the motionless footmen followed them as they passed.

The Prince of Wales remained standing. Deftly his glass of iced punch had been refilled, and he swallowed it. Once the shock had passed, drunkenness reeled and flowed back over him. He peeped down towards Mr. Sheridan, and looked very uncomfortable.

"Sherry. I say! Sherry!"

"Yes, sir?"

"You may be right, Sherry. I don't like this. Damme if I do!"

"Then stop it. There's time yet!"

"Can't stop it. Glenarvon can't speak if he spends a week or two in bed, while we decide what to do. He's a peer, Sherry; hard to get him jailed or transported. Got to be done, though, unless somebody plucks him in a duel. I've—"

Mr. Sheridan thrust out his neck and hissed like a snake.

"Sir! S-s-t! Take care what you say!"

"I've too many enemies," roared His Royal Highness. "Can't risk what he knows. All the same. Glenarvon's a sportsman. I'm a sportsman; never knew *he* was. Hate to send out that poor pigeon to fight the Bristol Smasher."

"Sir!" cried Mr. Sheridan.

There was a flurry among the headdress-plumes of the ladies. The Prince sat down heavily. Chloris, half-rising up, remembered cold prudence and sank back gracefully.

"This man Moggs," said Chloris. "He is a prize-fighter?"

Now why, the Prince seemed to be asking himself, in martyrdom, *must such troublesome matters fall forever upon me?*

"M-madam," he replied aloud, with tipsy grandeur, "the man Moggs is a m-member of the Fancy. Of whom, as Earl of Chester, I am proud to be a patron. All the same. Lady Glenarvon! I regret—!"

"You need not," said Chloris.

"I beg your pardon?"

"I adore my dearest Philip," breathed Chloris, closing her eyes. "I said before, and I say again, we are the happiest wed pair in all England!" She paused, and lifted her shoulders. "Still! If my husband will persist in these acts of folly, he must take his punishment."

"Must he, Lady Glenarvon?" demanded Jennifer.

Now it was Jennifer who leaped up, so abruptly that the red-upholstered chair crashed over behind her. A footman instantly retrieved it.

Jennifer's lips were open, but her face was without expression except for a light of partial memory in her eyes.

"Your Highness," she said, and swallowed hard, "may *I* ask permission to follow them?"

"Hey?"

"May I ask permission," repeated Jennifer in a clear voice, "to go after Colonel Thornton—and my lover?"

Chloris seized a tablespoon and tried violently to bend it.

The Prince, though shocked, was not so much shocked as completely astounded.

"C-come, madam!" he said, with a false ha-ha and a paternal air. "Your language ill becomes you. And such sights as that, my dear, are not for the pretty eyes of young ladies like yourself."

"Then, with your Highness's permission or without it, I am going none the less."

And, picking up her silk skirts, Jennifer scurried down towards the double doors of black and gold.

"*Madam!*"

It was not merely the Prince's voice which made her hesitate and half-turn; it was the intense pressure of so many eyes. Of all the company assembled, including the footmen, nobody remained unhorrified except wicked-minded Lady Oldham, who remembered George the Second and rubbed her hands with glee.

The Prince, stifling a hiccup, again heaved up his huge bulk. Deftly he was caught from behind and set straight.

"Madam," he began, in a terrifying bass like that of John Kemble, "I—"

Instinctively he stretched out his hand, received a glass of iced punch, and slowly drained it while the others waited. Backwards he flung the goblet, which was caught in mid-air from long practice.

"No, damme, let her go!" he bawled, making a gesture to the major-domo who had stepped in front of the double doors. "The gel's got pluck, too. But *I* never heard she was Glenarvon's light-Jane; Hanger, why don't you tell me these things? Now she'll see him half-killed by the Bristol Smasher, and she won't like it."

Jennifer's voice rang back clearly and sweetly.

"You need not be afeared, sir," she cried. "*He* will come to no harm. But may God help your Bristol Smasher."

Then she turned and ran.

vi

"Here's to the Maiden
of Bashful Fifteen . . . !"

Moggs, in bad trouble for nearly five minutes, never saw the blow that finished him.

The gardens, extending west as far as Marlborough House, east to a point well behind the middle of Warwick Street, and south to the Mall, were brilliantly lighted by the moon. But now other lights were creeping into it.

Flaming links, held high, moved very slowly round the eastern side of Carlton House, and touched the corner at the back of it. A servant had whispered, or a household tom-tom. Linkmen, linkboys, beggars, dice-throwers, all the throng, crushed round the front portico and waiting for the carriages to be called, heard the whisper and shuffled round to see.

Then their ears caught the thud and slither of the fight. They moved forward a little and stopped.

On cropped turf not four yards outside an open bow-window, Jemmy Moggs stood almost facing them. Torch-light ran across glimmering wet grass and up over the Bristol Smasher's white, shaven head. He stood with legs wide apart, foursquare, heavy fists raised to about the level of his shoulders, and elbows straight out before him. They saw his heavy shoulders in the woollen shirt, his mighty arms, and also his heavy belly.

He was too winded to shout defiance. He could not land a blow. Each time he lunged or swung, each time he closed in

75

for a wrestling-fall that would mark the end of a round and give him rest, either his fists mysteriously flew wide or he gripped empty air.

No man with such a stomach on him could take the punishment he was taking, always in the belly or under the heart. Viciously he lunged, and missed. His opponent hit him again. Mogg's knees were shaking; a brown froth of beer bubbled between his lips and dripped down over his shirt.

Then it flashed out—a left hook to the angle of the jaw, with full weight behind it and the risk of breaking a hand.

Mogg's knees collapsed. He pitched straight forward like a man pole-axed. Bright little flashes from the grass flew up round him as he landed and did not move. Now the spectators could hear only the hard breathing of his opponent, who stood still and looked down.

Philip Clavering, with sweat running into his eyes and down inside his shirt, gulped the cool, moist air. Dazedly he lifted his left hand, opening and shutting the fingers. Pain stabbed through it, and swelled up like the blood-drops over the knuckles. The hand was not broken, he decided. But, if he had attempted before then to put down Moggs with an attack to the jaw—

A shiver touched his wet shirt. He glanced round for the coat and waistcoat he had flung off. All about him lay the quiet gardens; and, a little distance out from the open bow-window, a marble pedestal with a marble statue of the great god Pan, leering sideways behind goat pipes and surveying the whole scene.

" 'E's knocked out of time," breathed an awed voice, out of a whole hissing of breath expelled. "Oh, so-and-so me so-and-so! The Smasher's knocked out of time!"

"Hold yer clack!" screamed another. "Knocked out of time with one fall?"

"So-and-so you. 'E can't come up to the scratch in thirty-eight minutes, much less thirty-eight seconds."

"But how'd the gent do it?"

"'Cos he can smash harder than the Smasher; wotdjer think?"

"'Tain't all of it, rot me guts! D'jever see anybody as milled like him? Sideways, like? In and out and all over the place? You! Sir!"

Philip turned round.

In the glare of torchlight, as they shuffled forward, they saw a pale-faced man who might actually have been a medium-weight member of the Fancy. His collar and neckcloth were gone. One diamond link had been lost from the sleeve of his cambric shirt, which was torn halfway out of his breeches.

And on his face was an uncanny stamp which might have been put there by the great god Pan, leering up white in the background against the trees.

"Sir," croaked one of the spectators, with great respect, "howdjer do it?"

Philip looked back at him blankly.

"I don't know," he said.

Along the whole great length of the house, every window seemed dark except for a little light spilling out past tasselled curtains in the open bow-window. Jennifer, without cloak or wrap, but holding up her skirts from the wet grass, hurried out to him.

"Put on your coat," she said. "You'll take your death of cold." Then she turned to the crowd. "Please go now!" she begged. "Please, please go!"

Someone cleared his throat. Out from the shadows of the house, where he had been waiting, marched a brisk, stout little man in a brown coat and mulberry-coloured small-clothes. Under a three-cornered hat his round, rosy, rather sly face was screwed up into a judicial expression. Holding

an open watch in his hand, he marched over to the long line
which Moggs's hobnailed heel had torn in the turf before
the fight.

"Thirty seconds' time," he announced. "Eight seconds
more to come up to the scratch." He looked down at the line
in the turf, and shut his watch. "My lord, I declare you the
winner."

"Philip! Please put on your coat!"

The stout little man bounced round to the spectators,
smiled at them, and clapped his hands together briskly.

"Be off, now!" he said. "Be off, like good people, or the
sentries will catch you. No; stay a moment! Two of you
carry Moggs out into the street. This is for your trouble."

Fishing in his pocket, he produced a shilling and threw it
on the ground.

The torchlight dipped and staggered. The biggest of the
spectators dived for the shilling and got it, crying that it
would be divided later. Ferociously, in silence, many hands
struggled at the unconscious Moggs and bore him away. All
of them were hungry and some were near to starving; they
would have scrabbled in the dust for three halfpence, much
less a shilling.

Slowly, amid sobs and curses, the torchlight wavered
round the corner of the house and died away. Only the
moon now shone down on three ghostly figures on the lawn.

"Dear, dear, dear!" chirped the stout little man, with
malicious relish. "What an uncommon rare eye-gouging and
throat-clawing there'll be, I warrant you, when they divide
that shilling! What a pity I can't be there to see it!"

He bounced round again, sweeping off his hat to Jennifer.

"And now, my lord—"

"Stop!" said Philip, who had got his breath back and was
sucking at his bleeding knuckles. "Weren't you here a while
ago? When—?"

"I was indeed here, Lord Glenarvon. Permit me. I am Samuel Horder, Esquire, at your service."

"Weren't you here when Colonel Thornton—?"

"Ah!" breathed Mr. Horder, ducking him another bow. "Let's do justice to Colonel Thornton! He wished your thrashing to be done with strict fairness. And I, Samuel Horder, if you please, was summoned as referee."

"But where's Thornton now? What happened to him?"

"Ah! He is a prudent gentleman, Lord Glenarvon. Much as he desired to witness your thrashing, he rightly thought it imprudent to remain long away from A Certain Person's table. He left, with regret, at the call of time. Colonel Thornton had no doubt of the outcome. Now *I*, on the other hand—"

In response to Jennifer's entreaties, Philip at last picked up waistcoat and coat, and struggled into them. He glanced round for his collar and neckcloth, but could see neither. Then he appealed to Jennifer.

"I knew, naturally," he said, "they were preparing for some kind of beating. But I hated Thornton too much to care. All the same! I felt a little sick when I saw Moggs."

Mr. Horder snickered, and his Cupid's eyebrows went up.

"You were surely not alarmed, my lord?"

"Alarmed? That's a mild word for it! After all, I've never been in a real fight since I was a schoolboy."

Perhaps it was an effect of the moonlight, but an almost shocking change went over Mr. Horder and even over Jennifer.

"Lord Glenarvon," said the former, "this is not a time for pleasantries."

"Pleasantries? I'm telling you the truth!"

"When yesterday, with these eyes of mine, I saw you floor the champion of England in his own sparring-saloon?"

"*What?*"

"You do not remember this, my lord?"

"I—I was drunk," Philip answered wildly. It seemed a reasonable enough excuse; everybody else appeared to be drunk a good part of the time.

" 'Gentleman' Jackson," said Mr. Horder, "was giving you a lesson in boxing. With the gloves on, to be sure. He protested against your manner of placing your feet and carrying your hands. You insisted. 'Gentleman' Jackson then did his best to hit you, and succeeded no more than Moggs."

"Mr. Horder," interrupted Jennifer. "If you will allow *me* to explain—"

"Madam," said Mr. Horder, with another bounce and another removing of his hat. "John Jackson," he added, not with relish, "is only twenty-five. He is elated by his victory over the Jewish Mendoza, on what some call the dirtiest of fouls. For all the Gentleman's manners, he can turn nasty. As he did."

"Well?"

" 'Come, my lord,' says Mr. Jackson, 'you need not fear to strike back; you will not hurt me.' In the next instant he was sitting on the floor, not knocked out of time, mark'ee, but with eyes as glazed as yours. And you—yes, somewhat fuddled, now I call it to mind!—were pulling off the mawleys and forcing your way out of the sparring-saloon, as though indeed you did not know how you were come there."

"But this is impossible!"

"Lord Glenarvon! You and I," proceeded Mr. Horder, significantly jingling coins in his pockets, "could make a vast deal of money together. I don't speak of that now."

Again Jennifer attempted to interrupt, but was silenced.

"Jackson," smoothly went on Mr. Horder, "is twenty-odd pounds over your fighting-weight, and in very good trim. As champion of England, he will not enjoy being laughed at. You have other and very highly placed enemies, too. In a short time, Lord Glenarvon, you will be in great trouble. When you are, be pleased to remember my name: Samuel

Horder, Esquire, always to be found at the Lion and Lamb public-house, in Wooburn Street over against Marquess Court and Drury Lane. Madam, your humblest admirer. Sir, your most obedient."

For the last time Mr. Horder lifted and replaced his three-cornered hat.

Over the smooth lawns, where in daytime peacocks strutted, now Mr. Horder strutted with his Cupid's face complacent under the eye of the great god Pan. He bounced round the eastern side of Carlton House and disappeared, whistling.

And Philip looked at Jennifer.

"Yes," she said in despair. "You can't remember it even now, can you? That's because you loathed and hated it so much your mind won't let you remember it."

"Jenny! Listen! Are you saying—?"

"A dozen times you tried to tell me. But you couldn't. I had to discover it for myself. And every time I had to go and see you fight. It was awful. But it was better than sitting at home wondering if you'd been hurt."

He did not speak; he was incapable of it.

"You wanted to be a historian, and have the leisure for it. To your mind—to your mind, darling—professional fighting was the only way to get what you wanted. *Because* you despised it so much, you worked and trained as few people ever have. *Because* you despised it so much, you went for every opponent as though you wanted to kill him. In a month's time, if something hadn't caught us and thrown us into the past—"

"Yes?"

"In a month's time," replied Jenny, "you'd probably have been middleweight champion of the world."

A breeze rustled and then stirred in a vast rushing through the trees. To the south of them, along an almost deserted

Mall, they could hear bearers trotting with a sedan-chair. Jennifer seized his arms.

"With you, Philip," she added, "there can't be any safe or prudent middle-course. You must be in heaven or in hell. And so must any woman who's fond of you."

He took her in his arms, though conscious of his dishevelled condition, and held her hard.

"It's not that I mind," Jennifer insisted, "I don't. Only— in the dining-room, now, they're piling up everything against you. They think, for their own safety, they must have you imprisoned or transported or killed in a duel. And Colonel Thornton will see to it, if no one else does."

"Will he, by God!"

"Oh, Philip!"

"And what else," he asked, with sardonic courtesy, "have you to add to the iniquities of my character?"

"You're easy-going. You're almost too easy-going. But you can't endure anyone who tries to act superior or be superior. If anyone attempts to lord it over you, you go berserk. And that doesn't make matters easy for me."

"Jenny, I'm sorry!" he said abruptly. "I should never have spoken like that. But there's something the matter with you, too. What is it?"

"Nothing. Nothing at all! But that horrible woman—!"

"Chloris? Oh."

"Why do you say 'oh' like that?" cried Jennifer, flinging her head back and up. "You would never hesitate for a minute to sleep with her. Would you?"

"In all honesty, I don't think I should hesitate. Wait; don't drag back. Listen to me! It's too complicated, and I can't explain."

"Let me go!"

"No! But if I ever did that, Jenny, it would be merely to prove that Chloris is as cold and fish-blooded as I think she is; and, though I don't think I've ever been with you in the same way, I'll take my oath *you're* not and never could be."

There was a silence. Whereupon Jennifer, like all the sisters of Eve, must become completely inconsistent.

"Then why don't you face your enemies?" she cried. "Colonel Thornton is in the dining-room now. He won't laugh, but he'll smile softly as he indicates how you're lying out here beaten to a pulp. Go in there; throw the door open; tell him what he can do with his challenges in future!"

"No."

"But why ever not?"

"Because it would be merely cheap. If you win, you stay silent. You don't crow."

"Oh, God," Jennifer blazed at him, "when will you ever stop being a gentleman? Especially with *me?* I hate you!"

Again she tried to wrench away, but he caught her wrist as she ran.

"Hate me all you like, for the time being—"

"I don't hate you. You know that. But there are times when I could kill you!"

"And make it unanimous? No, Jenny. Let's see you laugh!"

"You're—you're trying to coax me!"

"Of course I am. Hate me all you like, for the moment; but recall that we are not in the twentieth century, and mind you mend your speech in others' presences. We must leave here at once."

"How?"

"Through the house. Our outercoats and wraps are there."

"Philip! Your collar and neckcloth! I *won't* have anyone see you as you are."

He made remarks, about his missing collar and neckcloth, which would have horrified the Royal Society of Haberdashers. Jennifer, though in the past insistent on the point of his careless appearance, for once remained meek.

"For another thing," he went on, "Hopwith may have arrived with Mrs. Poppett and our coach for the country. It must be nearly midnight. I doubt that they'll try to hold me or put me under restraint tonight."

"You think they might?"

"They soon will. But tonight I don't think so. They're still at table, I make no doubt. We must slip past the doors unseen. Go gently, now!"

Jennifer put her hand over her mouth as, in the three sides of the bow-window, brighter light crept out under the heavy and looped scarlet curtains with their gold tassels. But they could do nothing but risk it.

The lower foyer, hung with His Royal Highness's pictures of the Dutch school, was empty except for a tall footman. White-wigged, in the red-and-gold livery much embossed and stamped with the Prince's crest of feathers, this footman was kindling many wax-lights on tables.

From behind the closed doors of the dining-room, at their left, rose a roar of voices in unintelligible speech. The footman, blowing out his thin wax lighting-paper, looked steadily at the two newcomers. He moved towards them without noise. When he spoke, it was without moving his lips and with electrifying effect.

"God bless you, sir. You done him up proper."

Philip nodded inquiringly towards the black-and-gold double doors.

"In a minute or so," continued the ventriloquial voice, "they'll be a-singing. That'll mean Sherry will call for a pianoforte, and His Royal Highness for the violincello so he can sing a bass solo. They'll be off for the music-room upstairs—"

Advice about the singing was unnecessary. Already, to a steady thumping of knife-handles on the table, the musical murmur was growing. Out burst Mr. Sheridan's rich tenor, upraised in the most rollicking of his own songs.

"Here's to the maiden of bashful fifteen,
    And here's to the woman of fifty—"

Every other voice swung in and took it up with him:

"Here's to the flaunting extravagant quean,
    And here's to the housewife who's thrifty!
Let the toast pass! Drink to the lass!
I'll warrant she'll prove an excuse for the glass!"

And all voices, except Mr. Sheridan's own, roared the
second verse.

"Here's to . . ."

"See?" asked the tall and impassive footman, without
seeming to move his lips. "Best make haste, sir. They
know."

"They know the outcome of the fight?"

"Oh, ah. 'Is Royal Highness sends out Major Hanger to
watch."

"But I didn't see Major Hanger!" whispered Jennifer.

"Maybe as not, miss. 'E was there, though. Comes back
and holds the doors open long enough to yell. 'Sir,' 'e shouts,
'Glenarvon's beat the Smasher and knocked him out of
time.' "

"And what did they say?"

"Nothink, sir. Stunned, like. Oh! Except for your lordship's wife, the pretty one. She stands up, in a giggly kind
of way. 'Did I not tell you?' says she, and touches her hair
all over as cool as cool. The doors closed then."

Jennifer's hands crisped and clasped in the air.

"See, sir?" pursued the ventriloquist-footman, staring ston-
ily over their heads. "They're expecting you back. 'Tisn't
etiquette to take your leave 'fore the Prince chooses to retire.
You'd best *hurry*."

"Yes, of course! Am I permitted to summon my coach, if it should happen to be there?"

"Leave this to me. Just follow. I'll—"

Abruptly the black-and-gold double-doors opened, and softly closed. Mr. Richard Brinsley Sheridan stood against them.

Though his heart rose up in his throat, Philip looked back at him. Mr. Sheridan's grizzled hair, tied at the back with a greasy bit of ribbon, stood straight up against the doors as though in terror. But his eye was partially sober. Picking out of his waistcoat-pocket a note folded into a pellet, he flicked it towards Philip so that it landed on the flowered carpet.

Then he reeled round, straightened up, and marched in again.

"Your Royal Highness," they heard him cry, "they are not yet returned."

"Sir!" hissed the footman.

Up the carpeted stairs they went, Jennifer clinging to Philip's arm and the footman moving poker-backed ahead, while Philip unfolded the note. Where Mr. Sheridan had obtained pen and ink he could not guess and never learned.

"You shack (shock?) me," ran the rolling scribble. "But be at the Lane tomorrow A.M. and trust. S."

At the top of the stairs stood Branley, the celebrated footman-in-chief, whose every word and gesture was said to resemble his master's. Also stout, fitted tightly into his scarlet-and-gold livery, he stood there as though he had just taken an invisible pinch of snuff from an elegantly invisible box.

"Lord Glenarvon's coach, Mr. Branley," said the poker-backed footman. "A sudden hindisposition—"

"Ah!" murmured Mr. Branley, with the faintest shadow of a smile under his puffy eyelids. "A great pity, my lord. Your lordship's antagonist, I feel, should have been revived with vinegar and burnt feathers. Lord Glenarvon's coach!"

At the flick of his nod, other servants hastened for his hat and cloak, for Jennifer's shoulder-wrap, under the crimson-shining wallpaper. At the door Philip hesitated, and glanced round at the footmen.

"I am much your debtor," he said, then added, "Gentlemen."

Not an eyelash stirred or a muscle moved. But he felt goodwill there, as palpable as a handshake; while, outside, the formidable voice of Big Ben, the porter, called out for Lord Glenarvon's coach.

Then he, drawing his cloak tightly round him and with *chapeau de bras* under his arm, stood outside under the breezy portico. Still the flames of torches curled up in brackets against a long stone-fronted façade, and the night hung crowded with its ghosts.

Jennifer raised her head.

"Don't laugh at me," she said quietly. "But I'll kill her, I swear I'll kill her, if tonight of all nights—"

"Jenny!"

"If, tonight of all nights, she seeks you. I swear that, Phil."

"You must not speak of this. What you tell me, about myself and my past life, seems so completely ridiculous."

"But it's true. Your father taught you boxing as a boy, though I can't say who your father was. You learned more at Cambridge. In the Army they 'discovered' you."

"But you, Jenny? Who are *you?*"

"I don't know."

"No remembrance at all?"

"No. But the disaster that's following you, if it's the same now as it was in our other lives—"

Out at the gate, before the outer colonnade, two sentries of the Grenadier Guards raised their muskets to salute. The heavy coach, its panels emblazoned with the star and falcon of the Glenarvon arms, swept through one of the outer gates, rumbled round the drive, and came to rest at the front steps. Much luggage was corded to its roof.

One of the two footmen sprang down to open door. Out ducked the smiling face of old Hopwith, Philip's manservant, with Mrs. Poppett asleep and snoring inside.

"The disaster in our other lives," Jennifer said through her teeth, "was murder."

"Murder!"

"Yes. You were accused of it. If it should happen here—"

With deftness Hopwith handed Jennifer into the coach, and then Philip. He himself bowed and climbed in. The door slammed; a whip cracked; they were off for the country, and the house called Widestairs beyond the village of Chelsea.

Distantly, the clock at St. James's Palace began to toll midnight. Just three hours later, there was murder done.

vii

"Yet I Have Been
Faithful to Thee . . ."

Bong trembled the heavy note of the clock over the stables, at Widestairs by the quiet river, on the single stroke of one.

Philip, in what they told him was his own bedroom at the front of the house one floor up, sat in a very small tin bath. Hopwith, in attendance, was talkative and cheerful. The present Earl of Glenarvon was not.

It had seemed to take hours for heavy buckets of hot water to be dragged up, from the cellar, by pale-faced girls untouched in sun or air. Philip first scalded himself in steam before he grew adjusted to it. The soap at least was excellent, though highly scented and in the form of a ball which flew out of your hand and bounced across the floor.

"Your lordship, I hope," Hopwith asked pointedly, "has had a sufficiency of water?"

"Yes. I daresay."

" 'Tis germ-laden, my lord."

"Not when it's boiled."

"My lord?"

"No matter." Philip jerked up his head. "Hopwith! Listen!"

He had been awaiting it. Clearly, in night stillness, he could hear the thump and jolt of a coach along the river

89

road; it could mean nothing but the return of Chloris, together with Lady Oldham and Chloris's maid, Molly.

"In a short time, Hopwith," he added, "there'll be a plaguy amount of recriminations and vapours to meet. I would meet 'em reasonably clad."

"But not yet for ten minutes, my lord. The coach, you hear, is passing the house? Her ladyship must deposit Colonel Thornton at his own door, at the Oaks, before she returns here. The towel, my lord?"

"Give it to me. I can dry myself," said Philip, and did. "Now, as touches this confounded bathtub—"

"Shall I allow it to remain, my lord? The water will serve well enough for tomorrow's bath, since you seem to desire one a day."

"The water? For tomorrow? Are you raving mad?"

"My lord?"

"Have them fetch it away, presently, and bring new hot water tomorrow morning. 'Fore gad, Hopwith!"

Hopwith closed his eyes.

"As your lordship pleases. Now the night-shift—no, my lord, it goes over the head—and the slippers. Finally, the dressing-robe, which I feel sure will please you. It is well quilted, as you observe, and its claret-colour well becomes you. As for the waist-cord, your lordship will permit—"

"No, curse it! *I* can tie the damn waist-cord. Am I a babe in arms?"

His temper, he knew in his heart, was not due to the proximity of Chloris and the scene which must ensue with her. It was not due to the friction with Hopwith which always arose over any matter of washing or dressing.

It was because this house, in some indefinable way at the back of his brain, was very familiar to him. He had been aware of that as soon as the coach galloped up to it. Widestairs—set back in gardens from the road, rising up square, massive, and Georgian-built, with its line of heavy pillars up

broad steps to the front door, its white stone hardly yet
turned grey—struck him not only with familiarity; but, for
the first time, with terror.

He stood in his own bedroom, dressed in night-shirt and
claret-coloured dressing-robe, and glanced round apprehensively.

Though the room was large and airy according to the
builder of 1770, it was lighted only by one candle in a glass
vase. Shadows thickened round the mahogany furniture
from the workshop of Mr. Sheraton, and round a heavy old-
fashioned four-poster bed unpleasantly suggestive of vermin.
Steam from the bath hung clammily, despite a bright fire,
and softened wallpaper in a design of green cabbages.

Jennifer, who must now also be indulging in what both
Hopwith and Mrs. Poppett called a hot-bathe, had shown
no sign of recognition. *She* never knew this house. But he—

"Hopwith!"

"My lord?"

"I am an ill-mannered cur, as you are well aware."

"No, my lord. Give me leave to differ."

The main door of the bedroom led out to the main landing
upstairs. There was another door in the wall to Philip's left,
near the angle of the other as he faced it. He knew, with
conviction, that this second door led to his dressing-room.

All the same he stalked over and opened it. The dressing-
room too had Sheraton mahogany and a full-length mirror,
murky too in the gleam of one candle. But this room was not
so large as the bedroom; it was severed by a partition on the
left, with another door.

"Hopwith, what does that partition close off?"

"An adjunct, my lord, containing your clothing. As also a
box-room for trunks, hatboxes, and the like."

Ahead of Philip, in the wall facing him, was still another
door. He went to it, found it bolted with a wooden bolt on

his side, and drew the bolt. But, when he turned the knob, it was also fastened on the other side.

"To where does this door lead?"

"To her ladyship's dressing-room," answered Hopwith. His eyelids lowered, and he looked at the floor. "It—my lord, you will recall it has been bolted, these last eighteen months, on both sides."

"And beyond her dressing-room?"

"Her ladyship's bedroom, my lord."

Philip spun round.

"Hopwith," he said out of a full heart, "what would you say if I were to tell you this is all a devilish and lying masquerade? That time itself has slipped its cogs and fallen over a mountainside? That I am not Earl of Glenarvon at all?"

Though Hopwith remained with his head down, he smiled as with the shadow of a shade.

"Indeed it is true," he murmured to the floor, "that your humours of recent days have been strange. It is of book-learning, too much of it. But—"

"Yes?"

"If your lordship were not apt to take cold after opening the pores with so much hot water—"

"I am not likely to take cold! What is it?"

Bowing, Hopwith backed away into the bedroom. There he took up an unlighted candle, in a tin dish with a tin fingerhold, on the chest of drawers by the door to the main landing. This he lighted with the flint from a tinder-box, and held up as he opened the door to the corridor.

Philip, in dressing-robe and slippers, marched out ahead of him. The corridor, on this side of the broad stair well, was full of cross-draughts; yet, to his disquiet, it was even more crowded with phantom memories.

He had not yet observed that dark portraits, two or three between each of the line of doors, hung on this wall. They were close to the front of the house, near the landing-window, and only one large picture hung here. Hopwith held up the candle, so that its light fell across a darkening canvas set in a heavy wooden frame.

And Philip's own face sprang out of the picture.

Though he glanced seldom into mirrors, there could be no mistaking the forehead, the nose, the mouth and chin; above all, the grave yet mocking and humorous mouth. It was enclosed in a long and heavy full-bottomed wig. A three-cornered laced hat pressed down on it, and, under the necklace, showed the dark gleam of a breastplate.

"That is your grandfather," said Hopwith, "the second earl."

Hopwith held the candle higher.

"He fought in Flanders with the Great Duke, my lord, and won much honour at the battle of Oudenarde. They called him Fighting Jack."

"But I can't believe—!"

"As a boy," said Hopwith, swallowing, "I saw him ride home through London streets after that campaign which ended the long war. I saw him ride behind the drums and fifes a-banging with 'The British Grenadiers.' There were not many cheers for Duke Marlborough's self, because his shrewish wife had undone him. But there were cheers for Jack Clavering. He would as soon pull off his coat to fight a street-porter as he would draw sword for duel against a general. But his purse was open to all men, and so was his heart. In you, my lord, I thank God that he is reborn."

Philip stared at the floor. By what tragic, incomprehensible mistake had this loyal old man been bound to an impostor?

"Hopwith! A truce to this!"

"I crave pardon, my lord," said Hopwith, without turning round, "for the liberty I take. Yet there in the corner of the portrait is his crest and motto: a star and falcon, above the

words, 'Et ego ad astra.' 'I also to the stars.' My lord, they
are your crest and motto now."

The candle flame fluttered in a draught.

Neither Philip nor Hopwith had heard coach wheels on
gravel outside. Only when wax-lights went hurrying into
the lower foyer, when the front door was unlocked and unchained, when the heavy tread of Lady Oldham came rolling
inside, did both Philip and his manservant awake with a
guilty start.

"God damme!" boomed Lady Oldham from below. "I'm
an old hag, m'gel, and this hurly-burly's not for me. I want
me bed."

"You shall have it, dear Lady Oldham," sang the calm,
lazy, contralto voice of Chloris. "Molly herself shall attend
you, ere she attends me."

Lady Oldham's waddling step, slow and asthmatic, began
to bang and bump up the oak staircase.

"Hey-day, though!" said Lady Oldham. "What a tidbit
for the news-sheets! Prinny's furious, scratch me! (And
scratch me's no figger o' speech, either; I've picked up a flea
or two somewhere.) But that husband of yours, m'gel!
Damme if he don't wallop over the Bristol Smasher, as flat
as a mustard-poultice, and I hear he done the same to John
Jackson yesterday. Ain't you proud of him, hey?"

"He did indeed do rather well." Chloris's voice remained
cool. "Yet his impertinence towards the Prince of Wales, in
more respects than one, will not lightly be forgiven."

Philip, temper rising again, gritted his teeth.

Up over the staircase well appeared the head of a footman, in the gold-and-grey Glenarvon livery, walking backwards and holding a candelabrum with five lights. Then
uprose the purple- and yellow-dyed ostrich plumes spread-
ing awry on Lady Oldham's head; the straight white plumes
of Chloris, her face repainted to vivid beauty; the pretty,
fresh-coloured countenance of Molly, and the not-so-pretty

countenance of another maid whose name Philip could not remember.

Hopwith, with a deep bow, handed the candle to Philip. Then he glided swiftly down the corridor and disappeared inside Philip's bedroom.

Philip, candle in hand, sauntered to the head of the stairs and met the rest of the party as they arrived there.

"Oh, rot me guts!" cried Lady Oldham, and went off into such a roar of laughter that she had to stop, breathless, and hold her sides. "Here's Tom Figg himself. And not a mark on him, as far as I can see. How'd you flatten 'em, lad?"

"For elucidation there," smiled Philip, "I fear you must ask my wife."

Chloris ignored him.

"Trina!" she said sharply to the not-so-pretty maid, who attempted a curtsey on the edge of the stairs. "The fires are mended? And the beds aired and warmed?"

"There's no bugs in 'em, is there?" Lady Oldham asked suspiciously. "I've picked up fleas already, either at Carlton House or in that coach, and somebody'll have to pick 'em off me. I won't suffer bugs on top of that."

"I do truly assure you," replied Chloris, not in anger but as a plain statement of fact, "you will find no objectionable creatures in any bed here."

"Now that, my love," observed Philip, "is a matter of opinion. For instance, should Colonel Thornton have spent the night here—"

"Trina!" shrieked Chloris, in such a way that Trina, attempting a deeper curtsey, almost tumbled backwards down the stairs.

"Yes, my lady?"

"Are all things as I have commanded them?"

"Yes, my lady."

"That is well. Holdsworth," and Chloris addressed the footman with the candelabrum, "you will light Lady Oldham to the Blue Room. Trina, accompany her. Molly, you may also go. But pray return soon; my head splits, and I would have my temples bathed in cologne-water. Is there aught else, Lady Oldham, you may require?"

"Well!" muttered that gentlewoman, turning down the corners of her broad mouth. "A pint o' mulled claret, maybe? To gimme sweet dreams?"

"Trina, go presently and fetch a pint of mulled claret. See that it be well spiced and hot. That is all."

Led by the footman in grey-and-gold, with five wavering flames held high, the procession straggled towards the back of the house and vanished.

Chloris took two or three steps after it, but she paused and turned round. Philip had put the tin candle-dish on the flat newel-post of the staircase. Only that thin burning taper lit the heavy, draughty darkness.

Chloris moved so close that he could have touched her, with her hazel eyes fixed on his face.

"Philip, you are a fool," she said in a different tone. She lowered her eyes. "But your sort of folly is—not displeasing. Do you understand?"

"No."

"No? Kiss me." Then, fiercely, after a pause, "No! Not in that fashion! Closely! Ah!"

He disliked the woman; it is sober fact that he did. He disliked her very cordially. And yet, whenever he was within touching distance of her . . .

After a minute or so Chloris tore herself loose and stood back. She was breathing hard; her nostrils were dilated; and her eyes again fixed on his face.

"I would lie with you, Philip. Do you know why?"

"Yes. Sheer curiosity."

"No! Again you are mistook, and again a fool. I am all but in love with you; I don't like it."

"And do you imagine, madam, that I like *you*? But there

are certain matters that must be discussed and decided between us. And tonight."

"No!" Chloris answered swiftly. "Not tonight. After that
—yes, and as soon as may be! But not this night. There are
reasons!"

"I did not speak of being abed together, madam. I spoke
of matters we must discuss."

"Did you, indeed?" murmured Chloris, lifting her arched
eyebrows. Her lips moved derisively, slowly, and desirably.
"Your mort is here, I suppose?"

"My what?"

"Your mopsy. Your light-Jane. Your whore."

Then Philip did what never, in his other life, would he
have dreamed of doing. With his open hand he whacked
Chloris so hard across the side of the face that she reeled
against the wall and tumbled down on her knees.

Just as he hit her, the door to the Blue Room opened
towards the rear of the hall. Holdsworth, the footman,
marched towards them with his wax-lights carried high.
Though he must have seen everything, he did not even
glance in their direction. Like a sleep-walker he descended
the stairs.

Chloris, jumping up, paused only to lift her skirts high
and make sure there was no rent in the knee of either stock-
ing. She ran to Philip, even closer, and her mouth widened
in a genuine smile.

"Now do you imagine," she whispered, in quick breathing,
"I am angered because you use me ill? No, no, no! I admire
the spirit; I would have had you do this long ago. One last
kiss, now!"

"Damn your soul, I said—"

"There!"

Chloris, breaking away, ran softly to the door of what
must be her dressing-room.

"Tomorrow night!" she called softly over her shoulder.

"Do I fear *any* rival at all, Philip, once you have been with me?"

The door closed. He heard a wooden bolt shot into its socket. Philip glared uneasily at a grotesque face which seemed to take form in the candle flame. Picking up the holder, he went to his bedroom, opened the door, and slammed it behind him.

Hopwith was there, hands outspread to the sea-coal fire, while a night wind stirred up round the house and rattled at the window frames.

"Hopwith, is there tobacco or brandy in the house?"

"My lord," said the startled Hopwith, "there is both, in plenty. But I did not know—"

"When I was in training," Philip retorted, cryptically and bitterly, "I was forbidden both. Now I want them; also in plenty."

"Your lordship does not own a pipe, to my knowledge. However, if you would deign to try one of mine—?"

"Yes, it would be an honour. Fetch them!"

While Hopwith hastened away, Philip sank down in the mahogany armchair before the fire. Though it was as hard as a rack, save for its green silk seat-pillow, he was growing used to minor inconveniences. Now that Hopwith had removed the candle, only one wax-light wavered and left soot stains inside its glass vase, in a damp dusky bedroom with a bed damp despite its warming-pan.

The door opened softly, and Jennifer came in.

She wore slippers and a pink quilted dressing-robe with collar turned up round her throat. The brown hair lay tumbled on her shoulders. Her left hand was tightly clenched against her breast, and she would not look at him.

From her left hand she took out a ring, a small, glittering circle of very fine diamonds. Jennifer held it out in the palm of her right hand. Philip sprang up.

"I found this in my luggage," she told him. "I must have

been wearing it when— Anyway, the shock of seeing it made me remember a little. Do you remember when you bought it?"

"No!"

"It was about seven weeks ago," she said, still not looking at him. "The morning after you met that Frenchman at Harringay. I can't remember his name, but he held both the European and the British Empire titles, and you knocked him out in the second round. Next day, while I still had to pretend I didn't know you were a professional fighter, I went with you to Garland's in Regent Street. You didn't say it was an engagement ring; you just said it was a present you wanted to give me. Please, Phil, I don't want it."

Still without looking at him, she dropped the glittering ring on the chest of drawers beside the door. It rattled and was still.

"If you want that woman," said Jennifer, still without looking at him, "then have her."

"But I don't—"

"Oh, Phil! That's what you think, I'm sure. You'd swear it, and honestly believe what you swore. In your heart it's different."

Then Jennifer flung the subject away. She partly opened the still tightened fingers of her left hand, and looked at something concealed there.

"The other ring," she said, "I'd like to keep."

"What other ring?"

"Please!" cried Jennifer, clenching her hand as though he might wrench the ring away. "It's not valuable, like the other one. It's only a keepsake. You gave it to me, I think, shortly after we first met, to hold as a keepsake. It's even got a little crest—"

"Crest? What crest?"

"It's nothing much." Jenny retreated. "You can hardly make it out anyway. Only a star, and some kind of bird,

over a Latin motto. 'I also to the stars.' And I have been,
Phil! I have been!"

Abruptly, with a choking feeling at his throat, he turned
his head away. When he turned back again, quickly, at the
creak of some noise, the door had closed and Jennifer was
gone.

He took two steps after her, but stopped. This was no
place to tell her how he meant to rid himself of Chloris,
forever.

The engagement ring sardonically winked its diamonds
from the top of the chest of drawers. He pulled open the top
drawer, flung the ring inside to get it out of sight, and saw
the dusty oblong box bound in leather with the gold-and-
grey of the Glenarvon arms.

That box had belonged to a young, hopeful-daring man.
Across its lid ran the gilt letters, Philip Maddern Clavering.
At the same instant he touched the box lid, a chink of memory from his other life opened: he heard men's voices bab-
bling under bright lamps, and saw a white poster. Memory
vanished. Opening the lid of the heavy wooden box, he
found the pair of duelling-pistols embedded in ruby velvet,
with a small ramrod embedded between.

Philip slammed the lid of the box, and heard its latch
click.

He *was* Lord Glenarvon. During his other life, at some
time or other, he had been the ninth or perhaps the tenth
Earl. In his veins, much as he hated or thought he hated
the prize-ring, ran the blood of Fighting Jack Clavering.
And he was proud of it.

In his mind curled out the American posters: "Phil Maddern vs. Al Rossi. For the middleweight championship of
the world."

Et ego ad astra!

"A noble motto, my lord," the voice of Hopwith broke

FEAR IS THE SAME

through his dreams, "but is it seemly to shout it aloud at this hour?"

"Was I shouting it aloud, Hopwith?"

"I fear so, my lord."

In marched Hopwith, deftly carrying a large tray laden with a tobacco bowl, three long pipes, a decanter of brandy, a water carafe, a heavy tumbler, and a glass of twisted paper-spills for lighting pipes. Behind him peered the shrivelled faces of the two kitchen maids who had dragged the bathtub upstairs.

With the air of a conjurer Hopwith floated up a small round mahogany table, and let it down beside the armchair as though the table had no weight at all. Across it he whipped a clean cloth, slid the tray across the table, and stood back to admire.

"It is well done, my lord?"

"Most excellent well! Hopwith, have I any money?"

Hopwith, who had been eyeing the two maidservants struggling out with the bathtub, clapped his hands for more speed.

"Money, my lord? Not on your person. Due to your—your absentmindedness, you recall, her ladyship bade me carry your purse."

"Did she so?" enquired Philip, in no pleasant tone. "You will return the purse tomorrow. In the meantime, give each of these two maids a crown-piece."

"*A crown-piece, my lord!*"

"Is it not enough? If not, give 'em—"

"My lord!" prayed Hopwith, nearly on his knees. "A four-penny-piece between them were far too much! Her ladyship well knows the value of money, and thinks—"

"What her ladyship thinks is no longer of import in this house. Is that plain?"

"Yes, my lord."

"Very well. Do as I bid, and take what you like for your-self. Good night; a sweet good night. That is all."

Again he was alone.

For the moment he distrusted both the tobacco and the clay pipes, nor did he dare drink any water. But he un-stoppered the decanter, poured out half a tumblerful of brandy, and drank it neat. At his first gulp he gasped and choked, with streaming eyes; afterwards he drank slowly until it was gone.

A warm mellowness spread through his innards, and he smiled.

Circling the chair, he took up from among the fire-arms a long and heavy iron poker. Still smiling without pleasure, he weighed it in his hand. Then he walked over to the door of his own dressing-room.

His own dressing-room, of course, was deserted and dark except for that single candle inside the glass vase. Chloris might be in her own dressing-room, just beyond the bolted door, or she might be in the bedroom beyond.

Philip seized the knob, turned it, and found it still bolted. But unquestionably Chloris was in the dressing-room near him. As the knob twisted and creaked, he heard the rustle of silk and a sharp *crick-crack* from the dressing-table bench.

"Who's there?" came the whisper.

"Your husband, madam. Open this door."

"No!" She sounded terrified.

"I have here," he said, "a good stout poker. Either you will open this door, madam, or I will smash it down. The choice is yours."

"*No!* Go away! Are you mad?"

The door, made of pinewood, was not very formidable.

Philip, balancing on his right foot, lashed forward. The crash of the poker against the middle panel exploded like a grenado in that little room. The poker's tip smashed altogether through, sending cracks and splinters starring across wood, and giving a shudder to the whole door.

Philip wrenched out the tip of the poker.

"Another blow or two, I think, will do the business. The next one—"

"No! Leave off! I'll unbolt it!"

Silk rustled swiftly towards him; he heard the slide and clack of the bolt shot back; then the sound of slippered feet running hard away. He threw the door open, but his wife's dressing-room was empty. He was just in time to see the flutter of a silk night-shift disappear round the corner of the door to Chloris's bedroom.

"There is no cause for fear!" he snapped. "I would merely have it understood, madam, that I mean what I say. If—"

Here he stalked through the open door of the bedroom, and stopped in astonishment.

The room was large and square, like his own, though heavily overdecorated with gilt, with a long mirror in each panel of the deep-scarlet wallpaper, and with muslin flounces. Its heavy smell was like that of a perfumer's shop, all the bottles open. Most of the space was taken up by an enormous bed, its curtains drawn back and a wax-light burning in a bracket on either side. At the left side of the bed hung a thin red bell-rope.

But Chloris was not there.

Instead, shrinking back from him in terror, her brown eyes wide open and her dark brown hair dressed like Chloris's, a certain woman wore a silk night-shift cut so high at the waist but so low at the bosom that long shoulder-straps were necessary to keep it up.

"Don't beat me," she screamed, backing away still further and nearly falling on the bed. " 'Twas none of my fault! Oh, God, don't beat me!"

She was Molly, Chloris's maid.

viii

"That Fellow's Got to Swing."

In that flash of astonishment near stupefaction, there formed in Philip's mind a single scene from early that evening.

He saw Chloris and Molly, together, in Chloris's dressing-room at Oldham House in London. He had noted idly that they were much the same height, and had much the same voice, in quality, in intonation, even in pronunciation. Now he could observe they had much the same figure.

If Molly were to pose as Chloris, speaking only through a locked door or seen briefly at a window, everyone would be deceived.

And Chloris would be free for—what?

Philip never recognized the harsh and murderous note in his own voice.

"Where is my wife?"

Molly's eyes, fear-distended and welling with tears, slid aside.

"She is—not here."

"So I observe. Where is she?"

"My lord, she is gone abroad."

"Gone ab— Oh! You mean she has gone from the house?"

There is a point at which terror inspires the wish to hit back. Gone was the fashionable quality of her accent; but it was warm, with a touch of Irish.

"Sure and what else would I mean? And the devil fly

104

away with you! If you beat me, it won't be the first time
from ladies' husbands."

She sat down on the bed, flung herself sideways, and burst
into tears.

Philip looked at her. Then he glanced over her shoulder
into the dressing-room where, on a well-lighted Queen-Anne
dressing-table, lay scattered under the mirror a jar of white-
lead cream, a bowl of powder, a hare's foot for reddening
the cheeks, and all other such gauds. Molly, alone, had been
dressing up even in Chloris's cosmetics and pretending she
was Chloris.

Philip searched round in the bedroom, heavier still in atmosphere with scented pastilles thrown into a fire which had
been allowed to go out. He found, obscurely tucked away,
a bowl and ewer of water. Though even the water was
dust-speckled, it would have to do.

Finding a rolled-up towel, he returned to the bedside with
a bowl of water.

"Sit up, Molly."

Molly, still sobbing on the bed, shivered but risked one
eye.

"If you beat me—"

"I'm not going to beat you, Molly, or hurt you in any way.
Why should I? Sit up."

Molly sat up, so abruptly that both shoulder-straps of her
night-shift tumbled down with predictable results. Crimson
with embarrassment, she hastened to pull them up together
with the bodice. As she did so, Philip studiously looked at
the floor and put down the basin of water.

"My lord! What is it?"

"Molly, do you know why so many women smear a thin
coat of white-lead cream on their faces, and cover it with
powder and all the rest of the daubings?"

" 'Tis—'tis the fashion!"

"Not exactly, no. They put on that cream, and heavy powder afterwards, because it fills and then hides the pits of smallpox scars. But you have not had smallpox. Nor has my wife. And white-lead is poison; it causes the blotches and skin diseases you must have seen so often. Sit still, Molly. I am going to take the filthy stuff off your face."

Molly suddenly reached out and grasped his left arm hard. But she did not look up for a few seconds.

He made her look up, but she closed her eyes. Because he tried to be gentle, it took some time. In the middle of it:

"My lord!" said Molly, without opening her eyes.

"Yes?"

"I've liked you," said Molly. "I liked you even when they said you was a ninnyhammer. I knew you weren't; I told her ladyship you were a proper man. But I never knew until now why I liked you so much. It's—"

"Sit still, can't you?"

He finished washing her face, which was pretty and fresh-coloured again, and handed her the towel to dry it. Still Molly spoke persistently, achingly, from out of the muffling folds of the towel.

"But I never told you before. I never told you that whenever we were at Widestairs, which has been very often, she would— Look at that!"

"That" appeared to be only rather a long cupboard, built out along the west wall from the northwest angle, and papered over in dull scarlet. Then he saw it was an unusual cupboard; its door was on the narrow side facing south.

"A staircase?" he demanded. "Going down to the ground floor?"

"Ay, that's it. Sometimes there's a horse; sometimes she goes on foot. But every night she creeps out to go abed with her fancy man, and not return till near morning. My lord, I did desire to tell you! But it would only have hurt you too much."

The basin of water shook in Philip's hand.

"Do you really conceive," he said between his teeth, "that my lady's behaviour could ever hurt *me?*"

"Oh, you think 'twill not. But I have watched you; I know!"

"Let us see, then."

"She thinks," cried Molly, flinging away the towel, "she has been most clever. Yet everybody at Widestairs knows: cook, and Holdsworth, and everybody. I'll warrant *she's* been passing the word for spite. Maybe in London, though, there's few that know about her and Colonel Thornton."

Philip stood motionless.

"Colonel Thornton?" he repeated.

"Ah, to be sure! She's been his for near on eighteen months, and my lady and the colonel take much pleasure in laughing at you behind your back. My lord! Did you not observe, at Lady Oldham's house early this night, how they spoke together almost as man and wife?"

"Yes. I observed it. But I never thought—"

Philip paused, moistening his lips.

"Tomorrow," he said, "Colonel Thornton means to engage me in a duel. He will be here bright and early, you may be sure, to demand 'satisfaction.' And, by the Face of Christ, he shall have it."

Suddenly Philip lifted high the heavy basin of water. He flung it down amid a crash of flying fragments and a swirl of water. Molly, terrified again, scrambled back on the bed.

"My lord, I warned you! This hurts! I told you 'twould!"

"It hurts. Yes. But not in the fashion you thought. To imagine that arrogant lout, a man nearly twice Chloris's age—!"

With a violent effort he conquered his outward behaviour. On a small table beside one of the closely curtained windows he saw a tray with a wine-glass and an opened wine bottle. Not until he had filled the glass and gulped at it did he find the wine was Madeira: heavy, sickly sweet, nauseating.

After the fashion of the time he poured out the rest on the floor, and filled the glass again. He was smiling.

"I forget my manners," he said. "Will you take wine, Molly?"

Molly took the glass, and slowly drained it. He was looking at one of the wax-lights on either side of the bed; it was painted with numbered rings, and showed it had been burning for just an hour.

"My lord!" cried Molly.

"How strange it seems to be called—no matter!"

"My lord, don't go. Stay with me!"

Philip took the glass from her hand and put it down on the table.

"Nay, I do not mean," said Molly, "what you will imagine I mean, though God He knows I would welcome such with you. But *she* will not return—"

Heavily, booming in the night, the clock over the stables struck two.

"—she will not return until three more hours. Sometimes she does not return until mid-morning. If she thinks she has been seen on the road, going to Colonel Thornton's house or returning from it, she will stay with her friends the Hallidays, who love her and will find some excuse, illness or the like, why she has come to their house. My lord, I am only your servant. But I would comfort you when you are sick at heart."

"And be found here," he said in disgust, "a cuckolded husband lying in wait to surprise her? No!"

"My lord, I do not understand."

"No. You are of good heart. You would not understand. Good night, Molly."

"My lord!"

He went out of the room, closing the bedroom door behind him as he heard her weeping. He closed behind him the half-wrecked door at the end of the dressing-room, then the door of his own dressing-room and finally his bedroom door.

The fire in his room was almost out. Hanging back the poker he had retrieved from the other bedroom, he poured coal on the fire. He sat down, and splashed brandy into the tumbler.

The only image which obsessed him blackly, and would not go away, was still that of Chloris in Colonel Thornton's arms.

Was that why he had hated Colonel Thornton from the first time they met? It was instinctive; he could not have guessed it with his conscious mind; but it was there, alive and astir. Thornton would have known, of course.

If all this were so, was he, Philip, more fond of Chloris than he would admit to himself? And was Jennifer right when she said so?

Thick black smoke poured up from the smothered fire. He got up, stirred it with the poker so that yellow flame glinted through. He sat down again, and put down the brandy glass.

No! Jenny was wrong!

He was tired, more tired and heavy-witted than he knew. Perhaps because of that weariness, the half-memories of this house—which had been plaguing him for several hours—grew a little less blurred.

This house, as he saw it in his other life, was bleak and mouldering; it was lost amid other houses pressing up round it. He had lived here. And Chloris, or someone very like Chloris, had lived here, too. His wife. Yes, Chloris was his wife! Dimly, as though through a cavern, he could hear her screaming and complaining about something. But he did not love her; quite the reverse, though something bound him to her.

Why didn't you tell me no money went with your title? Why didn't you tell me . . . ?

Abruptly Philip's head fell forward, and the untasted tumbler rolled from his hand. He had nearly plunged forward, in the literal sense, into sleep.

He rose to his feet. There was no time, or so it seemed, even to open windows or blow out the candle. He lurched over to the bed, kicked off his slippers, and rolled inside without taking off his dressing-robe. The bed was faintly damp even though warm. Pushing aside the warming-pan, he fell headlong into sleep.

What roused him, in the black middle of the night, was what he imagined to be a cry or a scream heard faintly. It must have been louder than he imagined; he raised himself on one elbow, still sleep-misted. It was at this time he heard the heavy clang of the stable-clock striking three. The small candle in its glass vase had burnt down, throwing blue uncanny shadows round the bed.

Memory afterwards gave back no more; he was again asleep.

That unconscious sense told him it was a long time before he woke. There were dreams pleasant and dreams foul. The pleasant dreams concerned Jennifer, whom he associated with Regent's Park or being in a theatre. The other sort concerned Chloris, to whom he was held and grasped by some kind of spell.

Then he seemed to be floating up towards wakefulness, with sights and sound at its edges. There was a smash as of china falling, suggesting his own destruction of the washbasin. Heavy footsteps waddled across the floor. He heard a rattle of wooden rings as of window-curtains thrown open.

And he sat up blinking, with a heavy headache.

Through three large windows, facing south, grey light painted the room from over thick countryside and broad river. Against the light, Lady Oldham, in a frilled cap and so hastily dressed that her stays were unfastened, stood with her hands on her hips.

Philip glanced to his left. Trina, the far-from-pretty maid, was standing back against the open door of his dressing-room, a silver tray dangling from one hand. On the floor lay a Sèvres-porcelain chocolate service, unbroken except for the pitcher, which was slowly oozing out chocolate on the carpet.

"I told that odious gel," said Lady Oldham, pointing a finger, "to take heed to the chocolate service. And so she did, too, until you sat up all of a sudden."

Here Lady Oldham waddled towards Philip, her broad face a pasty colour.

"You said you'd do it, Glenarvon. And now, damme, you've done it."

"Done what?"

"*You* don't know?"

"No!"

"In London," said Lady Oldham, "my first footman, Smithers, was outside the door when you said you wanted to wring her neck. When *I* asked you how you could wed me niece, you having a wife already, you showed your teeth and said that could be arranged. Why, damme! Even here last night, they tell me, you struck the poor woman across the face and knocked her down."

But in his heart, even when he demanded again to know what he had done, Philip knew the answer.

"You've strangled your wife, Glenarvon," said Lady Oldham. "Come and see."

ix

"If Thou Dost Love,
Pronounce It Faithfully."

In Chloris's bedroom, with two windows amid the red mirror-panels now having their curtains wide open, both light and thick-scented air seemed to press down on them, to accentuate the room's tawdriness and blotches.

Under the immense canopied bed, the gold-coloured bed-cover had been torn down towards the foot. The bed-clothes were much rumpled and disordered. She lay face downwards across the middle of the bed, her legs towards them and one leg drawn up. Though the rumpled bed-clothes nearly covered her body down its length, they could see the ripped silk night-shift. The head was almost covered, too. But the purple flesh of the neck showed, indented by a section of red cord—undoubtedly cut from the bell-cord in this room—twisted ever tighter and tighter until she died.

Lady Oldham spoke in a harsh voice like a croak.

"Hark'ee, lad!" she said.

Then, for some reason, she kept opening and shutting her hands until she put them behind her.

"I've stood your friend, and you know it. And there's parlous little *I* stick at. But—God damme! Murder!"

"I did not kill her."

"And, if you must kill the woman, why must you kill her so that everybody'd know you did it?"

112

"I did not kill her. Lady Oldham! Have you looked at her face?"

"Well! I—"

"Have you!"

"No. Where was the need?"

Philip, with horror as his only companion, circled round the foot of the bed to the other side. There the dead woman's head rested as she lay partly on one side. He sat down on the edge of the bed. Slipping his left arm under the bed-clothes so that he could reach across and support her back, he gently rolled her over until she lay on her back.

Then he heaved her up in his arms. Her head lolled against him, and the light ran across her face.

It was not Chloris, of course. It was Molly.

She was not pretty now, with her bluish and swollen face, her eyes rigidly half-closed. But Molly, or at least her memory, had become inexpressibly dear. He held her tightly, and put down his forehead against a forehead growing cold.

"Glenarvon!" screamed Lady Oldham. "If anyone should come now, they'd think you'd been a-wenching after her yourself. Let go! Have you no wits?"

"And have you, or your kind, ever any feeling of pity? Ever once? Ever at all?"

"Pity? Damme, I'm as kind-hearted a woman lives! But that slut?"

Philip looked up.

"She was no slut," he said, "and may your tongue rot for saying it. *She* was the one of kind heart; she wished only to comfort those who ill-deserved it. Can anyone say as much for the rest of us?"

Lady Oldham fell back a step, her hand at her capacious bosom.

"Well! Laws-a-me! Here's pretty thanks I get when I come to warn you!"

"To warn me of what?"

" 'Tis nine o'clock, man! They've sent for a magistrate to take you in charge, and he'll be here in an hour."

Gently he put back the hair from Molly's face. He stood up, lowered her, and covered her with a blanket. There should be a great reckoning for this. It took no common strength to wrench those red cords around her neck, to tighten and twist until Molly, kicking violently as the strangled will, presently died.

Meanwhile . . .

His eyes roved round the room. The first thing he noticed was what looked like the long built-out cupboard, papered over, which housed the staircase by which Chloris slipped in or out. Last night he had observed that the door, then partly open, had a stout wooden bolt both inside and outside.

That door was now shut and bolted on the inside.

And he guessed what Molly, whose heart had been won by a kind word, tried to do for him and in despite of Chloris. He knew this as clearly as though, somewhere, it had happened before.

Molly had bolted the door on the inside, so that Chloris should be locked out. Very vividly he recalled that cry or scream in the night, just before the stable-clock struck three. Undoubtedly that was the time of the murder, if—

"One moment, I beg!" he said.

He strode over to the fat candle in its wall-bracket at the left of the bed. When he last saw it, it had burned down to a point which indicated just a little past the hour of two. There was an extinguisher-cap on it now.

Philip reached up and took off the extinguisher-cap. It was burned down but little more than that. Hurrying round to the other side of the bed, he examined the second candle; it had burnt for just the same time.

Molly, then, had put out the lights and gone to bed at, say, two-fifteen or two-twenty. At three o'clock, the hour of suicides and bad dreams, this murderer had caught her in the dark.

Chloris, according to Molly, would not return until about five o'clock. No beatings on the door, no curses or honeyed whispers, could persuade Molly to open that bolted door. Molly was dead, and Chloris inexorably locked out. Chloris could not enter the house; downstairs the doors were barred and chained, the windows locked; she would not dare rouse the household, or she would have to explain her absence.

Therefore, in all probability—

"Madam," Philip said quietly, "where is my wife?"

He sensed rather than saw the formidable old woman start.

"Why, as to that!" Lady Oldham gulped, and pointed towards the bed. "I had thought her *there*. What could I think else?"

"Well, she is not there. Where is she?"

"Can *I* tell?"

"I think you can hazard a guess. After coming here and finding herself unable to make entrance, she took refuge with her friends the Hallidays. Doubtless a note will soon arrive, pleading that she was called abroad by illness or the like. I do not think it probable she would return to Colonel Thornton's."

It was a direct challenge, received with a hissing of breath.

"Then ye *knew!*"

No reply.

"Sometimes I thought ye did know; sometimes I thought ye didn't; 'twas of no purpose to let tongues wag. But ye knew!"

"I learned it all last night."

"Ay, and 'twill hang ye higher still!"

"As— How?"

"Foh! What changes a milksop into a lion, save the knowledge his wife has been cuckolding him for near two

years? You threw Toby Thornton downstairs; you fought
and beat his bully. Afterwards, as your intent was, you did
try to murder your wife."

"Come, madam! And killed my wife's maid instead?"

"Of a surety. You thought Chloris in her rooms. When
Molly would not suffer you to enter, you broke a panel of
the door. See it, there in the dressing-room! Molly, much
afeared, drew the bolt and let you enter. It was dark, as
black as hell. All know how Molly could affect Chloris's
voice. She dared not tell you. But, in the dark, you strangled her in error for your wife. Is aught more plain?"

Philip thrust his hands into the pockets of his crumpled
dressing-gown. He took a turn round the room, and then
faced her.

"Now mark what I say, madam! In this bloody century
of yours—"

Lady Oldham reared up her bust.

"Of mine, d'ye say? Not yours? What clack d'ye speak
now?"

"—in this bloody century, that man is a fool who lets himself be caught into the cruelty and stupidity of the law. And
I will not endure it."

"Then what can you do, pray?"

"I can cut and run; and let them find me if they can!"

Lady Oldham's pasty face sagged, and she clasped her
hands together.

"Lad," she pleaded, "be advised! There's no Newgate
awaiting you. A room at the Tower; a trial before the House
of Lords. Carry yourself well, and they'll acquit you.
There'll be little enough scandal then."

"You fear scandal, I apprehend?"

"God damme, who don't?" Lady Oldham was shaking all
over. "If you fly from the magistrate—"

"In passing, Lady Oldham, who sent for a magistrate to
take me in charge?"

"Dick Thornton."

"*Dick* Thornton? The son? Is *he* here?"

"He has been here," admitted Lady Oldham, "since very late last night. *I* knew nothing of this. Master Dick had determined to follow his father to the Oaks, it would appear, and stopped here in case Colonel Thornton should have stopped here."

"Well?"

"He was drunk," said Lady Oldham, with her eyes sliding away. "A footman named Holdsworth persuaded him it were best to lie the night here."

"Lest he interrupt his father's assignation? I am overjoyed, madam, at this concern for the poor colonel."

"Howbeit!" snarled Lady Oldham. "He was put to bed in the room over this one. At half-past eight this morning, Trina fetched up your wife's morning chocolate. She knocked at the corridor door to the bedroom; 'twas locked, and none answered. But the corridor door to your wife's dressing-room, this was unlocked. She found—"

"Yes, yes! But you were saying?"

"Chocolate dishes of Sèvres work," said Lady Oldham, outraged. "The wretched gel didn't drop 'em *then*. Lawk, no! She must come a-screaming and a-flying to me, and fetched me out half clad. Down the stairs, dressed and cheerful, came Master Dick. When *he* hears what's amiss: 'God,' says Master Dick, 'Glenarvon's done it.' And downstairs he bolted to pen a note to his friend Mr. Avery, the magistrate, some six miles beyond the Oaks on the river road. A groom carried the note, and one to his father too, not five minutes ago."

Time was passing; time grew ever more urgent.

Philip went to the corridor door out of the bedroom. It was now unlocked. He opened it, and went out into the big, dusky, white-painted hall.

"Hopwith!" he shouted. "Hopwith!"

He could not conjecture where the little elderly man had been hiding. Hopwith, as placid as ever, appeared at his elbow.

"Hopwith! Did you by chance overhear what Lady Oldham and I were saying?"

"Well, my lord, you and her ladyship did not trouble to speak in whispers."

"Do *you* believe I killed that woman?"

"No, my lord. Nor any woman."

"Good! Now I travel to London, and in great haste. Have we a light carriage here, perhaps a gig?"

"If I may suggest it, your lordship will travel much faster on horseback. Your own mare, Folly, can—"

"I can't ride horseback; I never learned. But as a boy I was taught to drive. Have we a trap or a gig?"

For the first time, as Hopwith shied a little, he saw a suspicion in the old man's eyes that his master really might be insane.

"There is in truth a gig, my lord," replied Hopwith, becoming himself again, "and a fine horse to draw it."

"Bid them make it ready as soon as may be. And a mouthful of breakfast in the dining-room. Meanwhile—"

"My lord! I must dress you properly! And the shaving? I alone can do it."

"The shaving must wait. I'll dress myself, if I can remember how to put the damned clothes on. Stay! Who are my bankers?"

"As always, my lord. Hookson's, between the Temple gates, and over against Mrs. Salmon's Waxwork."

"And—ah, yes," said Philip. "Is Mr. Richard Thornton," he added with pleasure, "still in the house?"

"No, my lord. As soon as he heard your lordship was risen, Mr. Thornton said he must take a stroll in the garden, and dashed most hurriedly from the house."

"A pity," said Philip, and dashed for his own bedroom.

There, after dousing his face and head into cool water from the ewer to help cure his headache, he rummaged in cupboards and drawers for clothes.

He could find no underwear; nobody seemed to wear it. But he found a tolerable shirt, with low collar and neckcloth. He found a somewhat old-style coat, curving down past shoulders and waist and thighs into a tail—dark-blue, with brass buttons down one side. He chose the red Tory waistcoat, the white doeskin breeches with short silk stockings attached to them, and heavy top-boots.

Though dressing was not so difficult, the neckcloth and the boots were devilish. He had no notion how to tie the former, so he made an artistic flourish and a hard knot, slipping the ends under his waistcoat. With the boots he stamped and danced and swore until they fitted him.

No very long time, that! Now only a comb, to give his hair what curves and twirls he could recall on others' heads and—

The door opened, and Chloris walked in.

Her turban and two plumes were gone, her face washed clean of cosmetics. A long grey cloak, ankle-length and fastened at the neck, concealed her gown of the night before. As she closed the door behind her and swept into the middle of the room, Philip passed her without a word. He began to comb his hair by the wall mirror over the chest of drawers beside the door.

"Philip," she began.

"Yes, my love?"

"If only you had waited!"

"Was I too precipitous, my dear, in killing your maid?"

Chloris, ignoring this, stamped her foot.

"If only you had *listened!*" she cried. "I told you there was a reason why we must not be together last night. And there was! There was!"

From the corner of his eye he watched her face in the

mirror. And he could have sworn she breathed sincerity. Her face, without cosmetics, was as he had seen it early yesterday evening—warm with the appeal of the long hazel eyes.

"I have but only five minutes returned," said Chloris, lowering her eyes, "from staying the night with my good friend Mrs. Halliday." Then her mood changed. "Nay, no lies!" she snapped, with a disgust of which he would never have believed her capable. "Doubtless they have already told you of . . . of . . ."

"Of your relations with the good Colonel Thornton? Yes, Molly told me."

"*Molly?*"

"Yes. No matter how or why."

Chloris kept her eyelids lowered, though colour crept up into her face.

"Now hear me!" she said in a low voice. "I went to the Oaks last night. That is truth. But it was for one reason only. It was to tell Toby Thornton that our—our relations, as you call them, were finished, ended, done with forever! Do you fancy there was love-making? God! It was a Billingsgate-match while he shouted at me and I screamed till near four in the morning, as any servant there may attest. Can you credit me?"

Philip put down the comb on the chest of drawers and turned round.

"I can credit," he replied politely, "that it must be a devilish odd household. Or is Thornton's wife as complacent as *I* am thought to be?"

"His *wife?*"

"Yes."

And now in Chloris's eyes, as he had seen it in the eyes of old Hopwith, flickered that suspicion as to his sanity.

"You profess not to know," she cried, "that his wife has been dead for years?"

"And as your husband, Chloris, have I ever been told *anything?*"

It was invented on the spur of the moment, not only to turn away suspicion, but deliberately and coldly to stop her dangerous appeal. Chloris hesitated, and pressed her hands to the sides of her face. Tears—real or easily assumed—glimmered on her lashes.

"Yes, you are right. Philip! If I have done you wrong or shame—"

"God's death, am I concerned with that?"

"Concerned with—"

"Any fool may hold your body. Who holds your heart?"

In the little space of silence, sunshine pressed through the grey air outside the southern windows. Chloris looked at the floor.

"I have told you that. I think you know."

"Good!" he retorted briskly. "Then I will apply a small test."

"Test?"

"Yes. I am leaving here—running away, if you prefer the term. I shall be in hiding until I can prove who killed that girl, and I challenge the present-day police to find me. Outside this house, now, is a gig which can carry two persons. Will you go with me?"

Again a silence. Chloris seemed about to cry yes, when another thought struck her.

"Philip! They may think—"

"Yes," he agreed. "They may well think you aided and abetted me in the murder of Molly—"

"*Philip!*"

"—and are near to being as guilty as I am. It will mean sensation, scandal, doggerel in the worst news-sheets. It will certainly mean danger; perhaps suffering as well. Will you go?"

"I can't! I daren't! 'Tis too much to ask, and you have no right to ask it!"

"None whatever. Madam, good day."

He opened the door, went out into the corridor, and closed the door firmly.

For an instant he heard her run forward, impulsively; then, as her mind clearly painted all the things she most abhorred, Chloris stopped. There was no time to think of her now. Hopwith was hurrying up the stairs.

"There is ample time for breakfast," said Hopwith, "if you be quick." Reaching the top of the stairs, he regarded Philip in consternation. "My lord! You have forgot the ribbon to tie your hair in a queue! And you have forgot your hat!"

"Upon my word, Hopwith, the hair did seem a trifle scraggly at the back. But no matter for the hat! I never wear a hat anyway."

Hopwith, though he did not much betray it, was as much shocked as though Philip had said he never wore his knee-breeches. And Philip, better accustomed to Hopwith now, guessed the old man's feelings and cursed himself.

He was blurting out too many anachronisms, both of speech and custom. He must cease to do it; he must not become nervous at the approach of danger.

"As also, my lord," pursued Hopwith, "I must pack your portmanteau. Pray, my lord, don't, *don't* appear downstairs with your hair untied."

Portmanteau! He had forgotten luggage, too.

Hopwith, in opening the door, disclosed Chloris. With a bow and a "By your leave, your ladyship," Hopwith scurried to work while Chloris remained motionless, breast heaving.

A bumping noise, from somewhere at the back of the hall, made Philip glance over his shoulder. The door opposite Chloris's bedroom door was open. Two housemaids were scuffling at a corded portmanteau, which they lifted and carried towards the front of the hall.

After them, rather defiantly and with head raised, walked Jennifer.

She was dressed, as though for travelling, in a white muslin dress sprigged with blue, and a grey pelisse drawn over her arms and shoulders. Her long-sided blue bonnet, with a knot of grey ribbons above the forehead, was bound to her head with a gauzy scarf tied under the chin.

He did not speak until he was almost face to face with her at the head of the stairs.

"Jenny?"

"Yes, Lord Glenarvon?" said Jenny, without looking at him.

"Where are you going?"

"Hopwith," she informed him, "was not the only person who heard your words to Lady Oldham. I am going with you. That is, if you desire me to do so?"

"Of course I do! But I can't involve you in this! The danger—"

Jennifer raised her head. Her mutinous under-lip contrasted with the expression in the dark-lashed grey eyes.

"Did I quit your side when you were in danger—the other time?" she asked. Her head went higher. "I further propose to become—what's the word?—your mopsy, and to make no secret of the fact."

Jennifer curtseyed. A shadow drifted across her eyes; when she spoke again, in quotation, it was wry, humorous self-mockery.

" 'If thou dost love,' " she said, " 'pronounce it faithfully. Or, if thou think'st I am too quickly won, I'll frown, and be perverse, and say thee nay. . . .' "

The beautiful voice, with its throb which could stir him

so much, died away. Jennifer woke up and made a small girl's gesture of wrath.

"I *will* go!" she cried.

"But last night you as good as told me you never wanted to see me again."

"Oh, why *must* you remember the things I say when you've hurt me and I'm in a beast's temper? Please forget I said that. May I go?"

"On one condition. That you take back the diamond ring."

"I hoped you would say that," replied Jennifer, looking away. "But I didn't dare ask."

"Jenny . . ."

"My lord!" interrupted the voice of Hopwith, almost under his ear. "My lord, the hair-ribbon! Have the goodness to remain still while I tie your hair."

"Oh, God damn it," shouted Philip, "why must all great moments in life be broken by some practical drivel or other?"

He saw laughter bubbling up in Jenny's face, and glared at her.

"Very well!" he said. "Tie the cursed queue if you must. But give me back my purse: the purse you said you were carrying."

"Your lordship, I fear," replied Hopwith, deftly transferring the purse from his coat-tail pocket to Philip's, "will not find it heavy. Still, it should suffice if you drive straightway to Hookson's."

Deftly he finished tying the queue, and stepped back to admire his work.

"As to the hat, my lord—"

"The ring!" said Philip.

From the top of the stairs he looked forward at the open door of his bedroom. He raced down the corridor, into the room, and again came face to face with Chloris.

Neither of them spoke. Neither of them moved. Chlo-

ris's expression—well, he had seen it once before, at Lady
Oldham's, when Chloris sat naked in the yellow-upholstered
chair, and looked at him steadily. But he could not remember just when.

Instead he swung round to the chest of drawers beside
him, opened the top drawer, and began a search which was
first casual and then frantic. He could swear he had put the
diamond ring somewhere here. But he couldn't find it.

"My lord!" said that pursuing voice of Hopwith in the
doorway. "I fear—"

"Wait! Wait!"

A dozen times Philip's hand had brushed the case of pistols bearing his own name. In a last effort, as a man looks
in some place he knows to be impossible, he opened the case.

And the ring was there. It lay glittering against ruby-
coloured velvet, between the two pistols with their beautiful
balance, their mother-of-pearl crust down the stocks, their
hair-triggers that would fire at the lightest touch. In some
freakish absence of mind he must have put it there himself.
As he snatched it up, he felt a stab of his old headache.

"My lord! You must have at least ten minutes' start before the magistrate arrives with his constables."

"They are sending constables? Am I so dangerous a character as that?"

"Report," Hopwith said dryly, "hath it very much so. My
lord! Be quick!"

Philip bowed to Chloris as he went out.

"Again good-bye, madam."

"Foh!" murmured Chloris, with lowered eyelids and a curling smile. "We shall be together again. And soon."

This time Hopwith was careful to close the door.

"The young lady's portmanteau," he reported, "is stowed
away in the gig. Your own will be packed and placed there
immediately. The young lady is downstairs."

"Hopwith! Miss Baird! We must order some breakfast for her."

"I had already commanded it, my lord," said Hopwith, with his eye on a corner of the ceiling, "when I commanded yours."

The dining-room, if Philip remembered correctly from last night, was on the left at the foot of the stairs. This time he had not forgotten the watch he found ticking in the drawer. It was cumbersome, and felt like half a brick in his waistcoat pocket. He was taking it out and opening it as he raced into the sun-flooded dining-room.

There he found Jennifer looking rather apprehensively from a long mahogany table, heavily silver-laden, to an immense mahogany sideboard as heavily food-laden.

"Phil—" she began.

"Good God," he said, "Hopwith was right. When Lady Oldham woke me, she said it was nine o'clock and that the magistrate would be here in an hour. If we're to have ten minutes' start of the beak—and don't correct my language; Sir John Fielding was called the beak years ago—we must hurry like the devil. It's nearly a quarter to ten. Eat!"

"Darling, that's just it. I'm trying to be as hardened as any woman. But I don't think I can face cold roast beef and a pint of small-beer at breakfast."

Philip, putting away the watch, inspected the table.

"There's tea, though. Hot and black. And here"—he lifted a silver dish-cover—"here, by all the gods, is buttered toast. I had never discovered they knew the witching secret of it. Tea, Jenny!"

Jennifer picked up a cup and saucer. Suddenly the cup and saucer began to clatter and tremble in her hands; she turned her head away.

"Jenny! You are not to be alarmed. What is there to frighten you now?"

"I—I know." She moistened her lips. "It's this house. If we were in London, or even on the edge of it, I'm certain we could make our escape. But, as long as we're here, I feel that something or somebody will catch us before we can leave."

"If you feel as strongly as that, we can leave at this minute."

"Yes! May we?" She looked back at him with intensity. "In two minutes we could be off in that gig."

"We can. And we will," said a very worried man. "It's only that you must not become frightened at shadows in your own mind. Lady Oldham said ten o'clock; there was no reason for her to lie. The magistrate and two bruisers are on their way. Who or what else could stop us?"

"I can't tell. But don't laugh at me: I *know*."

"Know what?"

"That, unless we leave this house immediately—"

Some distance behind Philip's back there was a discreet cough.

He had not heard the door open and close behind him. Sunlight from the three large windows, facing front, momentarily blinded him as it kindled a lofty room with walls painted light-green and with Ionic pillars, fluted in gold and white, half imbedded in the walls.

Then he saw the long nose, the rather unpleasant face, the grey-and-gold livery of the first footman, Holdsworth.

"I ask your pardon, my lord, but there are two gentlemen to see you."

Philip, who had been pouring tea from the very heavy urn, splashed milk into the cup.

"I can't see—" he was beginning. Then, as he lifted the cup to his lips, his eyes narrowed. "Who are these two gentlemen?"

"One is Colonel Thornton, my lord, who presents his compliments. Colonel Thornton bids me add that the other

gentleman is Sir Benedict Skene, who is to act as," the footman hesitated, "as his second."

"*No!*" cried Jennifer.

Philip, taking a sip of very hot tea, eyed Holdsworth over
the rim of the cup. He smiled, not very pleasantly.

"Beg the gentlemen to walk in."

X

"Shall It Be Pistols, Gentlemen?"

The empty cup and saucer so clattered together in Jennifer's hand that she put them down on the table.

"Phil! If this is what I think it is, you're mad! The magistrate will be here to arrest you before—"

"With luck, perhaps not. Jenny, do you trust me?"

"You know I do!"

"Then trust me now."

"Are you a good pistol-shot?"

Philip looked wry. "With a Service revol—that is to say, with a pistol—I was never more than average."

"Do you know swordplay?"

"To the best of my knowledge, I have never touched a foil or a sabre in my life."

"Darling! This man is a famous duellist with both! You haven't a chance!"

"Oh, some chance. You forget, Jenny—"

He was interrupted by the entrance of Holdsworth, who with much formality announced Colonel Thornton and Sir Benedict Skene, and hastily retired.

Colonel Thornton, in honour of the occasion, again wore full-dress uniform, speckless from each curl of his powdered head to the gold cords across his scarlet coat and the gold-hilted dress-sword bumping against jack-boots polished like a mirror. Though he spoke with some politeness, he was hollowed-eyed and angry.

His companion, clearly a retired naval officer in semi-official dress, was a stout man, half bald and good-natured. His blue coat, with buff facings and buttons, disclosed a buff waistcoat over white breeches and white stockings ending in blunt buckled shoes. Though he must have been a friend of Thornton, he eyed that gentleman with no favour.

"Your servant, gentlemen," bowed Philip over the teacup. He glanced at Sir Benedict Skene, and then at Jennifer. "Sir Benedict Skene, Miss Jennifer Baird."

"That's not necessary," snapped Colonel Thornton.

"Your pardon. It is most necessary," said Philip.

"Then *Rear-Admiral* Sir Benedict Skene," said the colonel, with a sneer.

Jennifer murmured and curtseyed, while Sir Benedict, after bowing as low as his corporation would allow, gave Colonel Thornton a glare of even less favour.

"And now, my dear," Philip smiled at Jennifer, "if you will leave us for a little while? And trust me?"

Jennifer marched out with her head high, and Philip's heart glowed to see it.

Colonel Thornton, eyeing the door as it closed, strolled forward with his thumbs hooked in his white-and-gold sword-belt.

" 'Morning, Glenarvon," he said casually. "See you brought your willing dame with you after all?"

"Is it so happy a time for *you*, Colonel Thornton, to discuss a willing dame?"

The colonel's face seemed to cave in, and his hand flew to his sword-hilt.

In very truth Chloris must have broken with him, and broken forever. Chloris had been telling the truth: all night she had screamed at him, adding such taunts as scratched his vanity raw. Thornton, on this morning of all mornings, was in no mood for anything but murder.

"Hey, now, hard your helm!" blurted out Sir Benedict

Skene, and bristled. "Never had the pleasure of meeting you before, Lord Glenarvon."

"The pleasure, sir," bowed Philip, "is entirely mine. I have heard much," he lied, "of your distinguished career, to say nothing of your fairness both as second and as arbitrator."

"Hem! Well!" said Sir Benedict, much pleased but so fussed that his half-bald head appeared to steam. "But this is all irregular. Irregular, damme if it ain't! A principal calls on a principal, *and* fetches his second with him. If that's not irregular, what is?"

"Let's cut the cackle," snapped Colonel Thornton in a different voice. "You know why we're here, Glenarvon. I'll pass over any question of who's challenger and who's challenged. What's it to be: swords or pistols?"

"Pistols," said Philip instantly.

"Good! We brought both, whatever your choice might be. I'll get—"

"No!" said Philip. "Since I am the challenged party, because of your attempted blow last night, you will use my pistols or none at all."

"As you like. There is much open ground hereabouts. The only remaining question," smiled Colonel Thornton, "is your own second. There's no gentleman in the house."

"There is your son. That is, if you call—"

"Dick," snapped Colonel Thornton, "is at home, where he should be. In any event, he can't act as second against his father. No; it is very simple. You have only to send a message to Chelsea half a mile away, to Major Thorpe or Mr. Hewelett or any of your friends, and the second can be here well within half an hour."

"Yes," said Philip. "So he can! Sir Benedict!"

He put the cup and saucer down on the table, again marvelling that his hands did not tremble. They would do so, presently.

"I am bound to tell you," he went on, "that this man does not wish and has never wished for a duel."

"Are you questioning?"

"Never your courage, Colonel Thornton. Only your small-minded caution. Sir Benedict!"

"Eh, lad? That's to say, under favour, my lord?"

"It is now"—Philip took out his watch, opened it, glanced at it, and replaced it—"it is now ten minutes to ten. I am bound to tell you, sir, that a justice and two constables are on their way to arrest me. They ride from the other direction, west. Long before I can procure a second, they will be here to take me. Colonel Thornton knew as much; his son sent him a note. And he might be ridiculed in his club if he shot such a pigeon as myself."

Colonel Thornton, though politely refraining from a jeer, laughed without noise.

"Then you cry off?" he asked. "All brag, all bounce, but you cry off!"

"I think not," said Philip. "I will meet you with pistols, according to Sir Benedict's ruling as arbitrator, if you accept my conditions as to time and place."

"What time? What place?"

"Here," said Philip, "and now. In this room, before anyone can arrive."

In the silence that followed, he could hear the watch ticking. How fast did the law ride? How far might "ten o'clock" be expanded, in one direction or the other?

"This table," and doggedly Philip tapped the mahogany, "is something over eight feet long. It is in the middle of the room, and it can be cleared."

"You suggest—" began Sir Benedict Skene.

"I suggest, sir, that Colonel Thornton and I stand at either end of the table. The loaded pistols, muzzle to muzzle and handles towards each of us, shall lie in the centre. When you drop the handkerchief, we pick up the pistols and fire."

Rear-Admiral Sir Benedict Skene hesitated. But his bulging brown eye slid up sideways towards Philip, with a look of something like respect.

Still without speaking, he went with his rolling walk towards the nearest of the three great windows. There he stood with his legs wide apart, staring out with his hand under his coat-tail and flapping it.

Time was passing, time was passing!

"Sir!" Philip appealed. "In the absence of another second, is this not entirely according to the duelling code?"

"Ay, it is that!" roared Sir Benedict, swinging round on one leg. "And I've seen it done. You apprehend, 'tis certain death for one or both? Do you, Colonel Thornton, favour firing point-blank across a table?"

Thornton did not favour it; so much was clear. But the veins stood out in his forehead under the white powder. For Philip's death, or Philip's capture, he would have charged a breach single-handed.

"Agreed!" he said curtly.

"Very well. You, Lord Glenarvon—?"

"Since neither the ladies nor the servants must know of this," said Philip, "I will go upstairs myself to fetch the pistols. In the meantime . . ."

"Come!" drawled Colonel Thornton, and smiled. "Now I remember it, there was a gig prepared outside for Lord Glenarvon and his woman. Should he go from the room unattended, it is in my mind—"

" 'Fore gad, Thornton," yelled the retired admiral, "I make no doubt it is in your mind. But it's not in the mind of any gentleman. Glenarvon, pray fetch the pistols!"

"I was about to suggest," said Philip, smiling back at Colonel Thornton, "that Sir Benedict should accompany me. He should judge the worth of the pistols ere he pronounces them fit. In the meantime, Colonel, will you oblige me by

ringing the bell and having the table cleared? You will find
refreshment on the sideboard, should you need it."

A moment later, he and the fuming Skene were out in the
hall. Hopwith was there, trembling all over. Jennifer was
there, not trembling, with her hand on Hopwith's shoulder.
Philip did not speak; he merely smiled reassuringly and put
a finger to his lips for silence.

Also in silence, Philip and Sir Benedict Skene went upstairs and into Philip's now-deserted bedroom. Bringing out
the box, he put it on top of the chest of drawers.

"The box is dusty, sir. But you will observe that the pistols are well-polished and fragrant. Also, there is a powder-
flask and a supply of ball in the pocket under the lid. Do
you find the pistols worthy, sir?"

Sir Benedict weighed one in his hand. There was a muffled melodious click as he drew back the hammer.

"Ay, they're beauties! I mind—"

"And now, sir, I have a request to make." Philip's heart
jumped up into his throat. "I ask you to hold secret what I
say, provided it be such a matter as any man of honour may
hold secret."

"Ah! Then there's something? Speak it!"

"You, as arbitrator, will load both pistols?"

"Ay, to be sure! What then?"

"I request, sir, that the pistol you give to Colonel Thornton shall be fully loaded, with powder, wad, and ball. I request that the pistol you give me shall be unloaded, save
perhaps for a paper wad."

Sir Benedict, reaching out for the other pistol, seemed to
roll round the back of his neck on the edge of the chest of
drawers as his bulging brown eyes came up.

"Lad! This madness o' yours—!"

"Sir! Have I the right, according to the duelling code, to
demand an unloaded pistol?"

"Ay, ye have." Sir Benedict swallowed. "A dozen times

they've done it. A fella don't want to hurt his man; he's
afeard the hair-trigger will jar and go off before he can lift to
fire in the air. Both seconds are obliged to know the secret,
and the other principal mustn't know. But, damme, man!
That was in a field; thirty-six paces apart; every chance the
other'd miss. Here you'll be firing all but straight into each
other's chests."

Again Philip drew out and consulted his watch. It was
six minutes to ten.

"Sir! Have I the right to call for an unloaded pistol?"

"Yes!"

"Then I do ask it, sir, upon your own honour."

The fat admiral, in his square-toed shoes with silver buckles, launched a savage kick at one leg of the chest of drawers. Afterwards he drew himself up.

"Lord Glenarvon." Out went his chest. " 'Tis none of my
business to question your motives or tactics. I'll load the
pistols here, if it please you. Have you an old news-sheet I
can tear up for wadding?"

"I saw one here somewhere. I'll bring it."

"Good. The powder is bone dry; that's as well. We need
a better weapon than these cursed flintlocks. And, by the
weight, there'll be no mistakening the weapons when I carry
'em downstairs. The news-sheet, Lord Glenarvon!"

He was incredibly swift and deft: with the powder-flask,
with the greased bullet, with the wad and the little ramrod.
Into the other pistol he pressed only a section of the *Morning Post*. Within thirty seconds they were going downstairs.

No stir seemed in the house. Nobody looked out at a door;
no servant scurried in corridor or foyer. But the whisper had
crept round; not a soul but knew. Widestairs was like a
house tunnelled and mined underneath, waiting to explode.

Only Hopwith, almost pitiable in his faithfulness, waited
in the lower foyer. The immense front door stood wide
open. Down the very broad stairs leading to the entrance,

past the wide gravelled drive branching east and west, stood
a hooded gig with blue-and-yellow wheel-spokes. A groom
held the head of its restive bay horse. And in the gig, her
hands in a muff, Jennifer sat waiting, as though already she
knew the outcome and remained unconcerned.

After all, Philip thought, *she's seen me fight often enough.*
But not like this.

In the dining-room, in which the table had been cleared
so that its mahogany surface gleamed dark under polish, the
air had turned grey. In that flighty weather, on the twenty-
first of April, the sun had again squeezed behind cloud.

Colonel Thornton, perfectly calm, was walking slowly up
and down. But he had removed his sword-belt and sabre,
his stiff scarlet coat with the braid, and his high black stock
as well. Over all these, on a chair, hung his white cross-belt
with the pouch.

"No call of foul?" he enquired, lifting his eyebrows and
touching his ruffled shirt.

"None at all," replied Philip, stripping off his own coat
and waistcoat. "I follow you."

"The Frenchies are right about one thing," Colonel Thornton remarked casually. "They say our cavalry jackets are so
tight-fitting we can't lift our sword-arms in a charge. It's
true, egad!"

"Gentlemen!" snapped Sir Benedict.

At the harsh note in his voice, the nerve-strain which
marks preliminaries for murder, the two contestants grew
rigid.

"These pistols are now loaded and ready. I see little difference in the light, as it is. Still! As challenger, Colonel,
you have the choice of position."

Colonel Thornton strolled to the south end of the table,
his back to the three great windows, and pressed against it.

"Well!" he said. "Have me back to what light there is."

Philip, his thighs and legs feeling light, went to the north end of the table and stood there.

The high Adam fireplace, of white marble, was in the east wall at Philip's left. In the back wall, some distance behind him, stood the sideboard still laden with food and drink, and, against the wall above it, hung an oil-painting of Madonna with Child. The two contestants were so close together that they could have leaned across the table and strangled each other.

Sir Benedict Skene, the loaded pistol in his left hand and the empty one in his right, stood with his back to the fireplace.

"Now, gentlemen—"

"Get on with it!" said Colonel Thornton, out of the side of his mouth.

Philip said nothing.

Sir Benedict took the loaded pistol, and put it on the table with its butt towards Colonel Thornton and its muzzle towards Philip. The empty pistol he placed opposite it, the muzzle only an inch or two from Colonel Thornton's own pistol.

Then Sir Benedict took up a position with his back to the empty fireplace.

"Next!" he said. "Each of you will pick up his pistol, and satisfy himself it is loaded according to his own wishes. Lord Glenarvon?"

Philip did as he was told.

"En-entirely so," he said.

"Colonel Thornton?"

"Yes, well enough," replied Colonel Thornton, weighing the weapon in his hand and admiring the mother-of-pearl inlay along the stock. "By Jove, yes!"

"Now, gentlemen, you will cock your pistols."

There was a soft, muffled, eerie-sounding click as two hammers were drawn back.

"Place the weapons," said Sir Benedict, "back on the table exactly where they were before. If there is any difference of position, I must correct it."

There was no difference; only a rattle on wood as the pistols were placed back.

"Finally!" said Sir Benedict, producing a very large red handkerchief with white spots all over it. Seen here, the handkerchief appeared grotesque; it was like a doll in a room of death, but nobody commented.

"Finally," repeated Sir Benedict, "I will count to three. At the third count, I will drop this handkerchief."

Unexpected, capricious as always, the April sun flooded out from behind clouds. Its light, thin but very bright, ran along pale-green walls and half-columns fluted in gilt and white. It dazzled across polished mahogany, and straight up into Philip's eyes.

Then Colonel Thornton drew back his lips over well-fitting false-teeth.

"You're done, Glenarvon," he whispered. "This time, God damme, you're done!"

"Colonel Thornton. Silence!"

The colonel laughed.

Still Philip did not speak.

"But, at the count of three," continued steady-speaking Sir Benedict, "you need not distract your eye by watching this handkerchief. When I say 'three,' you will pick up your pistols and use them as you see fit. Are you ready, then? *One!*"

You could almost feel the silence of the house. Colonel Thornton, thighs flat against the table, measured distances and watched the sun on his opponent's face.

"*Two!*"

Sir Benedict, alone of the three, showed moisture on his forehead as he held out the handkerchief and looked at the empty pistol in front of Philip.

Philip blinked and shifted his right leg a little, but not much.

"My lord!" suddenly screamed the voice of Hopwith, outside the door. "The justice and his men! They are—"

"*Three!*"

The spotted handkerchief fluttered down.

Already Philip Clavering had made a move of such blinding speed that Sir Benedict hardly followed it. Philip's body and right hand streaked out. He did not touch the pistol-handle; his hand flashed past it, gripped the steel muzzle of his own pistol, and swung it high.

Colonel Thornton had also lunged. He caught the butt of his own weapon. He was lifting elbow to fire when the butt of Philip's pistol crashed down on his thin-haired, powdered head.

And so the Colonel was a second-and-a-half too late to fire at all. But his elbow banged the table. His pistol exploded, firing wild. The heavy bullet chopped off a corner of the mantelpiece; then, with a twang like a high harpstring, it flew sideways and half-stuck in the wall beneath the painting of Madonna with Child.

Colonel Thornton fell face down on the table, with his black ribbon-bow neatly tied and an ooze of blood through his hair-powder. His pistol rattled on mahogany beside him. But his ruffled shirt slid sideways. He rolled off the edge of the table and fell heavily on his back, mouth open but high nose still dominant. Layers of the smoke from black-powder, so harsh as to be nearly unbreathable, stretched out across his body.

"Oh, God sink me," whispered Sir Benedict Skene.

Philip flung his empty pistol on the table.

"Have no fear, sir," he snapped. "Colonel Thornton is unhurt; I did not strike to kill. But you now see why I was compelled to use an empty pistol?"

Sir Benedict, purple in the face, could not speak at all.

And Philip, now the ordeal was finished and the reaction had come, Philip was trembling at the knees; sweat ran down him; he himself could scarcely speak.

"If I struck him on the head with a loaded weapon, the hair-trigger would have jarred and fired. As his did. And, from the manner in which I was obliged to hold it, my own bullet would have been fired back into my own body."

The dining-room door burst open. Hopwith, carrying a cloak and hat, gave only one glance at the beaten colonel.

"My lord," he cried, "the magistrate—"

"Yes," Philip agreed bitterly. "Against all Jenny's warnings, I put it off too long."

All his anger against Colonel Thornton boiled up again.

"Now hark'ee, sir," he said to Sir Benedict. "You have been a true sportsman, and I thank you. But, ere you begin prating of the duelling code, I would ask but a question." He pointed at Thornton. "Did that man have fair play?"

"Ay!" gulped Sir Benedict. "Fair play, to be sure, but the code—?"

"Who held the advantage? He or I?"

"He did, granted. But—"

"Then that is all of interest for me. No, stay! Once too often he has used his sneers and his attempts at humiliation. Should ever I meet him again, and wherever it may be, I swear before God I will kill him. Tell him this, when he awakes; and let him look to it henceforward!"

Philip whipped round.

"Now, Hopwith! The magistrate! The manacles! Where are they?"

"My lord, I have been attempting to tell you. Mr. Avery is not yet arrived."

"Not—arrived?"

"They would have been here long ere this. Howbeit, the magistrate's horse cast a shoe. Young Jared, on the roof with a telescope, can see them at Miller's Smithy. If you hurry and hurry and hurry, you have at least a chance to escape them even yet."

Into Philip's hands he thrust the cloak and hat. Also, in secret, he conveyed a folded note which Philip slipped into his waistcoat pocket.

"God bless you, Hopwith!"

"God speed you, my lord."

Out he ran, into the perfumed April day, with heart high again, to Jennifer and to the waiting gig. Indeed, it was an hour and a half before all his plans were again upset.

xi

"'Speed!' Echoed the Wall to Us Galloping Through."

Over half a mile of woods and trees, on the road by the river, the gig with the blue-and-yellow wheels flew behind a skittish bay mare at a high-stepping trot.

They raced into Cheyne Walk, the outermost street in the village of Chelsea. There were houses here, but only one line of houses on the left-hand side; the rest, beyond, was no more than a sea of meadows and of trees coming into leaf.

Jennifer, attempting to balance herself in an effort to stand up in the gig, looked round in bewilderment.

"But it's *all* country!" she said. "Have you any idea where we are?"

Philip lifted the reins and flicked them sharply on the horse's back.

"Roughly, yes. This is Cheyne Walk, and it leads into—"

"Royal Hospital Avenue, isn't it? Straight up towards the Chelsea Veterans' Hospital?"

"It will be called that in a hundred and fifty years. At the moment, according to Horwood's Plan of London in 1795, the whole street is called Paradise Row. Keep your eye out for white signboards stuck up at the roadside. If we get lost now—!"

Jenny, instead, was leaning out past the side of the gig and looking through the dust behind them.

"But that's just it! We're not going fast enough! Phil,

142

hadn't you better use your whip? They'll catch us at any minute."

"I don't think they will."

"And why not?" demanded Jennifer, turning round again.

"I seem to have acquired," he answered, and showed his teeth, "some considerable reputation as a desperado. They won't think two constables are enough to handle me."

"And they won't be, either," Jennifer retorted bitterly. "Phil, why *must* you take such insane risks whenever you get angry? Why *must* you show off your speed and timing by whacking Colonel Thornton over the head with that pistol, with the sun in your eyes and him a dead shot?"

"How the devil do you know what happened? You were sitting out in the gig!"

Jennifer looked at him past the long sides of her bonnet.

"Oh, darling, do you think I'm made of stone? Of course I ran out and peeped through the front windows. Phil, if I didn't care for you so much—" Jennifer fixed her teeth in her lower lip. "But what's this about nobody catching us? Why won't they catch us?"

"Because they'll think of a better plan. Jenny, I'll give you five to one that in another minute, perhaps two, a horseman will overtake us. He'll wear very plain clothes, and he'll ride a very fast horse. He'll fly past at the gallop, not even glancing at us."

As though uncanny prophecies were again becoming true, Jennifer could already hear the galloping hoof-beats behind them.

"But who—?"

"One of the magistrate's men. He'll ride straight to the chief magistrate at Bow Street. And the redbreasts will be out against us half an hour before we can get there."

"The redbreasts?"

"The Bow Street Runners! They're all armed with pistols, and they're all ugly customers. In fact—"

The heavy thud of hoof-beats grew louder and louder behind them. Clouds of dust billowed into their faces, making Jennifer close her eyes, as a horseman with rusty coat-tail buttons, bent low over the back of a fine Arab mare, flashed past at the gallop.

"In, for a fiver!" muttered Philip. "We haven't a chance against that speed."

"But Phil! I think everybody knows where we're going. Between you and Hopwith, you were shouting it all over the house: Hookson's Bank."

"I know I did," he said grimly. "That's why we're not going anywhere near the Bank."

"Then what—where *are* we going?"

"Straight to Sheridan at Drury Lane."

For the first time Philip drew the whip from its upright socket and lashed. The mare flew forward. Philip was half-standing up and peering towards the right.

"Yes, this is Paradise Row," he said. "There, beyond the brick wall on the right, are Sir Hans Sloane's botanical gardens. It's a comfort to reflect they'll still be there when we've been born and grown up. The next turning, I am sure, is to the left. Unless I can reach Hyde Park Turnpike before they turn out the Horse Patrol, then we're done. But I don't believe they will. A dozen redbreasts will watch Hookson's Bank until their necks are stiff."

"Phil," observed Jennifer in a small voice, and folded her hands in her lap.

"Yes?"

"You say we're going to Mr. Sheridan's at Drury Lane?"

"Yes! Can you think of a better place to hide than in an immense theatre?"

"I know! And I like him. But," Jenny lifted her eyes, "do you think you can trust him?"

"For the moment, yes. He's a quixotic Irishman. This sort of drama will delight him. And he sent me a note last night which you didn't see. The end of it ran something like, 'Be at the Lane tomorrow A.M. and trust—S.' Well! Unless he has realized the danger *he's* in—"

"Danger? Mr. Sheridan?"

Again Philip lashed out viciously at the mare. With a careful hand he replaced the whip in its socket.

Then he turned round.

"They're not going to take me, Jenny," he said. "I tell you now they're not going to take me alive."

"Phil! Stop it!"

"Stop what?"

"That look on your face. I've seen it there every time you went into the ring to fight, and it terrifies me!"

"If you are unduly upset at my facial contortions, madam, which undoubtedly would stop any clock at sixty paces—"

Now he was being elaborately polite, which was almost worse. Jennifer, figuratively, wrung her hands. What could you do with such a man?

"White signboard ahead!" she cried.

Wrenching at the left-hand rein, Philip sent the gig on one wheel on a left turn, and again they flew into the straight: still amid meadows, but with one row of houses on either side. Instantly Philip, all contritions and apologies, ripped off the veil that held her bonnet in place. He kissed the side of her neck thoroughly, letting the bonnet blow wild. Then, jamming back the bonnet skew-whiff, he tied the veil so tightly that she gasped. An instant later, very decorously, he was driving the gig like a young elder-statesman.

"Hem!" he said.

"Oh, Phil . . . really!"

"As I was about to say—"

"But I don't mind what you do. I never did and I never will."

"Then try to understand," he said, "the corner into which I've been forced. First, there's the murder of Molly; I'm supposed to have mistaken her for Chloris. Two witnesses, Lady Oldham and a footman called Smithers, heard me, apparently, utter threats against Chloris's life. Another witness saw me hit her in the face and knock her over. It's true I smashed down the door of her dressing-room when I thought she was there."

Now it was Jennifer's turn to grow irrational.

"You wanted *very* much to sleep with her, didn't you? Oh, Phil, why deny it? I heard you ask her!"

Philip lowered his head to cool it.

"Like every other witness," he said, "you are only repeating what you expected to hear and thought you heard. That's the trouble with all evidence!"

"But you said—"

"No! I said there were certain matters which must be discussed and decided between us, and on that night!"

"Well, really! What could you expect—"

"I know, I know. Chloris thought just as you did. If you're honest, you'll remember I corrected her. I said I did not mean being abed with her, but certain matters we must discuss."

"Well, what else *could* you discuss with that woman? Every time you see her, you grab her and kiss her. Physically, at least, you can't resist her. Isn't that true?"

"No. But there is just enough of a small element of truth in it—"

"That's why I hate her," said Jennifer, clenching her fists. "That's why I—" She paused, and her voice softened. "I repeat, what else could you have discussed with her?"

"Divorce," answered Philip.

The word hung in the air before them, in the rural road where children played and a milk-maid, her two pails of milk slung from the beam across her shoulders, made a face as they passed.

"Divorce?" echoed Jennifer. "In this age? That's not possible!"

"Oh, yes, it is! It takes an Act of Parliament and a very deep purse, but it can be done. Now apparently I have all the money I want, and I'd use my last farthing for it. I should allow Chloris to divorce me, if she would. On the other hand, her affair with Thornton gives me all the evidence to fight."

Again Philip took out the whip and lashed.

"But how can I fight now?" he asked. "I'm charged with murder and on the run. Finally, you don't see the whole trap. Early last night, at Carlton House, I made an accusation very damaging to the whole Whig cause."

"The Prince of Wales? His secret marriage? *He* would—"

"No," replied Philip. "The Prince is not cruel. He would never order secret assassination, and his advisers wouldn't dare. Everybody has heard about the secret marriage to Mrs. Fitzherbert. But nobody can prove it. What they fear is documentary evidence."

"But surely they could—"

"No, Jenny. It's a deadlock. If they proceed against me for libel, I should have to produce the clergyman who performed the ceremony (he's still alive) and most of the witnesses. The Whigs would never risk prosecuting me. But what about a straightforward, nonpolitical charge of murder? Do you see what will happen, if they catch me now?"

"I—"

"Apparently I tried to kill my wife and killed a servant instead. There's a very strong case against me. I threatened her, I hit her, I broke her door down and strangled her in the dark. All this is brought up in the House of Lords. The Whigs will use every bit of influence they have. The old King himself, mad as a hatter but inflexible about domestic virtues, will charge up from Windsor and make sure his

Lords vote as he directs. And they'll hang me in the Tower within a fortnight."

Philip lashed out savagely, his whip not even touching the mare's back.

"But they'll not take me, Jenny," he added. "I go into hiding until I can prove who really killed that girl. You know the odds against me. It would be—it would be very wise not to stay with me."

"Oh, you idiot!" cried Jenny. "Do you think I could leave you *now?*"

"Well. I felt bound to ask."

Right swung the gig into King's Road, with Philip's attention carefully on the driving.

"There is something else," he continued, clearing his throat, "I am bound to tell you. I have remembered much of my past life. I know what my name really was."

"*Phil!*"

"My dear," he said, "do you remember that dingy little ring I gave you, as a keepsake, shortly after we first met?"

"Remember it?" exclaimed Jenny. "But I've never ceased to wear it!"

Reaching down inside the bodice of her dress, she drew out the very thin gold chain on which the ring hung between her breasts.

"Didn't I tell you last night, Phil? It has some queer symbols for a crest, and a Latin motto."

"The crest," he said, "is a star and a falcon. The motto is, *Et Ego ad Astra*. They are the crest and motto of the Glenarvons. I *am* Lord Glenarvon, Jenny. My full name is Philip Maddern Clavering. I was Lord Glenarvon when you and I used to meet in Regent's Park, all those many years ago."

Still he did not dare look at her.

The whip was still in its socket. He drove fast but with great care, up the long stretch of rural greenery and cot-

tages of King's Road, while the changeful April sky darkened towards rain. After a time Philip risked a sideways
glance.

Jenny's head was bent forward, her lips were pressed
against the ring, and she was crying.

"And you never told me who you were?"

"Jenny! Don't!"

"You never told me?"

"What was the good of swanking it? I never used the title.
I had no money, except the little I could earn in the ring;
and I couldn't, physically couldn't, tell you about that. Does
it upset you so very much?"

"No. Not really."

"Then there are a few things more. If *they* upset you,
then curse my soul for good and all. But first let me ask
you a question. Have you remembered your other life?"

"N-no. Not much."

"For instance, were you an actress?"

"Why do you ask that?"

"Ever since we found each other last night, there have
been certain gestures, mannerisms, use of the voice—I don't
know! Perhaps it was your ease in assuming eighteenth-
century speech, how you walked at Carlton House as though
you had been there all your life. Also, somehow, I associated you with a theatre. And then, when you quoted the
speech from *Romeo and Juliet* this morning, I was almost
sure. Were you an actress?"

"Yes. I think I was. But I have no—associations, as you
have."

The sky grew darker. A few drops of rain splashed and
spattered on the hood of the gig.

Jenny still held the ring tightly, but the grey eyes looked
up with steady frankness as she asked quickly, "What else
have you to tell me?"

"That house, Widestairs. Was it familiar to you? Had you any recollection of being there before?"

"No, never. But I hated and feared it. I can't say why."

"In the old days when you and I were together, I lived there. The house has gone to rack and ruin; somebody's tennis-court is in front of it; and they've shoved out a wedge of buildings on the south side so that you can hardly see the river. But *I* recognized it."

Then Philip braced himself.

"I'm bound in fairness to tell you this, Jenny. I was married then. To Chloris, or someone very like Chloris."

Jennifer's steady gaze did not waver.

"Yes," she said quietly. "I supposed you were."

"You supposed—?"

"Oh, Phil, what else could it have been? You never made love to me, not properly, though I could tell you cared for me as much as I cared for you. How I wished you had! But you were being the perfect gentleman, as usual, so I knew—"

The rain was thickening and flying in their faces, but neither observed it.

"This other Chloris," said Jennifer with an effort. "The one in our modern life. Did you love her?"

"No. That is . . . a certain physical—"

"Yes, yes! We talked of all that. I meant—"

"No, I didn't. Since I had a title, she supposed I had money. So she married me. *I* never even thought of mentioning money; that's how naïve I was. When she discovered I was poor, she turned into a fish-blooded shrew. Listen, Jenny!"

Philip's voice was hoarse. As more chinks and glimmers opened in his memory, he held the reins in one hand and gripped Jenny's arm with the other.

"As soon as I saw that cupboard-staircase built against the wall, I began to remember. You were right: the whole story is being acted over again. Murder *will* be done a hundred and fifty years from now. Chloris—or whatever her name will be then—will have been creeping out at night to see some man whose name I can't even remember, and leaving her maid to impersonate her. Someone, attempting to strangle Chloris, will kill her maid. And they will blame me.

"Except that there were no great names in it, that's the same story! I'm the accused. Listen to the rain on the roof of the gig! You and I, together, are lost and fleeing in the rain just as we were in the other life."

"No, Phil," she said gently.

"*No?* Why not?"

"Because there's something else yet to come. That's the terror, though I can't think what it is. We're not yet lost or desperate; the terror isn't approaching yet. But, when we're running on foot near some steps, it will be on us."

"What will be on us?"

"I don't know!"

"Well," said Philip, sitting up grimly and taking both reins again. "Let it come, then. Whatever it is, be assured of this. As for Chloris in another life or particularly a much-bedecked Chloris in this life—"

"Y-yes?"

"Jenny, is there a fastening in that chain round your neck? Can you detach the little ring?"

"You're not going to take it from me?"

"No. Only for a moment."

Jennifer's fingers fumbled as she undid the tiny catch, and gave him the ring which to Philip was so mighty a symbol. Winding the reins round the whip-stock, he let the horse whirl them at her own pace as they crossed Sloane Square and up Sloane Street towards Knightsbridge. From his waistcoat pocket he took out the small, glittering circle of diamonds.

"Wear this," he said, pressing down the crest-and-motto ring on the third finger of her left hand, "until I can find you a better wedding ring. Wear *this*," and he pressed down the diamond circlet, "as a true engagement ring. If time tilts the world against us, we must make our own laws. From this moment you are my wife. Do you agree to this, my dear?"

"You know I do! Only—"

"You have doubts?"

"Not one. Only please don't speak for a moment! Just for a moment! Don't speak."

Philip nodded. He could not have spoken in any case, because of the lump in his throat. He unwound the reins from the whip-stock and stared straight ahead.

Jennifer, untying the gauze which held her bonnet in place, threw the bonnet into the back of the gig. Gently she put her head on his shoulder, as softly and gently as though she were asleep, and the lump in his throat increased.

Very little rain blew in at them now. The curved roof of the gig kept it off. But the rain was thickening, the unpaved road growing slippery.

Steady!

He rounded the right turn into Knightsbridge. All this strange, green alien world rushed out at him, from his left, in the immensity of Hyde Park. It was like no Hyde Park he had ever known; there were very few trees, and the grass lay in untidy hummocks.

Nevertheless, it was a very real world, with fangs to strike him. If ever he used his wits, he must use them on a problem in murder.

He had not killed Molly. Then who had?

It seemed to him, dimly, that in his other life he had *almost* found the solution to the other servant's murder; *almost* grasped everything, and yet . . .

Philip recreated, in every detail he could recall, the bedroom in which he had seen Molly last night. He pictured the gilt decorations, the long mirrors, the dull-scarlet wallpaper, the fire gone out. In particular he studied the immense canopied bed, with its gold-coloured bed-cover, its numbered and ringed wall-candles burning, and at the head of the bed—

That was where Philip suddenly sat up straight as though he had been burnt.

Jennifer still seemed half-asleep on his shoulder.

"Phil!" she murmured against his neck. "What is it? What are you thinking about?"

"Murder."

Now Jennifer sat up straight.

"I was thinking," he answered, "what a dolt and an imbecile I've been. To have had my whole defence in my hands from the first, yet never to have seen it!"

"What defence?"

"First," he said, staring at the past, "we'll think of what really happened. They say, loosely, that I 'smashed down the door.' That's not literally true, and it can be proved. I gave the door one heavy wallop with a poker, which split a panel. Then Molly drew the bolt and let me in.

"Actually, both bedroom and dressing-room were lighted at the time. But let's allow my accusers that both rooms were dark, and think of where that leads us.

"Molly, then, unbolted the door. In total darkness, mistaking her for Chloris, I strangled her. Now what must have happened, according to them? In this same total darkness, I never touched Molly *then*. I walked through a dark dressing-room, and into a dark bedroom cluttered with furniture. I circled round the bed, cut off a fairly long length of bell-rope, and was ready for business. I then found Molly, in darkness, while she obediently allowed herself to be strangled with it."

"But that—!"

"It's impossible, my dear," he said quietly. "No man on earth could have done it, without the woman running away or screaming the house down. Their whole case depends on all this happening in darkness; the slightest glimmer of light would have shown me it was Molly and not Chloris. And, if it *is* their whole case, they're done."

Rain splashed and drummed on the roof of the gig. Jennifer, her hands at her temples, was holding back her curls.

"Then we needn't have run away? This completely clears you?"

"Oh, no," he said with that same sardonic look. "If they see the flaw, as they will, they can turn the evidence in another direction. And that would be even worse."

"But how could they turn the evidence in another direction?"

"Well! What if I had prepared to cut the bell-rope beforehand?"

Jennifer opened her mouth to speak, but checked herself.

"You see? Before Chloris arrives at Widestairs, I go in and cut the bell-rope. I have it ready when I am ready. I make such a crashing at the door that anyone inside is certain to open it. Just then, in the dark, I spring forward and—"

"Stop! Please!"

"In any event, there is it."

"Then you haven't any defence after all?"

"Oh, yes, I have!" he retorted. "I can prove my innocence, completely, by proving just one point. That point, Jenny, is—"

Philip paused abruptly. Very slowly tightening the reins, he brought the horse down to an easy canter.

"Hyde Park Turnpike ahead," he muttered. "Look as innocent as possible while I pay the toll. If word has reached here from Bow Street—"

Evidently it had not. As the long white gate creaked open, Philip paid his sixpence to an affable elderly man, face covered in whiskers and with so unintelligible a country accent they barely understood a word he said. But he ap-

peared to be paying compliments to Jennifer, and bowed like
a dandy as he waved them on into the rural greenery of
Piccadilly.

"But about the evidence!" she insisted. "You were saying?"

"Sorry my dear. We can't speak of that now."

"Why ever not?"

Philip gave her a curious look.

"Up to now we have met very few wheeled vehicles.
About halfway along Piccadilly it will begin, and grow
steadily worse and worse. I haven't driven since I was a boy;
I don't want a collision or a street accident that would make
us conspicuous. Er—"

"Yes?"

"And don't let anything offend you, Jenny. Grit you teeth
and hold on."

"Offend me? How should anything offend me?"

He did not answer. But she soon learned.

That drive, which took just under an hour, Jennifer afterwards tried to blot from her mind as a smoky nightmare
which had never happened. But it was as real as the stone
paving-blocks, as vivid as the sewage-system.

She had heard and read, and even once or twice seen,
what are called slums. But she had never even imagined,
much less smelled, the slums that lay round Great Newport
Street. Though she never minded what people did, she
sometimes objected to what they said. The obscenity of the
street-language, shrilled or bellowed above the crashing of
iron wheels on cobbles, so embarrassed her that she could
not look at Philip, who was just as embarrassed as she was.

Nor were they without mishaps. For all his intensive
knowledge of maps, Philip had forgotten that there was now
no way through from Coventry Street into Leicester Square;
you must go round by way of Whitcomb Street.

Once, in the crush, they locked wheels with another gig.

Again, in the narrow way out on the east side of Leicester Square, Philip stood up and exchanged vicious whip-cuts with a hackney coachman who was trying to force him against the line of stone posts which marked the footpath.

Philip ended it by a slash across the coachman's mouth which drew blood and made one mouth seem to run across his face. Spectators roared with laughter. Philip, by pure luck, flung the gig into a gap between heavy drays and got away into the worst of the slums.

Jennifer closed her eyes. She felt like retching, and could not.

And yet, she swore, she would allow no fear or disgust to show. She opened her eyes and fully looked, but presently closed them again. As they moved farther east, the thick drizzle of chimney smoke grew darker and darker. Presently there seemed to be less noise about them; the horse could move at an easy trot.

For the second time she opened her eyes. Philip, a trifle shaken but holding the reins lightly and deftly, was smiling down at her in the old way.

"I trust, madam," he enquired in his most formal eighteenth-century manner, "you are not unwell?"

And now she must take up *her* role.

"Nay, sir, but what could make me unwell? 'Tis but a sight we see all our lives."

(And yet did they? Did the dainty ladies, with their milk-of-roses perfume, ever see what steamed within a mile or more of their own scrubbed doorsteps—save by night, on their way to the play, in glass-coaches or sedan-chairs?)

"Pray where are we, sir?"

"This is Long Acre, and we near the end of it. It leads into Drury Lane; presently, with a right turn, we are in Little Russell Street and before the Theatre Royal. However—"

Drury Lane, though not precisely a slum, loomed dreary

and smoky with its tall houses. Philip was biting at his lip as the gig rattled southwards.

"However," he went on, "there is an ill-report I must make. The nearer we go to the theatre, the nearer to Bow Street magistrate's court, which is the nest of the Bow Street Runners. Be pleased to watch for a red waistcoat and a pair of white gaiters, with a pistol stuck in its belt. If you see one—"

And, almost immediately, they did.

The mare, hardly blown at all after her six-mile drive, danced down the cobbles of Drury Lane. As they swung round into Little Russell Street, they saw an unshaven Runner trudging southwards ahead of them. He was eating an apple and fighting off a crowd of children who wanted to see the manacles he carried.

The gig whipped past him as he glanced round. Ahead on the left, in narrow Little Russell Street, loomed the Theatre Royal under its great dome.

"Philip." Jennifer spoke calmly, without moving her lips. "Surely they will have a description of the carriage, too?"

"What matter if they have? We passed a dozen gigs painted just like this one. But there are no hitching-posts here, and—"

They clattered to a stop. Instantly two wizened-faced boys, always lurking in chance of a horse to hold, darted out from under the portico. One of them ran to the horse's head. Philip jumped out on one side, and came round to hand down Jennifer on the other.

Always, through the very pores of his skin, he was conscious that the Bow Street Runner had hurried back to the mouth of Little Russell Street, and was looking at them. His bad teeth were bared above the apple he was eating.

"Gently!" Philip said to the urchins. "Is there a tolerable stables near here?"

Both screamed out and said yes.

"Barty's, guv'nor! In Wooburn Street, over against the Lion and Lamb public-house. That's yer place!"

"Can either of you drive?"

A double-scream said yes.

"Then here's a florin between you. Take her to Barty's, and have them give her a rub-down. Say—say his lordship sent you."

The florin was caught spinning by the older boy, who leaped into the gig and unwound the reins from the whip-socket. The other boy did not move. Diminutive, his hand high on the mare's bridle, he was standing with mouth open and staring upwards at the roof-top of a prim-looking house across the street.

" 'Ere! Guv-nor! Look out!"

Philip spun round and glanced upwards.

There was not much sun in the street. But clearly he could see the polished muzzle of a musket edge round one of the chimney-stacks. Then he saw another, and another.

Without a word he flung Jennifer down on the cobbles of the street, falling on top of her to shield her. The horse snorted with terror, rearing and almost bolting with the boy swinging at her head, as the muskets fired at once. There were not three muskets, but a dozen.

The volley of shots crashed and rattled in echoes above their heads, sending stone-chips flying from the façade of the Theatre Royal. At the east end of the street, the Bow Street Runner had thrown away his apple and stood motionless.

xii

"Once, Then, and in Old Drury . . ."

"Tush, now!" said the rich voice of Mr. Richard Brinsley Sheridan. "Tush, tush, tush!"

Philip glanced up over Jenny's shoulder.

Mr. Sheridan was whistle-drunk. Always recklessly courageous, he was not completely full of gin. He stood beaming in the broad doorway, one knee elegantly advanced, his snuff-box in his hand.

"'Tis ill suited to your dignity, my lord," he continued, taking snuff with the gold box vivid under his large red nose, "to remain in such a position. Besides, the shots were not meant for you. Observe how high they were fired."

He nodded his frizzy hair upwards, at the white bullet pocks and scars against the grey façade, including one which had chipped the nose from a stone Venus.

"But I'll have the ears, egad, of those who mishandled venerable Madam Drury. Inside, now!"

They rose up, Jennifer dusting herself mightily. The Bow Street Runner had disappeared.

"To say truth," continued their host, ushering them into a huge dim foyer hung with somewhat odorous red curtains, and barring the doors behind them, "the musket-balls were meant as a warning to me. Against sheltering ye, d'ye see?"

"Against sheltering us?" demanded Philip. He turned towards the doors. "Then we had better—"

"Stay!" said Mr. Sheridan.

159

Mr. Sheridan, like the Prince of Wales, had a tendency to be somewhat lofty and lordly in liquor.

"Am I so base a traitor," he cried, slapping his chest, "as to turn both of you away in your hour of need? No, damme! My Lord Glenarvon, your servant. My Lady Glenarvon," and he bent low to kiss Jennifer's hand, "'twould be worth cannon trained against Old Drury for one sight of your fetchin' eyes."

This, Jennifer thought, was rather overdoing it. But Mr. Sheridan, though drunk, was deeply sincere.

"Nevertheless," protested Philip, "that Bow Street Runner—!"

"Pish!" said Mr. Sheridan, without quite the right effect. "He took to his heels, like a sensible fellow, when he saw those marksmen were of the Grenadier Guards."

"The Grenadier Guards?"

"Ay, no less," agreed Mr. Sheridan, with a touch of complacence. "I'll not deny, my lord, that the affair at Carlton House has stirred up a deal o' trouble."

"Then the Prince of Wales—?"

"Tush, no! Prinny's forgot all about it, as he usually does. But others haven't. 'Twas my fault, more's the pity!"

"How was it your fault?"

"Someone—nay, not Major Hanger; Hanger's your friend—saw me write that note to you. They knew you'd be here, all of 'em did. Meanwhile, to business."

Taking more snuff, he turned round and snapped his fingers.

Out from the dusk of the unpleasant-smelling red curtains, lighted only by two tiny glass panels in the closed front doors, moved a young man of about Philip's size and a girl of much the same size as Jennifer.

"Mr. Throgmorton, sir! Miss Dalrymple, madam!"

The young man bowed. The girl curtseyed.

"You have taken good note, I trust, of our distinguished guests' dress?"

"We have, sir," replied the young man in a heavy stage baritone.

"Good! Then bid the Mistress of the Robes deck you out as much like them as may be. Climb out by the roof, across the dome, and down into Wooburn Street. They'll espy you, to be sure. They'll follow you, to be sure. No matter; they won't molest you. They will merely wish to see where you go. That is understood? Then be off!"

This time, as he turned round, Mr. Sheridan's pinch of snuff missed his nose altogether. But his beaming complacency remained.

"A small stratagem, my lord," he said, "which I trust will mislead the bloody villains for a few more hours at least."

"Mr. Sheridan," said Philip, now as deeply moved as Jennifer had been before, "I cannot allow such generosity. The risk to yourself—"

"And am I to be bullied, my lord," demanded the other, folding his arms, "in the foyer of me own theatre?"

"No, no! I meant only—"

"Then let us say no more about it. Yet you will be good enough, perhaps, to enlighten me on another small matter?"

"Yes, sir?"

"I hear report, my lord, that last night you strangled your wife in her bedroom at home, and this morning wed my lady here—your gracious hand, my lady!—on the road from Chelsea?"

For an instant Philip stood motionless, his hand round Jenny's waist.

"May I ask, sir, from what source you heard of a murder at Widestairs last night?"

"Ah, bah!" said Mr. Sheridan, coming off his dignity. "Have I not an idle pot boy who does little but sit at the Bow Street Police Office yonder? A horseman with this report arrived scarce a quarter-hour before you did. Well, my lord?"

Philip cleared his throat.

"On my word of honour, sir, I have committed no murder. But, as for marrying this young lady on the road—that, Mr. Sheridan, is God's truth. Do you credit me, sir?"

Again there was a silence amid the red curtains. Again Jennifer, to her horror, found her eyes brimming over. As for the eyes of Mr. Sheridan, ageing and tired yet with an edge of shrewdness round their bloodshot film, these held a faint twinkle.

"Do you credit me, sir?" repeated Philip.

"And did I not credit you, my lord, should you be so welcome in the bosom of venerable Madam Drury? No, by Venus's ears!" yelled Mr. Sheridan, and flung away his gold snuff-box with immense dramatic effect. "Let blackguards walk in this moonshine; it don't fool Dick Sheridan. *You* are married. The day after tomorrow, egad, *I* am married. 'Tis the very Genius of Love I am—"

"By your leave, Mr. Sheridan!" smote in another voice.

This voice, though not as strong as some claimed, had a clarity and purity of diction Philip had never heard before and was never to hear again.

In an aperture of the red curtains, holding them back, stood a strongly built man of very fashionable dress, including hair-powder. The hair-powder set off his face: swarthily handsome, prominent of nose and chin, with flashing dark eyes and broad mobile mouth. As soon as he saw the visitors, however, his expression changed, and he bowed.

"Your pardon, sir," observed the newcomer. "I was not aware—"

Mr. Sheridan's elegance now matched his own, despite unshaven chin.

"May I present my acting manager, Mr. John Philip Kemble?" he enquired of Philip and Jennifer. "Not less famed for his own dramatic skill than for that of his celebrated sister, Mrs. Sarah Siddons? Mr. Kemble: my Lord and Lady Glenarvon."

"Not *the* Mrs. Siddons?" Jennifer exclaimed.

Mr. Kemble smiled and elegantly bowed.

"Your ladyship is kind to say so," he observed. Then a black vertical line appeared between his eyebrows, like the presence of a black leopard. "Though," he continued to smile, "dear Sarah hath her detractors, as all genius must. She appears tomorrow evening as Lady Macbeth, to the Macbeth of your obedient servant."

"Her most famous role? And yours?"

"Again your ladyship is kind. Yet I recall how, ten years ago when dear Sarah first played the part in this very theatre"—the black eyes slid sideways—"Mr. Sheridan himself was doubtful and feared a fiasco."

"Hey?" said Mr. Sheridan.

He had been fishing in the tail-pocket of his coat for a bottle of gin that wasn't there. Abruptly he straightened up.

"He feared a fiasco," pursued Mr. Kemble, "because my sister chose a new conception of the role. Sarah chose to present Lady Macbeth as a dainty blonde."

"As a *what?*" blurted Jennifer.

"Your amazement, Lady Glenarvon, is not unnatural," smiled Mr. Kemble.

Indeed it was not. From all Jennifer had read of Mrs. Siddons, she had pictured this actress as a holy terror: all stoutness and thunder, with finger pointed towards doom and intoning it in every line.

But all her conceptions of the famous Sarah, she realized, had come from portraits and anecdotes when that tremendous figure was an elderly woman, full of conceits and scaring the waiter with, "You have brought me water, boy; I called for beer." As her brother pictured her ten years ago, she could not have been older than Jennifer herself.

Wildly Jennifer turned towards Philip for reassurance. But Philip had taken the first opportunity to snatch from his pocket and read the note Hopwith slipped into his hand before they left Widestairs.

Philip was gnawing at his under-lip. More danger on the way.

Jennifer swung back graciously to the handsome Mr. Kemble.

"As a dainty lady of blonde tresses," he continued, "who uses her—shall we say?—her woman's wiles to seduce her husband into power and murder. She is clever, she is ambitious. But, *au fond,* she has a conscience. She falters and fails. And her husband, like a wolf, goes out sword in hand to his death."

Though Mr. Kemble's last simile was a trifle mixed, Jennifer could almost see the sword in his hand as he acted it.

"But that's exactly how her part should be played!" cried Jennifer. "That's—"

"I say," complained Mr. Sheridan, introducing the practical note. "Don't anybody want a drink?"

"A drink, sir?" cried the outraged Mr. Kemble.

" 'Tis plaguy thirsty work, all this talk. And I had not known, Mr. Kemble, that a rehearsal was called for today."

"Nor is it, sir. Yet my dear sister, who is subject to chills, wishes merely to speak a dozen or two lines to test her voice." Mr. Kemble bowed again. "We should feel honoured if Lord and Lady Glenarvon would condescend to occupy a box and hear us."

"Pish and tush!" said Mr. Sheridan.

"Sir!" said Mr. Kemble.

"If that's the manner o' playing Macbeth," declared Mr. Sheridan, "he's the queerest Scotchman ever wore a kilt. If he desires to lie with his wife, why can't he lie with her without murdering everybody else in Scotland? Lord Glen-

arvon! 'Tis but a step or two through the private passage to
the Lion and Lamb. Come and take refreshment!"

It was Jennifer, instantly, who intervened.

"Mr. Sheridan," she pleaded, with her eyes upturned,
"may I ask yet another great favour?"

"My lady!" said Mr. Sheridan—at her feet in a gesture
which the envious Mr. Kemble could never have matched.

"My husband, I am sure," Jennifer told him roguishly,
"would be at your side in an instant. But I? Sir, I am in
sore need of my breakfast, of which I have not had one
mouthful. If you, Mr. Sheridan, would but go and fetch
something to eat from the public-house, you would earn even
more gratitude from one who already owes you too much."

You little devil, thought Philip.

Mr. Sheridan did not merely rise to his feet; he soared
there. He threw only one disdainful word over his shoulder.

"Keep guard on 'em, Kemble," he said, as the Prince of
Wales would have done. "Or, egad, my actor friend, I'll
wring your neck."

Then he was gone. Three minutes later, and Jennifer
again walked amid ghosts. The past, as chilly as it had been
at Lady Oldham's house, pressed round and against her.

She sat in the right-hand stage-box at Old Drury, as rebuilt by Mr. Sheridan in 1792. Dimly she saw its white
arches of boxes, built in a horseshoe shape all round the pit.
Dimly she saw its two thousand seats, up to an immense
dome. The great crystal chandelier, which could be lowered on ropes to be lighted, was only a muffled glimmer.
The only lights were the foot-floats, candles in glass vases,
stretching across the broad, eerie stage.

Nobody was on the stage. She saw only the grey background of Inverness Castle.

The merest whisper went out in hollow speech. And she,
who had read stage history and all her life dreamed of the

tuning fiddles and the thrown flowers, could think only of Philip sitting close beside and a little behind her.

Philip put his arm round her from the back, his fingers tightening.

"May I say, Jenny," he whispered, "that you were magnificent?"

"H-how?"

"Only what you did could have averted an open quarrel between Sheridan and Kemble, who always try to out-act each other. Bless you."

"Philip. What are you *really* thinking?"

"I?"

"Yes! That note you were reading a while ago—was it the same note Mr. Sheridan gave you last night?"

"No. It came from Hopwith, before I left Widestairs and you were outside. It even holds out a little of hope."

"What hope?"

"Wait!" And the pressure of his arm grew so tight that she felt almost stifled. "First, hear a few other matters. You are quite safe here tonight. Sheridan, God defend his sentimental soul, will even give you a dressing-room with a lock and no window. Because, for the first part of the night, I must go out."

"Go? Where?"

"Jenny, I must go back to Widestairs again tonight."

Pause.

All Jennifer's fears boiled up into a kind of stifled shriek. For a time she had felt warm, even comforted amid the dangers. Now she felt the terror was approaching; and she could not endure this much longer.

"Go back there?" she whispered, though her voice went out into the theatre. "Amid all your enemies? Openly?"

"No. In secret."

"But *why* must you do this? Why, *why*? Because of Hopwith's note?"

"No. That note may be very important. But I had already determined, before I read the note, that I must search the bedroom where Molly was murdered, and search it tonight."

"I still ask *why?*"

"Because by doing so, my dear, I can completely prove my innocence and set us both free. Does that mean nothing to you, Jenny?"

"No! No! No! Not if you must go back there and be caught! Let me go!"

She wrenched loose from his arm. Then, finding no refuge, she buried her face in the dingy plush of the box-rail, her arms out-thrown, and sobbed and sobbed her heart out into the emptiness of Old Drury.

"You mustn't go! I won't let you! Oh, God, I can't endure this any longer!"

She flinched, wishing nobody to touch her, until she realized someone was walking his fingers along the back of her neck amid the curls.

"Why, then," said Philip's calm, cheerful voice, "what's the reason for tears? I won't go."

"Wha-wha—?"

"If you don't wish it, there's an end to the matter," smiled Philip. "Now sit up, my dear, and watch the players. Some other time will do as well."

Dead silence.

Jennifer did not move. A red drapery fluttered in a draught against the great gilt-painted proscenium arch. Two voices argued backstage. It was ten seconds before Jennifer sat up, groped for her reticule, and found it.

Still without looking at him, she dried her eyes with a handkerchief and with great care repaired most of the damage with rice-powder. Then she flung round.

"Darling," she said fiercely, "if ever again I am such a stupid little idiot as that, please beat me as I deserve. Yes, go! Of course you must go to Widestairs. Go, and see them all to the devil!"

Philip's smile vanished.

He bent forward and kissed her lightly on the lips. Out on the stage, hand in hand, moved Mrs. Sarah Siddons and Mr. John Philip Kemble.

And at the same moment, stumbling amid a rattle of crockery and bottles, Mr. Richard Brinsley Sheridan emerged from the darkness with a loaded tray, and set down the tray on another chair. As he straightened up, Philip could again have sworn Mr. Sheridan had been stricken cold sober.

"Glenarvon," he said, "it's always a sour business to bear ill-tidings, rot me if it's not! But in this case—"

"Well?"

"We must take thought, egad, and find a better plan! My two cozen-pigeons, Sally Dalrymple and Tom Throgmorton, have been espied by the military. In ten minutes the Bow Street Runners will know you're both here!"

xiii

"There's One did Laugh in 's Sleep, and One Cried, 'Murder!'"

Jennifer had only one glimpse of the stage, as Sarah Siddons glided towards the stage-box, and made a curtsey to those she could not see.

She was still slim. But her figure, in a plain white gown, was growing voluptuous in her late thirties. Foot-floats softened the bold lines of her face, making it languorous in the black smouldering eyes like her brother's. There was even a naïveté about her, emphasized by the blonde wig whose curls slipped forward when she curtsied.

Her voice was singularly sweet, though without the power she later attained.

"By your gracious permission, my lord and lady," she said, "my brother and I will do rather more than the dozen lines we had intent to do. Bear with us, if it may please you, in a small scene from a great tragedy."

That was what Jennifer heard and saw.

It was all she heard and saw, because Mr. Sheridan's words blotted out everything else. Jennifer whirled round.

"Curse that gel Dalrymple," said Mr. Sheridan, sitting down gloomily beside the laden tray. "Pretty gel, too. But she'll never play a ghost again, so help me, as long as I live!"

Philip, despite all the bedevilments, could hardly keep a straight face here.

"A ghost?" he asked politely. "Is the young lady, then, so desirous of the spiritual state?"

"My lord!" said Mr. Sheridan, with reproach. "You well know, what with all this madness for tales of terror, you can't make a halfpenny on any play that don't have *Castle Something* in the title and ghosts all over the stage.

"Ghosts!" added Mr. Sheridan, soaring to a point of eloquence. "More trouble than they're worth. You must send 'em up on a trap door, in the gauze costume everybody knows ghosts wear. And this gel Dalrymple, my lord, must become affrighted because her costume caught in the machinery. And she floated up stark naked, damme if she didn't, just as the poor dyin' father spoke of his blameless life."

"Philip! Mr. Sheridan!" said Jennifer, in so terrified a whisper that the others broke off. "You say the Runners will know we're here. How was that?"

Mr. Sheridan spread out his hand.

"My lady, I was telling ye! This accurst mort Dalrymple—"

"But what of her?"

"She and her swain made escape well enough, ay. Then they must sit down a-boozing at a tavern in Fleet Street. A-boozing!" snapped Mr. Sheridan, angrily and absent-mindedly seizing a squat green bottle of gin from the tray, and taking a long pull at it.

"Abominable!" said Philip. "But what of that?"

"Their cloaks were dropped. Anyone could see their faces. You apprehend the plan of your enemies, I hope?"

"Not entirely, now."

"A platoon of the Guards, under a certain Whig leader, was appointed to follow you and observe your movements. Once you had gone to ground, they would withdraw with dignity and whistle up the Runners. Then the redbreasts would close in for the kill—either to arrest you, or to shoot you on sight. This is a most parlous situation, my lord. A drop of gin, perhaps?"

Ordinarily it would have horrified the old-time Philip to have taken drink on any occasion, especially before breakfast. But he also took a pull at the bottle.

"Where did you learn this, Mr. Sheridan?"

"At the Lion and Lamb next door. 'Tis all the gossip there!"

"Lion and Lamb!" repeated Philip. "Wooburn Street. Yes! Now I recall why those names are so familiar. Do *you* remember, Jenny?"

"Darling, you must *do* something!"

"So I will. But attend, Mr. Sheridan! Last night, after I fought the Bristol Smasher, out there strutted a plump little man, all benevolence and graces outside. He said I might soon be in trouble and that I must seek his help. He was insistent on his gentility, and named himself Samuel Horder, Esquire."

Against the green of the gin bottle, Mr. Sheridan's long face seemed to have acquired a tinge of green.

"Sam Horder?" he demanded.

"I think that was the name, yes."

"And what did he want of you?"

"He would not say. But I think he wants to match me in a bare-knuckle fight with 'Gentleman' Jackson, in a private view before, as he would say, the nobility and gentry."

"Could ye beat Jackson?"

"No. Never in the world. My hands would break in two or three rounds. Unless, of course—"

Mr. Sheridan put away the bottle and spoke soberly.

"Hark'ee, my lord. I love a rogue; nay, I can embrace a rogue. But not a rogue like Sam Horder. Have no dealing with him, on your life! He is all fangs and claws under that bump of benevolence. He'll undo ye; take care!"

Jennifer, desperate, could not seem to divert them. Behind her, as in a dream, she heard voices crying passion in the gloom of Drury Lane.

" 'This is a sorry sight.' "

" 'A foolish thought, to say a sorry sight.' "

" 'There's one did laugh in 's sleep, and one cried "Murder!" ' "

In Jennifer's consciousness, the voices were blotted away. She was desperate and frantic. Mr. Sheridan saw it, and with grace pushed forward the chair bearing the tray of food. It contained a plate of ham, with hunks of bread and cheese, together with a dubious-looking game-pie. There were several bottles, but only one glass.

"Be pleased to eat, my lady," their host said gruffly. "Your lord and I are not so much in cloud-cuckooland as you think. At worst, I can think of a place to hide you."

"No!" said Philip.

"And pray why not?"

"We have trespassed too far. The redbreasts will tear Madam Drury to pieces, and well you know it."

Philip was wolfishly eating, using his hands because there was not cutlery, and motioned Jennifer to do the same.

"It is true," admitted Mr. Sheridan in an odd voice, "that I much cherish what I scarcely own for debt." He rubbed his hand across his unshaven chin. "But you'll make no bargains with Sam Horder?"

"What choice have I? If he can hide criminals, he can hide us. The Runners will be here at any minute; you own it?"

" 'Infirm of purpose! Give me the daggers. The sleeping and the dead are but as pictures; 'tis the eye of childhood that fears a painted devil. If he do bleed, I'll gild the faces of the grooms withal . . .' "

The noise they heard then, from the stage, made everybody in the box jump and turn round. It was only the hollow, terrifying knocking at the gate which follows the exit

of Lady Macbeth. But, to Jennifer and Philip, it seemed to
presage their own fate.

On the stage, now, the scene had gone as far as the
players meant to take it. Sarah Siddons and John Kemble
were smiling, the one curtseying and the other bowing, towards the invisible box.

Irony was bitter in Jennifer's mouth. All her life she had
day-dreamed of seeing Sarah Siddons and John Kemble play
the murder scene from *Macbeth*. She had seen nothing
whatever, and had heard only a few words.

But Philip, who had kept half an eye on the stage even
when he argued or ate, leaped out of the box and on the
stage to congratulate the players.

"Sir and madam," he said, "I have never known the scene
so well done. It will never be so well done by any others."

Mr. Kemble bowed in his stately way. But Sarah Siddons,
a good-hearted soul who was most at home in her cottage at
Paddington, gabbled away lavishly.

"Did you in truth like it?" she asked. "I once thought it a
horrid play, and indeed I still think so. Once I told—was it
Mr. Walpole, John? Yes! Mr. Walpole!—I told him I should
never, *never* undertake the part. Lady Macbeth is *not* a
womanly woman. She lacks those domestic virtues which I
like to find in a heroine."

"Er—yes," agreed Philip. "But as you played her, madam,
she was all woman."

"Hey, damme," yelled Mr. Sheridan from the box, "but
d'ye mark the time, Glenarvon? Must you put courtesy before the safety of your own neck?"

Mr. Kemble cast one black look at the box, and then swept
a cloak round his sister's shoulders.

"For *your* graciousness, my lord, we are much in debt.
Yet I fear lest Sarah take a chill in this somewhat mouldy
air. Have we your leave to go?"

Philip bowed.

He watched them cross the stage, arguing in undertones because Mrs. Siddons wished to stay and chatter, before they disappeared into the wings.

"Are you eating, my lady?" he heard Mr. Sheridan say from the darkness. "The ham is good, and the bread new-baked. There is also a glass. When I am host, egad, no lady shall drink gin from a bottle! Pray make haste, then!"

Mr. Sheridan, who had been winding himself up with gin to his former lordliness, now leaped nimbly on the stage and strode towards Philip.

"Now hearken!" he said. "If you will be advised by me, there is yet time to go out by way of the stage-entrance."

"It is bad advice, my lord," chirped a voice from almost under their feet.

Both Philip and their host jumped back, until they realized where the voice came from.

In the orchestra pit, amid chairs and music-stands, stood Samuel Horder, Esquire. His three-cornered hat was still set neatly. The yellow glow of the foot-floats shone with halo-like effect on his round, red, benevolent face, with little sparrow eyes, upturned to them.

"*Very* bad advice," sighed Mr. Horder.

"Come, Glenarvon," Mr. Sheridan said lazily. "I never knew Madam Drury was infested with vermin. When I call the stage-hands to pitch this fellow into the street—"

Samuel Horder, Esquire, shook his head sadly. His Cupid's bow mouth, so grotesque because nature had really formed it like that, was pursed up.

"Mr. Sheridan, Mr. Sheridan! You have only one stage hand on duty today, and he an ancient watchman. Can you deny this?"

"I—"

"Your talk is bounce, Mr. Sheridan, as it so often is. Whereas I am perhaps better protected."

He made a slight gesture behind his back. Up from one

of the benches in the pit, unobserved until now, rose four
young men with white, cropped heads. All were larger or
smaller versions of the Bristol Smasher. Each held a pistol,
negligently, but with hammer back to fire.

For the first time Philip realized that the air of Old Drury
was mouldy, as John Kemble had said, and filled with the
ghosts of unwashed bodies.

"My lord," pursued Mr. Horder, regarding him like a dis-
approving but indulgent father, "I warned you of something
like this. Now you are wanted on a charge of murder. And
I, Samuel Horder at your service, am the only man who can
conceal you undetectably."

"How?"

"Upstairs, in my large quarters above the Lion and Lamb,
there is a secret door. No man has ever found that door.
No man ever will. Harken, my lord! I harboured Handsome
Nell, who cut her lover's throat; yet she safely took ship
abroad. I harboured Jerry Bains, who cracked more houses
than any fogelman in London, yet lived to a serene old age
in Jamaica. I can offer you and your good lady a comfort-
able room. Who else can do that?"

"And your price for this hospitality?"

"Money?" said Mr. Horder, with a slight shudder. "Please,
among gentlemen, let us not mention money!"

Mr. Sheridan laughed aloud. It was this, perhaps, which
cut a sneer into Mr. Horder's Cupid's bow mouth and made
him snap.

"I have you where I want you, my lord," he said with
immense superiority. "But make haste, if you please, or even
I cannot save you."

Jennifer, in the box, went cold all over. This was the one
tone you must never use with Philip Clavering.

"Now what," said Philip, "if I were minded not to accept
your offer?"

"My lord?"

"What," snarled Philip, "if I were minded to give myself up to the law—and your whole damned thieves' nest with me?"

"You would be prevented, my lord," Mr. Horder said gently.

"As—how, for instance?"

"Dolly!" said Mr. Horder.

Jennifer screamed as a large dark shape lunged past her, spilling the plate, and sprang over the foot-floats on the stage.

What Philip saw, as he glanced over his left shoulder, was another crop-headed bruiser in fustian clothes and woollen stockings. But Dolly was in good condition, without a paunch, half a stone over Philip's weight; and in his right hand he held a pistol cocked and ready.

Even so, Dolly approached warily. A bead of sweat ran down his temple.

Philip, full of gin and the devil, merely watched him and did not move.

Dolly, with a sudden run, whirled round in front of Philip and jabbed the muzzle of the pistol against his opponent's left waistcoat-pocket.

"We know yer can 'it, melord," said Dolly, in a hoarse, husky voice. "But there's no arguing with this barker, is there?"

"Shall I raise my hands?" enquired Philip, politely lifting them.

"No need for that. But best do what the guv'nor tells you. He's a hard cove, the guv'nor is."

"And are *you* a hard cove, Dolly?"

"I—"

Once more Mr. Sheridan skipped back, this time with a ringing oath.

Philip's left arm, like a butcher's cleaver, chopped down inside Dolly's right elbow, jerking the pistol away from his body just as Dolly pulled the trigger. The flash and bang whacked out in that enclosed space. Dolly had involuntarily half-turned, leaving his left side wide open. Philip's vicious right-cross, catching him in the soft flesh just under the ear, sent him spinning over the edge of the stage into the orchestra pit.

Two foot-floats exploded with a loud pop. Dolly crashed and clattered amid chairs and music-stands at Mr. Horder's feet. There he lay stunned, with one upright music-stand gently waving over him.

Mr. Sheridan was casually examining the black rent torn by the pistol-ball in the sleeve of his coat.

"Devilish bad shootin', if you ask me," he remarked.

"Mr. Horder," Philip said politely, "I do beg of you to be reasonable. Your object, I conjecture, is to match me against 'Gentleman' Jackson in a private mill before certain sporting and perhaps noble gentlemen?"

"Hem!" said Mr. Horder.

"If you have me shot, I shall be in no condition to meet Jackson or anyone else. If you set your bruisers on me, they will be badly mauled and so shall I, being again in very poor condition for a mill. *Your* talk is bounce, sir. I will not meet your terms at all. You shall meet mine."

"Then be quick! What are these terms of yours?"

"First, I must have twenty-four hours to consider whether I dare meet Jackson at all. If he'd consent to use gloves—"

"Gloves?" echoed Mr. Horder, with cherubic horror.

"No matter. Do I have that twenty-four hours?"

"Indeed you have!" chirped Mr. Horder, all benevolence again. "It will take almost as much time to apprise, as your lordship says, certain sporting gentlemen of the noble match I prepare for tomorrow night. It will take place, most poetically, in an abandoned church with most of the pews gone."

"Second," interrupted Philip, "I must leave your secret lodging for a time tonight."

"Oh?"

"I have a gig, with our luggage in it, at Barty's stables near the Lion and Lamb. But an open gig is too dangerous. You shall provide me with a closed carriage and a trusted driver. I leave at midnight, and return in perhaps three hours. No, never fear I'll run away! Where could I hide?"

"And besides," said Jennifer, who had mysteriously appeared at Philip's side, "I remain as a hostage. Would he desert me?"

"Dear madam!" breathed Mr. Horder, seeming to swim on a cherubic cloud as he swept off his hat. "There is truth in what you say, as usual. Agree! Is there another condition?"

"No."

"Then we must be off, through the passage from the theatre into the Lion and Lamb."

"Glenarvon!" Mr. Sheridan said sharply.

"Take care, sir!" cried Samuel Horder, Esquire. "If the full extent of your debts were known to all—"

"If you must do this, Glenarvon," said Mr. Sheridan, ignoring him, "then a word aside with you." He dragged Philip over under the arch of Inverness Castle. There he spoke in a husky whisper. "Ask to see the prize-ring," he whispered, "at three o'clock tomorrow afternoon. Do you understand?"

"No!"

"Speak no word of it now. But ask to see the prize-ring at three o'clock tomorrow afternoon!"

Bang! went a heavy kick or knock against the outer doors of the theatre. It was followed by a whole volley of heavy knocks, echoing through this painted shell.

"The Runners are on us," screamed Mr. Horder. "Hesitate now and you are undone! Lord Glenarvon! What ails ye?"

Philip, in fact, was staring into space and lost in thought, even while the knocks smote harder at the outer door.

"Lord Glenarvon!"

"Those knocks," Philip said blankly. "Like the knocking in the play. And that accursed clock over the stables at Widestairs; I can't put it out of mind."

"Philip!" cried Jennifer.

"Yes, you are in the right!" he said, and flung away dreams. "The door to the Lion and Lamb, and run! But keep up your heart, Jenny. I may have the evidence to disprove a charge of murder before that stable-clock again strikes three."

xiv

"Out of the Night
That Covers Me . . ."

Bong trembled the heavy note of the clock over the stables, at Widestairs by the quiet river, on the single stroke of one in the morning.

Philip, in the closed carriage with one window lowered now that they were rattling along the deserted river-road under a still-bright moon, heard the sound clearly.

They could not be fifty yards from Widestairs now. Philip closed the slide of the dark-lantern. For twenty times, on that drive, he had reread Hopwith's note. Putting the dark-lantern on the floor, because he always picked it up in the wrong way and it burnt his fingers, he could almost read that message in the air.

"Beg favor to fay," it ran in Hopwith's old-fashioned spelling, "old Morecambe, groom, was awake all laft night with raging toothache. Has feen fomething from hif window. Fhall be all night at ftables if yr. lordfhip can be there. Refpectfully, J. Hopwith."

Philip had no idea who old Morecambe might be. But the grooms, who slept above the stables, had rooms with windows facing the back of the house at less than fifty feet. And Chloris's bedroom was at the back of the house.

If old Morecambe had seen something—

Leaning out of the open window, Philip hissed at the driver.

180

"This is close enough," he called softly. "Pull over to the side of the road and stop."

Instantly the driver obeyed. Philip wrapped his cloak round him, and drew up its collar to hide part of his face. Gingerly he took up the dark lantern, just as the driver jumped down and hastened to open the door.

"Sir!" he whispered. "Going to crack the 'ouse?"

"In a sense, I suppose I am."

"I could 'elp," the driver suggested wistfully. "I knows silver, what's the real stuff and what ain't."

This driver—a thick-set man who swore he was the living image of Sir John Lade, the famous whip; ay, and could handle the ribbons as well as Jack Lade or anybody else— shivered with eagerness in the cool night air. But, since he had only one eye and a cast in the other, Philip doubted the closeness of the resemblance.

"This is no burglary in your meaning of it! You've had your orders. Stay here until I return. If anything should happen to me—"

"Ay, sir?"

"I don't know," Philip admitted. "None the less, don't bolt even if you hear a commotion. Can I entrust you?"

"Ay, you can. But take heed o' the dogs!"

"There are no dogs. My—the lady of the house does not like them."

Widestairs, when Philip reached it, loomed up grey-white and stark under the moon. Nothing stirred. There was no light. To walk on gravel without noise was the very devil, but he circled round the house without too much crunching.

The long, high line of the stables also seemed lightless. Here the ground was hard earth. Philip turned slowly round, his heart bumping. Then Hopwith, with the moon on his thin white hair, materialized out of nowhere at his side.

"It was good of your lordship to come," he whispered.

"Hopwith! Is there news?"

Hopwith, with a murmured apology, drew him over into the shadow of the stables.

"There is news, my lord," he said sadly. "But none, I fear, that will greatly assist us."

Philip's heart sank again. Always to be beaten! Always to clutch at walls that slipped and hopes that vanished!

"I made mention of Morecambe, my lord, who sat at his window until near dawn. There is also his wife, who sat up as nurse to him. All they can say is that lights were burning in her ladyship's bedroom at three o'clock in the morning, and that—" Hopwith broke off, startled. "Is aught wrong, my lord?"

Philip's hand was shaking badly as he set the dark lantern on the ground. Its pungent hot-metal smell seemed to have got into his nostrils forever. Then he seized Hopwith by the shoulders.

"Attend to me carefully. All day, I have no doubt, the magistrate has been at his questioning of witnesses? And you have heard it?"

"Truly, my lord, I heard it."

"All witnesses agree, do they not, that Molly's murder occurred at or about three in the morning?"

"They do so agree, my lord. Lady Oldham and young Mr. Richard Thornton were most positive."

"Now consider! Their entire case against me—the whole of it, Hopwith!—rests on but one point: that this murder took place in the dark. Thus, they say, I mistook Molly for my wife and strangled her. If lights were on in that room at three o'clock, I could not have mistaken Molly for Chloris even in the dressing-room. The murder of Molly becomes ridiculous, and their case is smashed and destroyed. You apprehend this?"

Hopwith lowered his head and remained silent for a moment.

"My lord," he said, "up to this time, in my long life, I had

never counted myself a fool. I count myself one now. You
are right. Besides—"

"They saw something else?"

Hopwith moistened his lips.

"At just before three, which Morecambe's wife marked by
the notes of the stable-clock immediately afterwards, Molly
herself partly opened one window-curtain and peeped out.
They have known Molly since she was a child; they would
know her anywhere. Whereupon she turned back, as though
she would speak with someone behind her, and let fall the
curtain."

"Stay!" said Philip.

"My lord, your grip on my shoulders is somewhat painful.
If you would be good enough to—"

Philip dropped his hands. He tried to clear from his mind
that grisly picture of Molly at the lighted window, and the
murderer lurking just behind her.

Were all his calculations about time, as evidenced by the
burning down of the candles, upset by this new testimony?
No, not in the least. Molly, according to his theory, puts out
the candles and goes to bed about fifteen minutes past two.

But the murderer, slipping in by that mysteriously unlocked corridor door of the dressing-room, must not alarm
her. The candles must be relighted, in all friendliness. Murder, after all, takes very little time. If afterwards the lights
were extinguished when the murderer crept away, that little
space of evil could scarcely show on the rough-painted rings
of the candles.

And, if this were so—

"Hopwith!"

"My lord?"

"How came your witnesses to mark lights in the windows,
save when Molly raised one curtain? The curtains, I recall,
were drawn."

"Not so closely drawn, my lord, that glimmers did not stream through. Moreover—"

"Well?"

"Morecambe, my lord, was in great pain from his tooth. Today they held him down and drew it with pincers. But last night he marked the whole affair only because the lights sprang up, in windows hitherto dark, shortly before Molly peeped out; and afterwards, in a few minutes or so, they were gone."

"*So!*"

"You breathe as hard, my lord, as though you had run a mile."

"So I do, and with reason. One more question, and for God's sake tell me the truth. This man and his wife—is their word to be relied upon?"

Hopwith nodded towards a door behind him.

"I have them there," he said, "to wait upon you if you wish to question them. They speak only the country speech; I feared you would not understand them. But this I know. They would stand scrutiny by the sternest judge in Christendom, and he would believe them."

"Then that is all." Philip paced up and down in the shadows. "Hopwith, have you any relatives in London? Anyone, for instance, who could house you and perhaps two others for a day or more?"

He could almost feel the old servant's start of understanding.

"I have a married grandson in Lambeth, my lord. His quarters are small, but no doubt it could be managed. You would—?"

"Yes! There is a closed carriage awaiting me in the road. I would send you and my two witnesses into hiding until I can produce them and cry, 'Deuce, ace.' I am much in your debt, man. But would you do me this favour? Would you go? All of you? Now?"

"It is a small favour, my lord."

Philip, conquering the feelings that overcame him, began to say something and changed his mind.

"Then go and bid them make ready. I must accompany you as far as the carriage, or the coachman might refuse you."

"I would only ask, my lord, whether the carriage is large enough to hold us all?"

"It is scarce large enough for the three of you. I can walk back. Nay, no protest! Only the Charlies will be abroad at that hour; I need not fear to be taken by sixty-year-old watchmen with rattles. Moreover," and Philip's gaze strayed up to the dark bedroom windows, "this matter must be proved to the hilt."

"The bedroom? You'd not—?"

"Come, Hopwith!" Philip said dryly. "Don't tell me my Lady Glenarvon would lie in a room where a murder has just been done. Pray don't tell me so!"

"No, my lord. The room is not occupied—save by Molly's body."

"I see."

"The crowner's quest is to be held here tomorrow," said Hopwith, meaning the coroner's inquest. "To visit that room, at the turn of the night—"

"Now a truce to your superstitious clack! Go and fetch the others!"

It was less than fifteen minutes before Philip and Hopwith, together with a large sheepish man and a small eager woman who seldom ceased talking, stood in the soft glow of the carriage-lamps along the river-road. The one-eyed driver, infuriated by this change of plan, was quietened only with the entire contents of Philip's purse.

"Ay, I'll drive 'em to Lambeth," he growled, as Hopwith gave Philip the written address. "But what do I tell 'is nibs if he asks arter *you*?"

"Horder? Tell him I return before sunrise. To enter his house at any hour, as I understand it, I have only to knock softly and announce that I have the wings of a dove?"

"Ay, that's Sam. Well, me good people, 'op in."

In silence Philip watched the others climb into the carriage. By the glimmer of one lamp he saw the three old, tired faces, two of them so puzzled that he should allow them to ride. Morecambe's great hands hung between his knees, and his jaw was still swollen from that wicked toothdrawing. Mrs. Morecambe, who once had been very pretty, sat between Hopwith and her husband.

Suddenly, as Philip was about to close the door, she leaned forward and poured out to him in gratitude a long speech of which he could not understand three words.

"Hopwith! What did she say?"

"It is nothing, my lord," answered Hopwith, looking steadily at the floor of the carriage.

"What did she say? Tell me!"

"Did you never guess, my lord," said Hopwith, without raising his eyes, "that the girl Molly worshipped you? And had done so for above a year? And would hear no word against you? And even said she would tell— Nay, no matter."

"But Mrs. Morecambe?"

"The woman Morecambe, who knew Molly since she was a child, says she is glad you were always kind to her."

"She shall be avenged, Mrs. Morecambe. Good night."

For some time, with his cloak drawn up close against the cold breeze off the river, Philip stood and watched the carriage rattle away until its lights dwindled and died amid the trees. *The river glideth*, he thought. And, *This is madness. If it means what I think it means, we have only a new problem.* Then, doggedly, he hurried back to Widestairs and to his work.

It would have been very easy to enter by the front door,

which Hopwith had left on the latch. But one slip or stumble there would betray him. It was better to try the outside staircase, at the back, leading straight up to the bedroom.

At the back of the house he found his dark lantern. After some groping along the back wall at the western end of the house, he discovered the outer door to the bedroom staircase. It was not locked.

He opened the door softly, slipped inside, and closed it behind him. He breathed the damp, musty air of that enclosed space. He opened the slide of the dark lantern an inch or two, not caring now whether it burnt his fingers, and let the beam of light play up the stairs and along the narrow walls.

And fear seized him like a strangler, and all but made him turn back.

It was no superstitious terror that Molly might walk. It was not even his intense repugnance at seeing or touching anything in the bedroom above. But this staircase would exist in his own time, a hundred and fifty years from now; by some illusion, the walls seemed to be covered with the same damp wallpaper.

Shaking away such notions, at least partly overcoming fear, he went on up.

The stairs were of stone, and he made no sound. The door to the bedroom was still bolted on the inside, but this, as he had already noticed with such a loose-fitting door and loose-fitting bolt, presented no difficulty at all.

With a pocket-knife, provided like the lantern by the genius of Mr. Horder, he thrust the blade through the door-frame, caught the knob of the bolt, and shot it back with a woodeny rasp magnified to a screech in his ears.

The door creaked open on a dark bedroom, and a dark dressing-room. He had made no real noise. All in the house were fast asleep.

"There's one did laugh in 's sleep, and one cried, 'Murder!'"

Stop this!

But let him admit it. At the back of his mind there *was* some seed of superstitious dread, such as he had scorned in Hopwith, about that silent body on the bed. To admit this dread was to conquer it, or did life really make things as easy as all that? He had never found it so. But he must go on.

Very quietly he closed the door. The dim beam of his candle-lantern, moving round to the left, dazzled back from several mirrors before it touched the great canopied bed. Molly's body, completely covered by a sheet, lay face upwards in peace.

It lessened dread merely to see her there. After all, there was only one object he sought here—if it still remained.

The light moved over the bed, past the cut bell-rope, across one shrouded window, and touched the polish of a table underneath it. Particularly, it rested on a squat wine bottle, dark red in colour and still open, with one wine-glass beside it.

Still there!

He hurried round the bed. A board squeaked sharply underfoot. He stood still, listening. Then he went forward softly. Setting down the lantern on the table so that it lighted both bottle and glass, he studied them.

"Last night," he said to himself, "after I had quietened Molly and was myself in a rage, I saw the wine bottle and the glass. To show a composure I didn't feel, I poured out a glass of wine for myself. In addition to being Madeira and sickly-sweet, it had somehow a nauseating taste. I took only a gulp at it, less than a third of the contents, and then threw the rest down on the carpet."

He peered down. The wine-stain was there.

And after that? Vividly he saw the picture, with Molly

warm and alive. He had apologized for his lack of manners, and filled the same glass for Molly. Again he saw her, the brown eyes grateful, as she drank it; he had taken back the empty glass, and set it down where it was now. And this had occurred at about—

Bong! smote the heavy note of the stable-clock, quivering out. It made him start and sweat in an instant, as there was another heavy note for the hour of two.

Yes! It had happened at just about this time.

But he was not now half-crazed, as he had been last night. He was alert; he could think and judge.

Philip picked up the bottle and inhaled the scent of the wine that was left. He tilted it to his lips, tasting a few drops. Carefully he set down the bottle again. What he suspected this morning was true.

But if that were so, then what must have been—?

Philip, his hands pressed to his head, stood amid furtive gleams on mirrors and scarlet wallpaper, amid the stale odour of perfumes, and brought to mind every scene that had been enacted before him. Then, by a combination of deduction and remembrance of his other life, he saw the whole truth in a flash.

"Oh, my God," he said softly, as though he were praying.

Something dazzled at the corner of his eye. A floor-board creaked and cracked. Philip swung round.

In the doorway of the dressing-room, malevolently, a lighted candle and candlestick in her hand, stood Lady Old-ham.

XV

"And All That Mighty Heart . . ."

"Well, lad," she barked at him, though not in too
loud a voice, "you've gallowsed yourself this time."

Philip only smiled at her, not pleasantly.

Lady Oldham, her white hair in curl-papers, her stoutness
heightened by a black bedgown over her night-shift, waddled forward on creaky slippers. She stood at the foot of the
bed, holding her light high.

"There's three constables sleeping in the house," she said,
"for the crowner's quest tomorrow. I've but to shriek out
loud enough—"

"You won't."

"Hey? And why shouldn't I?"

"In blunt language, madam, because I can always bribe
you. By the by, recently I met a cherubic gentleman who
seems able to contrive all things. The five thousand pounds
I promised you, for forbidding Jenny's marriage to young
Thornton, were paid into your account at Groller's Bank
late this afternoon. You may draw on them when you like."

"Hey-dey!" muttered Lady Oldham, and bit at her under-
lip. "I hold no malice towards you, boy! You've learned
that?"

His slight gesture stopped her. He was a cloaked figure,
the collar drawn up almost to his eyes. But Lady Oldham
could see the eyes, and did not like their look.

"Be advised!" he said. "You aspire to stand high in the
190

world of fashion. Be sure you don't put your money on the wrong horse."

"Foh! What would ye tell me?"

"That I can now prove my innocence beyond any doubt. Tomorrow, if I can writhe out of another scape into which I have got myself, I propose to lay my evidence before the Lord Chief Justice. And there is more." He nodded towards the bed. "This morning, in your presence, I promised myself there should be a reckoning for that girl's death. I will see her murderer hanged on Tyburn Tree, and never think I can't prove who it is."

Lady Oldham, holding her candle steady, also glanced at the bed and shuddered. Philip turned slightly, picked up the wine bottle from the table, and looked round for a cork. He saw one on the window-ledge, between the curtains. Corking the bottle, and shifting back his cloak, he fitted the squat bottle into his back pocket of his coat, and let the cloak fall again.

Lady Oldham watched him.

"But what d'ye *do* here?" she asked, as though in a suppressed passion of curiosity. "What d'ye want o' that wine bottle?"

"Let us say I need stimulant. Meanwhile, madam, since I have bribery as a weapon against you—"

"Can you bribe *me*, dearest Philip?" asked the cool voice of Chloris, who stood in the doorway to the dressing-room and also held a light.

Chloris's tawny-yellow curls, unpowdered, hung down on the shoulders of the same dressing-robe—pink and quilted, sewn with many coloured ribbons—he had first seen her wear at Oldham House. Now she had wrapped it tightly round herself.

"Philip!" she said reproachfully, with that same slow and curling smile. "Do you imagine that there could be so many voices and steps round the house without rousing a light sleeper like me? Or do you imagine *I* should cry out and give you away to the constables?"

Giving her soundless little laugh, behind closed teeth, she moved forward on bare feet.

"As you said, we must have speech together," she went on. "Come with me to the Grey Chamber, where I now lodge, and we shall talk now."

"Thank you, Chloris. But I have another person, in London, with whom I prefer to . . . have speech."

Chloris stopped, the lids drooping over her long hazel eyes.

"Dearest Emma!" she gushed to Lady Oldham, "pray return to bed. Let me have speech with my poor husband, even here."

"But, rot my guts—" began Lady Oldham, with an incautious boom.

"Go."

Lady Oldham nodded reluctantly at Philip, but spoke over her shoulder to Chloris as she waddled out.

"If you were roused," she spoke sourly, "you had at least time to paint your mouth. I'm an old woman. I'll back to me dreams."

Philip, his gaze moving between Lady Oldham and the cut bell-rope, watched her go in silence. Chloris, catlike, glided round the foot of the bed. With the utmost coolness she sat down on the side of it, facing Philip, with Molly's covered body at her back. There she held up the candle to illumine him, and she laughed again.

"You have not shaved since yesterday, my husband," she said mockingly, and gave a simulated grimace of distaste. "Foh! An unshaven cheek is ill-mannerly and displeasing to me, under the circumstances."

"Under what circumstances?"

Chloris gave him a quick look. Lazily she crossed her knees, holding the light sideways for a better view. Some-

thing remained in his eyes which made her flinch; therefore,
instantly, she attacked.

"Faugh!" she said. "You think me callous, do you, because
I sit down beside a dead wench's body? Why? God knows
I had no hand in her death."

"No," he admitted, "you had no hand in her death. But
have you no fastidiousness, no sense of delicacy at all, in that
handsome carcass of yours?"

"None whatever. If I had ever possessed such, my husband, would you have been enamoured of me?"

Philip remained silent.

"Touché, I think?" asked Chloris.

"Admitted; a palpable hit. And yet, madam, if you had
not been absent on the night Molly died—"

"Come, this goes too far! On that night, Philip, I was
guiltless of adultery; I was guiltless of crime. Of what else,
my husband, would you have me guiltless?"

"Only of being what you are. Do you favour sweet wines,
Chloris?"

"Nay, I abominate them. Why?"

"Did Molly favour sweet wines?"

"She adored them, and could never resist them. Again,
why?"

Chloris leaned forward, and set down the candlestick on
the table behind him, as Philip moved towards her. There
was a smile between her closed teeth as he tilted up her chin.
Then the smile changed as he gripped her chin too hard.

"A moment ago, Chloris, you said you had no fear of
sitting down by Molly's body."

"Nor have I. Do I fear her ghost?"

"No. If there are any ghosts in this room, madam, they
are you and I."

Again she shied back, but he held her.

"You are no fool or madman, Philip. I never believed that,
even when I said so. You half-gulled even me." Chloris

breathed hard. "Never did I admire you so much, I swear, as when I heard how you fought Toby Thornton with an empty pistol, and struck him senseless on the dining-room floor. But take care, my sweetest; he is not done with. Should he force you to meet him with swords, then you are a dead man. And I could not bear the thought of that."

She lifted her lips.

He ignored them.

"You have no consciousness, I suppose, of any life in the future, a hundred and fifty years from now? No, I see you have not. None the less, I will tell you.

"In this room, Chloris, you and I will quarrel most bitterly. You will have a maid; I will give you everything you want, though I have not a penny except what I can earn—with my hands. Oh, the room will be different! There will be a tennis-court in front, and a tenement behind.

"But you, madam, will slip up and down those stairs to meet your lover, just as you do today. He will live in what they will then call a block of flats in Chelsea. One night, when you are away and your maid is killed, there will be witnesses in the tenement to say what happened. They—"

Philip, dazed, felt memory flash and flicker away. The eerie bedroom was dark except for candle and dark lantern. He saw only Chloris's red mouth, and her upturned eyes.

"You cannot remember that, Chloris. Yet it touches you like a feather across the gulf of time, and you are affrighted. One more fable, and I leave you."

"Leave me?" cried Chloris.

"Every man on earth has had at least once the same experience. There is one woman he loves. There is another he desires. In youth, in stupidity, he thinks these qualities may never exist in the same woman. The woman he desires, the touch of whose flesh he cannot resist—"

Chloris smiled a peculiar smile, like a razor-cut, and lounged back.

"He sees through her very clearly. He sees her for an empty-headed rattle, despite an outward cleverness. He sees her snobbery, her greed, her small-minded caution as to what the world will say, her wish, most inexplicably, for 'his name.' But still he cannot resist her. Until something crosses it, and the spell is snapped."

"You are very poetical, my husband."

"I am heartened above the world, madam. And don't call me 'husband.' Though you don't know it, you are already divorced."

Chloris sprang to her feet.

"Is this your country bumpkin?"

"If you wish to call her so. Today, from mid-afternoon until the time I set forth tonight, I was with her in a room customarily used by hunted criminals. I discovered what a less stupid man would have discovered long ago, that love and tenderness and passion may all exist in the same woman. Now proceed against me for divorce, Chloris, or I shall proceed against you. Be easy. You shall have what money you need."

"Philip!"

"Good night, Chloris."

Picking up the dark lantern from the table, he lowered the collar of his cloak and strolled across to the bedroom-staircase.

Chloris's pink dressing-robe had fallen open. Hatred overflowed her so much that he hardly recognized her face. Her hand flashed up to the red bell-rope, which she could just reach.

Philip glanced over his shoulder.

"Ay, ring the bell," he said. "Summon your damned constables! I had rather be taken as a felon—though I think, in my present exalted mood, it would need more than three to subdue me—than suffer more embraces from you or your future counterpart. Again good night."

"I will see you hanged!"

"Come!" mused Philip. "What happened to my witnesses, from the tenement, a hundred and fifty years from now? I can't call it to mind. What an irony it is, madam, that a man can't remember the future!"

He opened the door, closed it behind him, and walked downstairs without the least hurry.

The candle, burning low, shed its beam from the dark lantern before him. Still there appeared to be no jangle of the bell from the bedroom, but he would not have heard it from there. Only a storm of weeping, which made him hesitate. But he went on.

He opened and closed the outer door. Marching across the stable yard and then round the drive without troubling to conceal the crunch of his footsteps on gravel, he heard the bang of the stable-cloak strike three. Even yet there was no alarm, the house sealed up in sleep. Then he began the long walk back to London.

The moon was dying, and then it faded. Several times Philip lost his way in the five-mile tramp between Widestairs and Hyde Park Turnpike. But, in his present exalted mood, he blew out the dark lantern, thrust it into a pocket of his cloak, slung the cloak over his arm, and went forward whistling.

The long white Turnpike gate lay across the road, its keeper asleep. Ducking under it, he walked on into Piccadilly and past the weird white tombstone factory on the right. Henceforward he met only the Charlies, those elderly watchmen who cried the hours of the night with lanterns and rattles. After one glance at his fine clothes, they gave him only friendly grins.

"Lost yer last chair 'ome, sir?"

" 'Fraid so, old boy."

"Well, good luck!"

"And to you, old boy!"

"Half-past four," hair-raisingly rose that unmelodious cry, "of a fine, dry morning!"

It was not until he reached Leicester Square, behind which lay the region of the brothels, that Philip saw any sign of life. Only a few dram-shops remained open, and these were far from gay. When a fuddled figure reeled out from one of them, bumping along the wall to keep its balance, ten to one that man would wear bedraggled mourning.

At past five o'clock, in the darkest hour before dawn, Philip knocked at the door of Mr. Samuel Horder's house beside the Lion and Lamb public-house in Wooburn Street. Mr. Horder's own quarters, except privately, did not communicate with the Lion and Lamb which, as Philip and Jenny passed through it that afternoon, proved to be a tolerably filthy pub with, at the rear, a sparring-saloon.

Philip knocked at the outer, polished door. He knocked, and knocked again. When at length he heard someone stir inside, he announced clearly that he had the wings of a dove. Then he sang it, together with a regrettable modern parody of the words.

The door was unbolted and unchained by Samuel Horder, in a long tasselled night-cap and a woollen night-shirt. Not until he had locked the door behind his guest did Mr. Horder, carrying a taper in a dish, turn angry sparrow eyes on Philip.

"You are very late, my lord."

"True, but I am here. Did you really imagine I would break my word?"

"No," said Mr. Horder, after a pause. "I give you that." He lighted another taper in a tin dish. "Now up to the secret room with you. You may sleep late tomorrow; afterwards, there is much to be done."

"Before I sleep, sir, I must indite two letters. Have you pen, ink, and paper?"

"You will find all," said Mr. Horder, "in the hidden room. Up with you, now!"

Up he went, four flights to the top, on neat red Turkey carpet with brass stair-rods. Only halfway up, when he stumbled, did he know how tired he was. His head swam, and a ghost of the candle flame rose above itself.

At the top, nevertheless, he was home. You opened the secret door by pressing very hard on one of a straggle of nail-heads, as though for pictures, along a dark-panelled wall. The hidden entrance, backed with stone and felt to withstand sounding, rolled open. Philip slipped inside, pulled the door shut on rollers behind him, and for some time leaned with his back to it.

Outside two dusty windows there was a hint and illusion of dawn, like a mere breath on the panes. By what quirk of his odd nature, Philip wondered dully, had Samuel Horder chosen to deck out this small room so handsomely? Save for scrawled pencillings and crude drawings round the walls, from the obscene to the deeply devout, it might have been a small bedroom at Carlton House.

From the shadow on the other side of the fireplace between the windows, where Jenny lay in the narrow bed, he could hear her breathing gently in sleep. A great surge of tenderness and gratitude rose up in him, but he did not go to look at her just yet.

Instead he went over to the Sheraton writing-desk at the left-hand side. Setting down his taper in its dish, he found all the writing-materials Mr. Horder had promised. He wrote one letter to Mr. Richard Brinsley Sheridan, in care of the Theatre Royal, Drury Lane. He wrote another to the Lord Chief Justice, old Lord Mansfield, at his house in, Philip thought, Ken Wood, Hampstead. The sealing-wax dripped as bright as blood when the wax fell. Having no crest in star-and-falcon, he stamped both letters with a plain seal on the desk.

Last of all, he took the squat red wine bottle from his pocket. Scribbling "Don't touch" on a sheet of paper, he tore it over the neck of the bottle and left it there.

Grey daylight was at the dusty windows, out of which he could not see.

Philip stumbled to his feet, blowing out the candle, and went over to the bed where Jennifer lay.

She lay on her side, smiling in dreams. The coverlet was drawn almost up to her bare shoulders.

His gaze wandered to the narrow wall above her head. Some forgotten felon, crouching here in terror of the law, had scrawled above it those words which simplicity has written for all ages.

> Now I lay me down to sleep;
> I pray the Lord my soul to keep.
> If I should die before I wake . . .

Philip looked down at Jenny again. Because he was very tired and overwrought, a heavy lump was in his throat and tears stung his eyes. Gently he reached out and touched one curl which lay across her cheek.

Once more he glanced round him in the dim, deathly light. Their clothes, from the two portmanteaux neatly stacked in a corner, Jenny had put away in cupboards and a chest of drawers as carefully as though she believed they meant to occupy this thieves' hideaway for all time.

Then, because there was no room to lie beside her without waking her, Philip stretched himself out on the Turkey carpet beside the bed, rolled over, and fell headlong into sleep.

There were no dreams. There were no pursuing horrors, or remembrances of things left undone. An hour, a day, a century might have passed quietly in darkness. Afterwards, gently, someone plucked at his sleeve.

"Phil! Phil!"

He was not shocked awake. He roused himself, clear-eyed and refreshed. In some mysterious fashion he was now in bed, minus his coat and top-boots, with the coverlet over him. Jennifer, fully dressed, was bending above him.

"Phil! It's half-past two in the afternoon. You must get up now, or you'll be too late after all!"

XVI

"From the Hag
and the Hungry Goblin . . ."

Philip half-sat up on his elbows.

"How—how did I get in here?"

"Well! I woke up at about seven o'clock in the morning, and found you lying on the floor. I couldn't handle you. You seemed to think I was—well, that woman, and you fought me."

Jennifer, though she tossed her head, did not seem in the least ill-pleased.

"So I woke up Mr. Horder, who was positively furious," she continued. "But two of his men hoisted you up so that you could sleep comfortably."

Slowly he looked round. Though the two windows were still heavily grimy, he saw the padded Oriental chairs, the gold-framed mirror above the chest of drawers. It was marred only by those scrawls round the walls. Beside the mirror was a crude drawing of a man being hanged, with the word "me" underneath it; and over the desk, as he had not observed before, another drawing of an ecstatic man apparently scattering money in a tropical paradise.

"Jenny," he said in disgust, "this room—"

"The room? But I love it!" she said in a different kind of voice, her eyes widening. "Phil," she added, bending over him, "do you love me?"

Now this is the sort of conversation which can go on for

hours, and generally does. Presently Jennifer, with flushed cheeks, drew back.

"My dear," she told him, "I shouldn't mention it, and I don't really mind at all, but—"

"But what?"

"Your whiskers. They're *awful*."

"Yes, they do seem a bit on the bristly side."

"Well, your shaving-tackle's laid out on the chest of drawers. Also, there's a can of hot water, a basin, and a towel."

"Any chance of a bath?"

"No, I tried that." She looked wry. "Even Mr. Horder says it's unsanitary. But there's a big bucket of hot water, and another you can sluice yourself down in. I did. I've put out a change of clothes for you. Hurry, please, while I go and find you some food."

"But why hurry?"

The colour drained out of Jennifer's face.

"You kept telling me to remind you. For some reason, Mr. Sheridan insisted you must ask to see the prize-ring at three o'clock today, and it's going on for that already."

Now Jenny was whiter than ever.

"Phil. Can't you get out of this fight with Jackson, some-how?"

"No. At least, I don't see how."

"What are the rules of the London prize-ring in this age?"

"Never mind; it doesn't matter!"

"Tell me! Please! I shall have to learn anyway!"

"It's with bare knuckles, to a finish. A 'round' may last two seconds or twenty minutes; it ends only when somebody is knocked down or thrown with a wrestling-fall. Then you have thirty seconds rest; eight seconds more to come up to scratch. It may go on for twenty, thirty, forty rounds; even more. Or it may be over," he snapped his fingers, "like that."

Jennifer did not speak. She only looked.

"Now don't worry!" he urged. "I'll make him miss as much as possible; that's the trick they don't know. I'll carry the fight to his body, and try to save my hands as much as I can. In about the twentieth round, when my legs begin to go, he can knock me out. With that we've paid our debt to Horder."

"And afterwards?"

"Afterwards, Jenny, we're free."

"Free?"

"Of Horder and even of the law! On that desk over there—" Philip craned round the ledge of the fireplace. "Jenny! Where are the two letters I left propped against the candlestick?"

"It's all right, I think," she answered, swallowing hard. "Mr. Horder opened and read them. Afterwards he stuck down the seals again and took them away."

"Then we've nothing to fear. No word in those letters concerned *him;* they've been posted. But that wine bottle! You didn't drink from it, I hope?"

"Good heavens, no! With your warning jabbed over the neck? But why shouldn't I have? What's in it?"

"The wine is full of powdered opium. I learned more than I ever hoped at Widestairs, Jenny. With that wine bottle and two witnesses now at Lambeth," his hand flew to his waistcoat pocket, finding the address safely there on a crumple of paper, "I can show I'm innocent and prove who killed Molly. There's another river to cross, and one hell of an explosion ahead. After that, my dear, there will be no terror to follow us."

"Phil."

"Yes?"

"Mr. Horder," answered Jenny, the pupils of her eyes dilating with fear as she backed towards the door. "Look out for him! He's—he's different today. Beware of him."

Fear Sam Horder?

Yet Jenny's eyes were such, as she moved out of the door and closed it, that a cold pang went through Philip's stomach. He must forget it; he must be very quick!

Within ten minutes he had shaved, despite a cut-throat razor which nicked him under the jaw. He had sluiced himself down, and dressed, after a fashion, in much the same sort of clothes he had worn yesterday, except for a flowered waistcoat (Jenny's choice) which he disliked. He was combing his hair before the mirror when the door slid back. Samuel Horder, Esquire, softly entered.

He looked at Philip, and Philip looked back. Neither of them spoke.

It was a dark, overcast day, unnaturally hot for this time of year, and straining with a storm which would not break. Due to the closed windows, which not even leverage with a poker would pry open one inch, the atmosphere had grown unbearable.

Mr. Horder's round red face, a darker red as from some emotion, was topped with carefully dressed hair-powder. He still wore the brown coat and mulberry-coloured small-clothes in which Philip had first seen him. But his silver links were of fine quality, and he carried a jewelled watch-fob. He sat down in an Oriental chair, crossing his legs.

"Lord Glenarvon," he said, "since yesterday you have made very free of my hospitality."

Philip looked at him again, but did not speak.

"Also you have chosen to 'dictate terms,'" said Mr. Horder.

For a moment he contemplated the toe of one buckled shoe.

"Now I don't need you, Lord Glenarvon," he went on. "It is true that every gentleman who sees this match will pay a hundred guineas to do so. It is true I have bet very heavily on Jackson; he will knock you out of time as soon as that curious guard of yours is broken by his blows. But I am

far from being a poor man, sir. The match could be can-
celled without worry to me. Indeed—"

Here his lips pursed up.

"Indeed, several times during the night I wondered
whether it might not be simpler to have your throat cut, and
your woman's as well. You could then be disposed of without fuss."

The plump little man meant every word he said.

His elbow was on the arm of the chair; his hand, thoughtfully at his chin. Still he turned this matter over in his mind,
and looked up.

"I am a gentleman, sir," said Mr. Horder. "Perhaps that
is what rankles most. My father owned broad acres; my
mother's name is in the peerage. I was a famous swordsman,
before the sword went out of fashion. You will treat me, sir,
as one gentleman to another. Or—"

Philip flung down the comb and turned round. His own
temper shot up to the boil.

"Or—?" he enquired.

The other did not reply; did not even seem to hear.

"First," he said, looking Philip up and down without
seeming to see him, "you should not have shaved. A half-
beard is a half-disguise. Second, you cannot wear that coat
or waistcoat or neckcloth; they are too fine. I will provide
others."

He rose up, and went to the door. Rolling it open and
calling some words outside, he remained there looking at
Philip. Philip could not meet his eyes, but lowered them.
He was frightened, and he had better admit it. He and
Jenny were in a house crawling with killers, who would not
hesitate one flick to use a knife. The hazard of a prize-fight
seemed very small now.

Still Mr. Horder waited. Then past him into the room
came Dolly, the bruiser whom Philip had knocked into the
orchestra pit. Over Dolly's left arm he carried what looked

like a black leather jacket, waist-long, as well as a very dirty
flowered waistcoat and a bright red-coloured neckcloth. In
Dolly's right hand he held a long knife, blade upwards.

Behind him lumbered a larger and bulkier man, himself
with a half-beard, who carried nothing but another knife.
And beyond them moved Jennifer, bearing a large tray.

Jennifer's tray contained a smoking underdone steak, fried
eggs, wedges of black bread with much butter. But her arms
trembled so much that the crockery rattled together.

"My dear!" chirruped Mr. Horder, with such a sudden
change to benevolence that the effect verged on the horrible.
"You are far too kind to your—your young man. And the
tray is much too heavy. Put it down on the centre table,
pray."

There was another rattle as Jennifer thumped down the
tray on the Sheraton table. She ran quickly towards Philip,
but their host motioned her back as he rolled shut the secret door.

"Now, sir!" pursued Mr. Horder to Philip, no longer benevolent. "Strip to your shirt and put on these clothes.
You hesitate?"

"No."

"Very well. Wind the red muffler round your neck as
though you wore no shirt under it. Good! Now the waistcoat. It is not overclean, but, since you have ceased to be a
gentleman—"

Philip's head went up and his shoulders back. Up flashed
the knives of Dolly and Half-Beard. Mr. Horder laughed in
Philip's face.

"Since you have ceased to be a gentleman, you need not
dress or bear yourself like one. Next, the leather jacket.
Come, this is an admirable fit! Now, sir, sit down, across the
table from me, and take your breakfast. Dolly! MacAdam!
stand close behind him, with your knives. Lord Glenarvon

has many faults, but he moves fast and he hits hard. Beware of him."

Mr. Horder himself sat down in the same Oriental chair as before. He raised his fingers and put their tips together. Then he glanced at Jennifer.

Jennifer, who had backed away against the wardrobe, understood—in one glance—how this ruthless little Cupid-figure ruled the snarling dogs about him.

"There is no tea or coffee for the breakfast tray. Why?"

"At the Lion and Lamb," Jennifer cleared her throat, "they said it was the wrong time of day for them. A dreadful woman offered me beer or brandy."

"You will not call her by any such name. That is Flash Kate, who serves our clients in other ways than drawing strong waters, and would slit your nose if she heard. You'll not deny she is handsome?"

"I—"

"No matter. Lord Glenarvon, eat."

Philip's appetite, once prodigious, had dwindled to a shrinkage in his innards. But the plump little man was right, he must eat. For a time, in that hot darkened room with tempers held in check, there was no noise but the clacking of his knife and fork.

"And now," pursued Mr. Horder, "a final word of warning. Three times I have seen you make use of your fists. You floored John Jackson with your left hand—in a glove. You knocked the Bristol Smasher out of time with that same left. You sent Dolly into the orchestra pit with a right hand. But a right hand under the ear."

Mr. Horder paused, tapping his finger tips together.

"Where you learned this curious guard and attack, Lord Glenarvon, I do not know and I don't care. It has so fired the imaginations of our sporting gentlemen that they will pay a hundred guineas each to see you use it again. But *I* marked in you a strange reluctance to go with your fists for any man's head. Was this so?"

"Yes."

"But it will not be so tonight, in your match with Jackson. Our spectators care nothing for speed or for skill. They would have giant's blows and they would have blood."

"How truly you speak it!" snapped Philip, staring past him into the future and loathing what he saw.

"Ah? Then you recognize this? Very well. You will carry your attack to Jackson's head as well as his body."

"Let Jackson fight in his style. I fight in mine."

"Say you so? I think not. You will carry the fight to his head. Or afterwards, when the lights are out, you will be no longer alive. There will be no further use for you in any case."

Now it was the turn of Philip to laugh in Horder's face.

And the pink complexion of the other man went a dark, deadly red.

"You think you can outwit me?" asked Mr. Horder. "It may be. But one thing you cannot do or prevent. During the match, as is but natural, your," he looked at Jennifer, "your woman will remain in this room. Three of my men remain here, too. Should I send up report that you are not fighting as I desire, let me picture to you what will happen to her."

Mr. Horder pictured what would happen, in detail. It was worse than anything of which Philip had ever dreamed, and it almost sickened him physically.

"After that," shrugged Mr. Horder, "she may find a living, of sorts, on the streets. Yet I doubt it."

Philip's left hand shot down, to hurl the table sideways and get at Samuel Horder, Esquire. Instantly, as he leaped up, two knives dug a quarter-inch into his back and twisted sideways.

"If he does that again," Mr. Horder said to Dolly and Mac-

Adam, "send the knives to his heart and make an end of this. I repeat that I am weary of parleying."

Then he looked at Philip.

"Glenarvon, Glenarvon!" he said sadly. "Let me make known to you how stupid you have been in all things!"

Mr. Horder's wicked little Cupid's eyes moved over towards the writing-table.

"Last night," he continued, "you wrote two letters. Sometimes, sir, your ignorance amazes me. You appear to think that old Lord Mansfield, who died fully two years ago, is still Lord Chief Justice of England. Until I write the proper name on that letter, it cannot be sent and your masterly analysis would not reach him. Nor would your letter to Mr. Sheridan, if sent by post; early tomorrow he departs for his marriage in the country. And as sport, sir, purely as sport, we might smash that bottle of Madeira wine by which you appear to set such store. What do you say?"

Philip stood still, his head down.

He might, perhaps, save Jenny by smashing his hands to flinders against Jackson's bullet head, and he would do so. But if his evidence against the murderer, so long sought and so bitterly won, ran down the drain like the contents of a broken bottle—

"And by the by!" sang Mr. Horder, stabbing him again. "Yesterday you 'demanded' to see the ring in which you would fight. It would have been a reasonable request, if properly spoken. Do you still 'demand' to see the ring, Glenarvon? Or do you most courteously request it, as of one gentleman to another?"

And Philip was beaten.

Not only was he beaten, but he must humiliate himself and crawl before the Cupid against whom Sheridan had warned him.

"Sir," he replied, clearing his throat, "I courteously request it, as of one gentleman to another."

"Come!" beamed Mr. Horder, clapping his hands together softly. "This is much better. And I, as one gentleman to another, courteously allow it. You will fight as I do wish?"

"I will."

"Better and better!" His face changed. "We come down a peg, I think? As for your woman—"

Then Jennifer, white faced but not daunted, cried out at them.

"Do you think I care what happens to me?" she asked contemptuously. "Phil, Phil, don't let them overcome you because of *me!*" She whirled towards Mr. Horder. "*I* demand to be with him as long as may be! *I* demand to see this ring of yours!"

Again their host softly clapped his hands together.

"In woman, my friends," he declared, "spirit is a most proper excellent thing. As in Flash Kate, for instance." He frowned. "But those clothes of yours, in such a district as this—"

"It is the plainest gown I own! Besides, I have to wear over it a grey pelisse much stained where I fell yesterday in the dirt. Look, here in the wardrobe!"

"Why, then," smiled Mr. Horder, "I allow it."

He bounced to his feet. Caressing the jewelled watch-fob at his hip, he drew out the watch and consulted it.

"Lord Glenarvon, Lord Glenarvon!" he said. "Had I in my hand a well-balanced small-sword, light yet as deadly as an adder, held only between the thumb and forefinger of the right hand—!" Out pinched his thumb and forefinger, his little legs twinkling. "I vow, sir, I could make you flinch as even Jackson may not. Yet you know no swordplay, or so I think?"

"None."

"A pity! Yet I bear," said Mr. Horder, with a wicked look in his eyes, "no malice. Dear, dear, no! Dolly! MacAdam?"

Two voices behind Philip growled out a response.

"Have you still pistols in your belt, besides the knives? I can't see."

The two voices said they had.

"Good! It is past three, and we must be off. As we pass the side door to the Lion and Lamb, Dolly, seek out Cobb in the snuggery—No, madam, no bonnet; you must go hatless like Glenarvon!—and bid Cobb follow us, equally armed. Now!"

Distantly Philip thought he heard thunder, in this close-pressed day. But the secret door rolled open.

A few seconds more, and they were walking downstairs in cleaner air. Philip, who had snatched up the wine bottle without comment or even malicious smile from their host, went first with Jenny. Dolly and MacAdam followed, knives half-showing. Last skipped their host, on the neat Turkey carpet with stair-rods, his voice still a-din.

"The mill will take place," he said, "in an abandoned church. Come, I should have said Presbyterian chapel, but let it pass! I prefer the word church."

"No doubt," said Philip.

"The platform," said Mr. Horder, with pleasure, "still remains, with the pulpit in the middle of it. Behind it are half a dozen once-impressive chairs. In front of the platform, turned round backwards against it, are two rows of pews for distinguished guests. Otherwise the pews have been ripped out. There is ample space, noble space, for a full-sized ring and many spectators. Take care, now!"

While Dolly darted away into the side door of the Lion and Lamb, evidently to find the man named Cobb, Mr. Horder opened the front door and peered out.

A high wind whooped along Wooburn Street, odorously stirring and sending rolling the refuse in the kennel. The sky was curdled and blackish.

Mr. Horder closed the door.

"There are few here," he announced. "The church is very close; I do not think any Runners will see you."

"Many thanks," said Philip.

Nobody, not even Jennifer, could distinguish his tone of voice. Mr. Horder glanced at him sharply.

"My best course, last night," observed Mr. Horder in smooth accents, "would have been to hand you over to the chief magistrate at Bow Street. I misliked this, since you knew of my secret room and a little of my affairs. But I can always do it, as a last resort."

"No doubt."

Still that level, unpredictable voice. Mr. Horder would have added a question, if out of the Lion and Lamb had not stalked a big red-headed man, in a reek of gin and profanity from an interrupted game at cards. They could see no pistol buttoned under his grimy leather jacket, but the point of the knife jabbed through his jacket-pocket.

"Cobb!"

"Ay, sir?"

"We go to church. Dolly and MacAdam will follow the man close. Do you follow the woman."

"Ay, ecod, but that I will!"

"Silence, you scum!"

"Nay," muttered the deflated Mr. Cobb, "I but meant she's a tasty mort, and—"

"Be silent!"

Mr. Horder went out, closing and locking his front door after that small procession. Still the wind sailed high, carrying chimney-smoke and dust as well as refuse.

On the south side of the street stretched nothing but Mr. Horder's lodgings, out and above the Lion and Lamb, next door, and Barty's Stables beyond. The rest was only the blank back wall, grey bricks, of Drury Lane Theatre.

There was nobody in sight except a prostitute, leaning against the wall of the theatre and letting her skirts blow.

Though she was not old, she had raddled her face into such a mask of paint that, to Jennifer and Philip, at least, she seemed only a grotesque of a woman.

Samuel Horder, Esquire, led them across the street, into a broad opening, and up a narrow, dingy little alley which he said was still Wooburn Street. He turned right, and then left again. Though this was a solider street, you could have shaken hands from its upper windows; it held mud and debris days after any rain had fallen.

"Russell Court," grunted Mr. Horder. "We have but to turn left, fifty yards ahead, and—"

There they found it, as you may still find such curiosities, tucked away behind the squalor of the houses in Drury Lane. The long-past had flowed over it, mummifying the wood; even the windows seemed unbroken. Producing a large key, Mr. Horder opened the door. When he pressed them all inside, the clang of the iron bar shot into its socket went up with rattling echoes.

"It has been unused, save by us, since Oliver's time," said Mr. Horder. "Come! Cromwell himself may have prayed here. Yet observe, Lord Glenarvon, that the floor is hard wood. You will not fall soft."

"Whenever I have so fallen, Mr. Horder, it has been on a floor as hard as this. There was canvas over it, of course."

"And not on turf?" suddenly rasped out the man called Cobb. His voice went high. "Where was that, cully? And when?"

"A hundred and fifty years from now, when all your grand-sires are rotting in their graves. Yes! And long, long after our greatest bare-knuckle fighter, Jem Mace, has beaten Tom Allen in Louisiana."

" 'Ere!" cried Dolly.

A soft voice spoke dryly. "Do you think to affright us, Lord Glenarvon?"

"I may yet affright you badly, Mr. Horder."

Straining his eyes in the gloom as they all walked forward over the echoing floor, Philip could see little except shadows and vague outlines. Though someone had cleaned the windows, at least on the inside, these gave little light.

No figures of saints or angels adorned the windows of this chapel. The windows were of very thick coloured glass, lozenges of red or blue or purple or yellow, so that the procession seemed to shuffle forward through the dimness of a great lantern done into gleams of coloured glass.

Then Mr. Horder stopped abruptly. His voice was soft, but very quick and cool.

"Dolly! Cobb! MacAdam!"

"Ay, guv?"

"Spread out and look to your pistols. MacAdam!"

"Well?"

"Glenarvon can't get out; the door is locked as well as bolted. Here is the key. Take it."

"Ay, but what—?"

"There is someone in this church beside ourselves."

MacAdam, the Scot in the Scots chapel, uttered a ringing cry which was half-oath and half-prayer. Mr. Horder remained coolly contemptuous.

"Come, they are men like ourselves. Look forward to the platform, with the pulpit in the middle. Five men are sitting in the tall chairs behind the pulpit."

From the platform, now, they all heard the *whick* from the striker of a tinder-box.

At the same moment Philip seized Jennifer's arm, dragged her back ten feet, and threw her behind him. Dolly whipping round and jumping after them, lashed out left-handed with his knife—and missed by inches.

Now Dolly, Cobb, and MacAdam must all turn towards the pulpit, ahead and perhaps two feet above them. The flame of the tinder-box ignited the wick of a candle, standing on the pulpit in a bright, new silver candlestick.

Up behind the pulpit, as though he meant to preach a sermon, loomed a man Philip had never dreamed of seeing there. He was tightened into a green surcoat, much frogged and furred, and the Star of the Garter glimmered against his chest.

"Come, you interest me!" rang out a throaty, familiar bass voice. "Would you fire on the Prince of Wales?"

"Oh, Come Ye in Peace Here, or Come Ye in War?"

During that pause while nobody spoke, Philip glanced quickly between two faces.

One was the Prince's, as his bulky body hung above the pulpit in the green surcoat. He was cold sober. But his face was red and puffy under the brown wig and the cocked hat jammed down on it. His grey, bulging eyes were angry, bitterly angry, as he stared down at Mr. Horder beyond the two rows of pews.

The other face was that of Mr. Horder himself. It was as though Cupid's countenance, like a wax Cupid in the heat, had melted and run together so that only teeth and malice remained. As the blinking eyes flashed towards Philip, the latter had never known until then just how much Samuel Horder hated him.

"Now hear me!" boomed the Prince.

He slammed his hand down on the pulpit, between the jumping candle flame and an ancient hour-glass standing there.

"There will be no match here tonight," he said. "I do not mark the fact that John Jackson, with whom I have donned the gloves myself, is near two stone over Lord Glenarvon's weight and champion of England as well. But that gentleman, Mr. Horder," and he nodded towards Philip, "is a peer of this realm; you insult *me*. He will meet no professional

216

bruiser save with gloves in a sparring-go. That is my ruling, Mr. Horder; you will ignore it at your cost."

Samuel Horder, Esquire, bowed obsequiously. His voice was oily. Yet insolence flowed underneath, and the Prince knew it.

"If I might have permission to speak, Your Royal Highness—?"

"Well?"

"I might remind you, sir, when you go abroad on these adventures, under your title as Earl of Chester, you are still subject to the law of England."

"Damn the law," said the Prince briefly.

"I would further remind you, this house is my property. No man, however exalted, may enter it without my permission." Up went Mr. Horder's voice. "I would finally remind you, these three men are my servants, and they are all armed."

The Prince regarded him with real interest.

"Are they, by God!" he said softly. "Then perhaps, sir, they would care for pitched battle with *my* followers? Permit me to introduce them."

With much grace and dignity the Prince moved round his balloon-bulk towards the tall chair farthest away on his left.

"Fred, my dear fellow!"

Up rose a tall, heavy man, long-cloaked to his neck, whose cocked hat was squashed down over heavily powdered hair tied with a black military ribbon at the back. Though his face was red and somewhat resembled the Prince's, he looked a good deal more formidable.

"My brother Frederick," said the Prince. "His Royal Highness the Duke of York. He commands the Army, as may be known to you, and some count him the best shot among his own officers. Are *you* armed, Fred?"

"Oh, two barkers," growled the Duke of York.

He looked slowly out and down over Horder, over Dolly and MacAdam and Cobb. Then the Duke of York shook his head.

"Rum lot, you know," he declared, and unexpectedly grinned and sat down.

"Sir John Lade!" said the Prince.

Philip started. Jennifer had moved round beside him, and was tightly holding his hand.

Up behind the Prince, peering past his shoulder, rose a stockily built man, also caped and with one of the new flat-crowned hats, immediate predecessor of the top-hat, stuck on the side of his head. Though facially he did not resemble the one-eyed coachman of last night, his voice and manner might have been the same.

"Ay, sir, I remember the clouts!" he said. "My own wife was once a kept woman to a high-toby cove from these parts. He departed this life by way of Tyburn, rot him, and I got the filly. You, Frank Cobb! I grassed you twice, in a mill behind Wills's Coffee House, and you couldn't have come up if your pals hadn't tipped the privy over on me. But I admit," he slapped the sides of his cloak, "the poppers are best for a job like this."

And he sat down.

Urbanely the Prince turned a little towards his left.

"Mr. Brinsley Sheridan," he said. "Mr. Sheridan, I believe, was one of the last men to fight a duel with swords, and stabbed his man on the ground when his own blade broke. He is at least a tolerable shot if his hands be steady. Are they steady, Sherry?"

Mr. Sheridan, though he winked broadly at Philip, pulled a long face as he rose up.

"Your Royal Highness well knows," he replied in his Carlton-House manner, "that tomorrow I am to wed my sweetest Hecca. The ladies, bless 'em, don't like a bridegroom who

arrives owl drunk at their nuptials. I can't say why, but
they don't."

Both hands came out from under his cloak. Two pistols
spun high in the air, the polish of their barrels a flash by the
light of the one candle. Deftly Mr. Sheridan caught them
cross-handed, and he bowed as he subsided.

"Sir," he replied, "I am quite sober."

The Prince turned a little further to the left.

"Major George Hanger!" he said. "Once brevetted colonel, distinguished among our officers for his bravery and
striking power during the American War. Major Hanger
has chosen to bring two Brown Bess muskets and a cavalry
sabre. Eh, Hanger?"

"Ah, bejasus," growled Major Hanger, showing only a
little of his hooked nose and blue chin. "When one thing
don't serve another will. That's the first principle of war,
sorr."

The Prince turned back to Samuel Horder, Esquire, and
looked down at him without favour.

"Those are the cards in my hand," he said. "D'ye play?"

"Your Royal Highness, I am quite unarmed!"

"So am I. *D'ye play?*"

The plump little man hesitated.

Then he gave swift, hissing instructions, in an undertone
to two of his companions.

"You know what to do," he screeched, "and where to go.
Run!"

Dolly and MacAdam, thrusting their firearms into their
belts, turned and bolted hard for the front doors of the
empty church. Their running footfalls clacked loudly on the
hard wood. They were nearly disappearing in a gloom of
red, yellow, blue, purple touches from dusty windows.

Instantly the Duke of York was on his feet. The wings
of his cloak were thrown back. He stood sideways, his right

arm out rigid; his left hand carelessly carrying the other pistol high.

"George! Want me to pick 'em off?"

"No, now, that's unsportin'!" protested Sir John Lade, also jumping up. "Can't shoot 'em in the back can we?" Then he yelled through the echoing church. "Turn and show your fire, slumgullions! Turn and show fire!"

Dolly and MacAdam had no disposition to show fire. There was a crash as the iron bar was shot back. You could hear the key tremble with clashing noises round the lock before MacAdam fitted it in. The lock snapped; the doors opened; the fugitives disappeared.

"Mr. Horder!" snapped the Prince. "Where have those men gone?"

Samuel Horder, Esquire, smirked as he bowed.

"In candour, Your Royal Highness—"

"Speak, I say!"

"Why, sir, they are gone to fetch the chief magistrate at Bow Street and all his Runners. Against fifty redbreasts, I fear even your noble followers would have small chance. Lord Glenarvon shall not escape what he deserves. He will be taken and hanged, whether Your Highness wills it or no."

"Now will he, bejasus?" breathed Major Hanger, standing up to his full height.

The Prince of Wales motioned him to silence. The Prince looked down sternly at Philip and Jennifer, who had approached hand in hand almost to the front row of pews.

Taking a good grip on the sides of the pulpit, he eyed the hour-glass as though wondering how long his sermon ought to go on. By some illusion he seemed to expand and grow larger.

"My Lord Glenarvon. Miss Baird." The throaty boom grew sterner. "There are some matters, I hope, upon which it is not necessary to dwell. I need not say how the conduct of you both, in the past two days, has shocked and grieved me."

"Hey! George!" said the Duke of York.

"What's that, Fred?"

"You're only Earl of Chester today, dammit. Need you go on spoutin' sermons like the Old Man himself?"

"Hem! Well!" observed the Prince, much struck with this. "It is true that I need not bear myself as my position requires. However!"

Now he spoke so gravely, and with such curious dignity, that the whole platform fell silent.

"Lord Glenarvon." He bowed. "It has come to my ears that two nights ago, at Carlton House, you and I exchanged words somewhat sharp. Indeed, I remember little of this. But I thank you, sir, for another reason. You reminded me of something I had been apt to forget." His eyes clouded. "I hold you in high esteem, for—for causes I dare not explain even here. When Mr. Sheridan came to plead your cause, I was only too happy to appear here in your time of need. Major Hanger, I remind you, is a wizard with locks."

Philip bowed in his turn.

"Your Royal Highness—" he began.

"Stay!" the Prince interposed sharply. "I would further, sir, offer you apology. Yesterday a dozen men from the platoon of Grenadier Guards, assigned to protect Carlton House, were borrowed without my knowledge by a Whig gentleman so high placed that we need not mention his name. A treacherous footman informed him of a note written by Sheridan. These men were to follow you, and affright any who would give you shelter. For this, Lord Glenarvon, I offer you full and free apology."

Again Philip bowed, warm with gratitude.

"Sir! This apology is so needless that—"

"Forgive me. It is very needful."

"May I ask why, sir?"

"You may. Because there are other matters not so easily condoned. Because— Damme, man," added the Prince, breaking down a little and with his eye on Philip's black leather jacket, "are you so thirsty a tippler you must carry a wine bottle forever in your pocket?"

"This bottle, sir, is necessary to my evidence. Mr. Sheridan! Will you take it in your charge, as also (here!) this note of an address in Lambeth?"

"Ay, truly," answered Mr. Sheridan, getting up and leaning over the platform, as Philip stretched over the pews to give him the bottle and the note. "This bottle, stab me," and he eyed it longingly, "shall be well secure in my care."

"No!" Philip cried in alarm. "Don't drink it. For God's sake don't drink! It's full of poison!"

"Poison, is it?" demanded Mr. Sheridan, greener than he had already been.

"In a great sense, yes. You'll oblige me?"

"Indeed," agreed Mr. Sheridan, hastily thrusting bottle and note into his inside pocket of the cloak, " 'twill hold me to my resolution that no strong waters shall pass these lips until I am wed to my sweetest Hecca. Ouf!"

And he bowed to the Prince and sat down.

It was as though this pause had again pumped up the Prince, with a sort of elocutionary bellows, to immensity and sternness.

"Lord Glenarvon!" he said. "There are other matters, I repeat, not so easily condoned or explained away. You are accused of running away with Miss Baird here."

"That, sir, is true."

"Hem! Well! We can't be too hard on you for doing as much. But it is also stated, in order to be off with Miss Baird, you strangled to death your lady's maid in mistake for your lady. As your Prince and your future King, I ask you, is that charge true or false?"

Now Philip almost yelled.

"It is false, sir. As I hope soon to show."

It was Jennifer, pressing Philip's hand to keep him silent, who moved past. She turned up her most appealing look, and spoke in her sweetest voice.

"Your Royal Highness, may *I* be given leave to say a word?"

"Oh, damme," muttered the Prince, disconcerted again. He glanced over his shoulder, muttering to Sir John Lade, "Gel's got pluck too, didn't I tell you?" He turned back to Jennifer with overpowering dignity.

"Madam," he said, "this is most unwomanly. You should not be here amid men rough and—er—lustful. However, since you are here, speak your mind!"

"I believe, sir," continued Jennifer, her face upraised, "you are accounted one of the very authorities on English law? That you could sit with any red-robed judge on his bench, and render a decision as good as his?"

"Hum! Well!" said the Prince, and polished his finger-nails on his coat with some complacence. "If so many say it, no doubt 'tis true. Indeed, madam, *I* so account it. But what of this?"

"Then might Philip," said Jennifer, "plead his cause before *you?*"

"Madam?" exclaimed the startled Prince.

"Might Philip," repeated Jennifer in that same clear voice, "plead his cause before *you?*"

"Ay; so he might. But I would warn you, madam, I was so interested in this affair that I called for a copy of the depositions from a magistrate, one Mr. Avery. I got them; I read them; they have a black ugly sound. And I flatter myself I am a difficult man to hoodwink. Should I not be convinced—"

"And yet sir, should you be convinced?"

The Prince smote his hand on the desk.

"In that event, madam, I should inform the proper au-

thorities; Lord Glenarvon should go free in an instant. And
no man in this realm—save only the King my father, a gentleman unlikely to intrude—might touch him or lay hand on
him henceforward. I promise you this, upon my honour. Do
you, Lord Glenarvon, having been warned, desire to plead
your cause before me?"

"I desire it, sir, above all things."

Once more the Prince smote the pulpit.

"Then, egad, so you shall! And at Carlton House, and this
very afternoon!"

Here he paused. For a moment he seemed to look into his
own heart, and not to like what he saw. The red, puffy,
bloated face would not turn towards those below him.

Yet he did speak, after difficulty.

"Miss Baird," he said, "I am no longer a very young man.
Much of the scandal they tell of me, I fear, is true. My
motto, 'I serve,' has never once been fulfilled, and let no liar
or flatterer about me say it has!"

Nobody spoke.

"Yet those men are very stupid," said the Prince of Wales,
"who take me for a fool. As Prince or as King, I will see
justice done. I will see justice done, by God's grace and
my own forbears. And no man before me shall plead honourable cause in vain."

Though there was a moisture of self-pity in the grey eyes,
it was impossible to dislike the man or doubt his sincerity
in this.

Mr. Sheridan stared at the floor. Major Hanger fidgetted.
Sir John Lade, embarrassed, was silent. The Duke of York,
though hesitant and doubtful, cleared his throat. Then out
from the dimness at the back of the church, amid coloured
gleams, rose up a high, strident, arrogant voice which most
of them knew.

"Then will you hear my honourable cause, Your Royal
Highness?"

It was Colonel Thornton.

They heard his jack-boots creaking long before he emerged into the light of the solitary candle. His cocked hat, with the tuft of white feathers, he wore almost over one ear. His black military cloak was closed, except for what projected from it about the height of his chest.

But, when Jennifer saw this, all the fear-fangs closed on her once more. From the golden hand-guards, oblong and slightly curved, to the wire-woven grip and the golden pommel, Colonel Thornton carried under his arm a pair of small-swords.

"You know me, gentlemen, I think?"

"Ay, we know you," growled the Duke of York. "Young Glenarvon tried to teach you manners with an empty pistol. 'Tis only the Almighty can do that."

Completely ignoring the Duke of York, Colonel Thornton addressed himself to the Prince.

"It was this matter of the empty pistol," he said, "which compelled me to seek out Your Royal Highness here."

"And pray how, sir, did you find me?"

"An agent of this—this creature's," the colonel's eyes strayed briefly towards Samuel Horder, who had gone white, "asked me this morning, in my rooms, the sum of a hundred guineas to witness a prize-fight tonight. I have no money for such expenses," he hesitated, "until Glenarvon is taken and hanged. But a small outlay of silver, at Carlton House, disclosed the whereabouts of Your Royal Highness."

"Ay. Well, what then?"

"This," answered Colonel Thornton.

From under his arm, with a rattle of steel, he drew out the two small-swords and held them cradled in the arms. The bright blades flashed wickedly; they were not overlong and had no cutting edges, but the blades were ground needle-sharp.

"I would have fought the man fairly, with pistol," Colonel

Thornton bleated out. "He tricked and cheated me. It was a violation of the duelling code, as well you gentlemen know. Shall *I* be made laughing stock? I claim the right to meet him, here and now, with swords. Your Royal Highness, being incognito, may witness and judge."

"Stay, now!" said a voice they hardly recognized. "Under Your Royal Highness's indulgence, I crave one word!"

It was Samuel Horder. His Cupid's face had been again adjusted, his hands clasped.

"I too am a gentleman," he called softly. "If any of you remember, I was once a noted swordsman. As for my gentility, on my mother's side—"

"I was aware of it, Mr. Horder." The Prince spoke coldly. "Else I had not addressed you as 'sir.' What then?"

"By the many cheats and insults done me by Lord Glenarvon," snapped Mr. Horder, "*I* claim the right to meet him with small-swords! Here and now!"

Philip Clavering, with a half-smile on his face, strolled forward.

Jennifer, at the depth of despair, ran to stop him. But it was too late. Philip's voice rang loudly.

"Gentlemen," he called, "would you see good sport?"

Dead silence.

"In this room, as I understand it, can be set up immediately a twenty-four-foot ring, with stakes and posts. Doubtless there will be lights as well."

"Well, my dear sir?" demanded the Prince.

"My opponent," said Philip, "may go into that ring with his sword, and use it as he likes. I want no sword; I know no swordplay; I shall wear on my hands only boxing-gloves. I shall not attempt to seize his blade, or take any unfair advantage. Should he kill me—good, he is welcome! But, should *he* be knocked out of time for thirty-eight seconds, I claim the victory. Agreed?"

Up jumped the Duke of York.

"Damme, Glenarvon," he yelled, "this won't do!"

"And why not, sir?"

"You can't win! No boxer can win against a swordsman!"

The Duke of York's own boots creaked as he stood there; his cloak flopped round him in illustration, and his black eyebrows stood out against a redder, more bulging face.

"I've seen it too often, boxer against swordsman. The boxer stands four-square, like this, his fists straight up at the sides. When the swordsman lunges, d'ye see, the boxer can't avoid being pierced except by jumping back or tryin' to strike the blade away."

"This is very learned, Fred—" began his brother.

"Boo!" said the Duke of York, and turned back to Philip. "Well, by usual the boxer misses the blade and gets stuck. When he tries to hit back, the swordsman's out of reach. In a few minutes the boxer's covered with blood. The swordsman runs him through the calf of the leg, once or twice, and topples him over. After, if the swordsman's a good feller, he kicks his man and says, 'Let be.' If he ain't a good feller—"

Here the Duke of York made a vivid pantomime sword-thrust at the ground.

"What have ye got to say to that, hey?" he demanded, with all the insistence of a son of George the Third.

"Fred!"

"Hey, George?"

"Be pleased to sit down and shut up."

The Duke of York subsided.

The Prince of Wales, his immense chest puffed out and glimmering with the Star of the Garter, once more whacked his hand on the pulpit.

"I suppose I shall have to permit this," he said, concealing the fact that he loved it. His tone grew dry. "Yet you seem, Lord Glenarvon, to suffer from too many enemies. Colonel Thornton would meet you. Mr. Horder screams to meet you.

Yet the choice must be yours. Which one of them will you fight?"

Philip drew a deep breath.

"Both of them," he said. "Together, and at once."

And again the dead silence seemed to stretch out interminably, like a fiddle string which must crack or snap. And it did.

"Oh, damme!" moaned Mr. Sheridan, and put his head in his hands.

It is a sober fact that Sir John Lade removed his low-crowned hat, and savagely struck his forehead three times against the edge of the pulpit. He had done this before; he came to no harm.

"Glenarvon, you're mad!" yelled the Duke of York.

Now it was Major Hanger who stood up.

"Mad he may be," declared Major Hanger, "but, bejasus and the howly angels, 'tis the sort of madness I like. Gentlemen, I'll give any of ye a hundred pounds, even money, on Glenarvon."

"Done!" said the Duke of York, startling everyone because the Duke was rather tight-fisted and seldom made a bet. "I favour the lad, to be sure; but business is business."

"As for me," calmly and casually remarked the Prince, "I offer six to one on my friend Glenarvon, in any sum the taker may care to name."

"Done for a thousand guineas!" snapped Sir John Lade. "York's right. He can't meet one sword, let alone two."

"As for meself," intoned Mr. Sheridan, "I own no farthing save for me wedding. But I'll swallow this bottle of poison, I vow, if Glenarvon don't knock 'em both out of time."

"Speaking of that," said the Prince uneasily, "I should not serve as timekeeper, having a wager on the matter. Still, if you will permit me to hold the watch by virtue of my position, this match shall go on no longer than half an hour, if as long—"

A chorus of voices bellowed out and urged him to hold the watch.

Jennifer had groped her way to the front bench, and sat down. She could no longer even see Philip, who was searching for boxing-gloves. And Jennifer, now as once before, felt she could endure no more.

With incredible rapidity Cobb, under Mr. Horder's direction, was setting up the ring. The heavy oaken posts were first worked and hammered deep into holes into the floor; the hammering seemed to strike on Jennifer's brain.

Coloured ropes were run taut between the posts; Jennifer could have reached out and touched the nearest rope. From hooks at one side of the church, Cobb lowered two large stable-lanterns, oblong slides of glass bound in brass fittings and burning oil. As they were kindled, first a blue and then a yellow glare sprang out over the ring. Hoisting them to about ten feet above the ring, Cobb hooked them there.

Jennifer, pressing her hands over her ears, tried to shut out the cries of betting behind her. It was their utter callousness which made her wince, though this was only a custom of the time and should not have troubled her.

Now Colonel Thornton, in the middle of the ring, uplifted his own insufferable tones.

"Would you humiliate me further, gentlemen? Would you have me fight side by side with this—this—" He looked in a frenzy of contempt at Mr. Horder, who returned the look.

"Colonel Thornton, sir!" called Mr. Sheridan.

"Yes, Mr. Sheridan?"

"To the best of my knowledge, Mr. Horder has been thief, pimp, receiver of stolen goods, hider of criminals or exposer of them if it suits him better. He has been liar, false matchmaker, and half a dozen times murderer. But he *is* the grandson of a duke."

Colonel Thornton's hard face altered.

"The grandson of a duke? You swear this, sir?"

"You have only to ask His Royal Highness."

After a struggle within himself, Colonel Thornton turned to Mr. Horder, who was drawing a scratch-line in chalk across the right.

"Mr. Horder," he bowed, satisfied but not liking the man any better, "I have much misunderstood you. Will you honour me by fighting beside me, and further accepting one of these blades, on which you may rely?"

"The honour, sir," replied Mr. Horder, with an oily dislike, "is entirely mine."

Colonel Thornton stood sideways, offering the two hilts over his arm. Mr. Horder whipped out one of them. Each man saluted the other, the blades flashing upright under the bright yellow lights. Then both began pulling off their outer clothes, flinging them over the ring-ropes.

And Philip, with gloves on his hands, slid into the pew beside Jennifer.

"Phil!"

"It's all right," he whispered, putting his arm round her. "It's all right."

"It's not all right. Phil! Why? Why must you do this? You were all but out of danger; all but free—"

"Jenny," he interrupted softly, "haven't you always found some method in my madness?" .

"Well—"

"The first reason—no, it can wait. If those two swordsmen could work together, and time their lunges together, they'd finish me soon. But they can't; they detest each other. Each will fight in his own style, and get in each other's way.

"I still wear the heavy leather jacket; it impedes arms and shoulders, but it'll turn a light sword-thrust. The gloves are good—smoothly stuffed with felt and not straw, about eight ounces; I can go all out in them. All the same, I wish the Duke of York hadn't babbled. If those two think to go for my legs, which are the hardest to guard—Jenny!"

She did not speak. She felt with all her instinct, he would tell her something he had guarded before.

"Yesterday morning, Jenny, I did not tell you everything I knew about fencing."

"You *can* use the sword, then?"

"No, I've never touched a foil; that was true. But I've watched fencing. Watched it day after day, because I loved it—the speed, the skill, the subtlety. That was how I, as a boy, thought boxing ought to be. That's how I fight even now."

He unwound one arm from Jennifer's shoulder, and stared at the two gloves.

"But a deity called the crown, then or now, doesn't want that at all. They want the killer with the Big Punch. And because my wife of the old days taunted me about money, and jeered at me for not being able to make it, I must turn myself into a so-called heavy puncher to earn my bread and butter.

"Do you guess now why I hated my work? It was 'the crowd.' Every time I landed a solid punch, I was hitting 'the crowd.' Every time I knocked out a man, and knew he was gone the second he hit the canvas, for an instant I had knocked out 'the crowd.' Those two swordsmen in the ring now, whom I own I hate, are 'the crowd.' What's a championship, Jenny? It's only murdering 'the crowd.' "

And, pale of face, he sprang up.

"Phil!" Jennifer cried. "You mustn't lose your head now! You mustn't—"

"Lord Glenarvon!" said a voice, up and a little behind them.

"Yes, Your Royal Highness?"

"The hand of my watch hovers near four. The other contestants are ready. Are you?"

"Quite ready, sir!"

But Philip had not lost his head. As he climbed through the ropes, he turned back his head and smiled wryly at Jennifer.

"Pray for me, sweet," he said. "This is the hardest fight of all."

xviii

"Vengeance, My Lords!"

Jennifer, sitting with her head back over the back of the pew, did not see the first full lunge of the sword, or the vicious glove blow in reply.

She was peering, through a chink in the past, at some memory that startled her. The clear glow of the lanterns lit up the church to its farthest end. It set gleaming the red, yellow, blue, and purple lozenges in the window, outlining even their shape. It showed the rotted wooden planks of the walls, run together by dirt.

Then, by some illusion, it became her church, the church she had known as a girl. It was of some other dissenting Protestant sect; despite the voice of her father, heard behind a crackling newspaper, she was not sure what.

Yet distinctly she could see a ghostly congregation, over a floor where she had dreamed there was a prize-ring and a long open space to the front doors. She could hear the minister's footsteps creak on the platform behind her. The ghostly congregation rose up, to a rustling and a crackling of hymn books, and they sang to the wheezy notes of the organ.

"Lead, Kindly Light." That was the hymn. They sang it, and sat down with more rustling. The minister cleared his throat. Was it for sermon, or for prayers?

No. Someone had called on her, Jenny Baird, to pray. Her lips moved soundlessly.

"O, Thou," it was a trembling through her, "bid us go from

233

this cage in which we are held. Lead us back to our own space and time. Set us free from this dirt, and cruelty, and snobbishness. Was it not marked, only a moment ago, how the worst of men was called worthy because he was the grandson of a duke, and no man laughed, or even smiled?

"Is my lover, my husband, forever to be beaten to his knees? He stands up again; he defeats them, and I am glad. But there is much blood on his head; he is changing every hour before my eyes, and I am afraid. Let him go! And, if I be considered at all worthy, let me go too."

"Got him! Got him! Got him!"

The shout pierced through a roar of applause and acclaim from the platform.

Jennifer, her dream gone, sat up straight and looked at the ring.

What had happened there, since Philip ducked through the ropes, had gone fast and gone murderously.

Philip had walked across, toed the scratch, and slipped back with his guard up. His left glove was carried high, but the right arm carried almost as high, too.

His two adversaries, rather wide apart, faced him from beyond the scratch. Colonel Thornton was on his right. Colonel Thornton, right knee bent and out, toe pointing forward, had his left knee behind and bent, toe sideways, crouched in orthodox position. His blade, its grip held hard between thumb and two fingers, slanted outwards; his left arm was behind him, forearm up from the elbow, as though to balance him.

On the left side Mr. Samuel Horder, the only one Philip really feared, appeared more careless. His shirt, though be-ruffled, was fairly dirty. Though he crouched in much the same position as Colonel Thornton, he lightly held the wire-woven grip of the blade between thumb and forefinger.

Out boomed a familiar, throaty voice.

"Time!"

The lantern light flashed on the motionless blades. For a second nobody moved. The platform was dead quiet.

Philip, his eyes flickering, decided that Colonel Thornton would strike first. And he was right.

Thornton, supple for all his years, streaked out at full-length lunge in tierce for the right side of Philip's chest. Philip's right arm, leather-clad, jerked up under the sword halfway down. He turned it flat, and the blade flashed wide as Philip gave Colonel Thornton a hard left jab in the face. Colonel Thornton, a little rocked, jumped back to guard position.

Even as the colonel moved back, Mr. Horder's blade drove in at full-length lunge in quarte for Philip's heart.

Philip, who had gone in, had barely time to strike the blade aside with his left hand and dance back. There was no chance to hit in reply. Slipping to the left, he met the chubby little man face to face.

Mr. Horder's Cupid face still wore that sly, triumphant smile. He moved the point of his blade in little circles, light-stung. His smile broadened. He darted out in a feint, in high quarte; that was a boxer's trick. When the lunge came, again straight for the heart, Philip parried it easily—and went out in a right cross to the jaw. But again the little man, faster than any cat, bounced so far back to guard position that Philip's blow missed him by two feet.

The *clack-stamp* of booted feet raised heavy dust, floating as high as the waist. Mr. Horder, with care, was ready to lunge again. Then Colonel Thornton, jumping too far to his own right and jarring his partner away, made his great bid.

His long length shot out in low second, for the extended side of Philip's leg just above the knee and the top-boot.

Philip leaped back. There was no way to parry this. But the lunge, a bad one and ill-directed, caught him none the less.

The blade ripped through the side of his left calf and

stabbed deep. Agony pierced up through Philip from his calf through his whole body to his head. Colonel Thornton was dragging to get the sword out. He did get it out, with a last yank that nearly upset his opponent.

But Philip, with murder in his heart, could still use two legs for a time. He surged up on both of them. His right upper-cut travelled less than fifteen inches. But it landed so hard under Colonel Thornton's jaw that the spectators did not hear the thud of the glove.

The colonel pitched forward. He landed flat on his face with a crash which raised dust-puffs from the floor, instinctively throwing out his right arm to avoid falling on his own sword. He twitched once or twice, like a cut snake. Then he lay still.

Mr. Horder, again about to lunge for Philip's heart, stopped at the roar of applause and acclaim from the platform. Through it pierced the voice of Mr. Sheridan:

"Got him! Got him! Got him!"

"Gentlemen!" called the authoritative voice of the Prince. "You in the ring will wait, and the others will wait, for a count of time on Colonel Thornton."

There was such a stillness that they could hear the heavy ticking of the watch. It had no second-hand, and the Prince was obliged to screw up his eyes and peer closely to judge.

Philip Clavering needed that. The agony in his leg had a little subsided; he felt a numbness, a swelling up, but the blood still trickled down into his top-boot. It was very heavy as he lifted it tentatively. He wondered how long it would uphold him now.

And of course, he was thinking, *there's a parry for that lunge in seconde, even if it comes at you sideways. Strike it back towards your opponent! If it comes at you from in front, strike the blade sideways to the right or the left. It's simple, but we never think of holding our guards low. That's it! That's it!*

". . . thirty-six, thirty-seven, thirty-eight," intoned the Prince of Wales. He shut up his watch with a click, and opened it again. "Hanger!"

"Sir?"

"Carry Colonel Thornton out of the ring. No, drag him; it is more suitable."

All waited, with a babble of talk, while this was done.

"Gentlemen in the ring!" said the Prince. "You will toe the scratch, I shall cry, 'Time!' and you shall resume your contest. Now!"

Carefully Philip walked back to toe the scratch, stumbling only once. Mr. Horder's Cupid face wore a faintly scornful, faintly leering smile.

"Time!"

Instantly Mr. Horder's point flashed out for the heart. Philip blocked it, feeling the intense heat from friction as the side of the blade whipped along leather. Twice again this happened. But each time Philip could not hit back; he lumbered, and once nearly fell.

My God, he thought, *suppose I can't hit the fellow at all?*

All power remained in arms and shoulders. But his famous speed was gone. And so, *I need only fall once. They're permitted to finish you on the floor.*

Look out!

Something flickered in Horder's eyes. It meant a feint, and a different attack, as a boxer telegraphs a punch. Horder was moving, moving slightly sideways. He wouldn't try—?

But he did.

Out went Horder, back bent, in full-length lunge for the calf of Philip's right leg, the other leg, to bring him down. Philip slapped at the sword wildly—and missed. Again the blade pierced and stabbed agony through him; deftly the blade flew out, and blood flowed into the top-boot. Mr. Horder was well back at guard position, his Cupid face laughing behind the stained sword.

There was a roar from the platform as Philip, tottering, dropped down on one knee.

And Mr. Horder darted in for the kill.

It was only then, when for the first time panic took him in the ring, that Philip remembered. He remembered Mr. Horder's hand, with finger and thumb pinched too lightly against the wire-woven grip of the sword.

In that desperation of strength he had known before, Philip surged to his feet. As the sword came in for his heart, he whacked sideways with his left arm. It caught the sword midway down, and tore the blade from Horder's fingers. The blade swung away over the ropes, whirling until it clanged, hilt down, a dozen feet beyond.

Philip's left glove whipped over and up. It was his best blow: the left hook which had knocked out Henri Duchêne at Harringay, and it landed with full power on Mr. Horder's jaw.

Afterwards there were arguments, even bets, as to whether the feet of Samuel Horder, Esquire, had completely left the floor as he sailed over backwards. But nobody doubted he was clean knocked out. He landed on his back with a sodden flop, his face wet with sweat, his shirt clinging to him, his Cupid's mouth open like a dead man's.

The babble along the platform had grown deafening. The Duke of York was arguing with Major Hanger, who waved his hand. Mr. Sheridan was loudly singing one of his own airs. Glumly Sir John Lade wrote an I.O.U. Only the Prince remained still, after counting and closing up his watch.

As for Philip, he had gone off balance with that blow. He leaned on his right knee, very close to Horder, and his head was down. Presently he looked instinctively round for Jenny.

He saw her sitting in the pew, paralyzed, unable to move, but with her large eyes on him.

Philip staggered to his feet. He crossed the ring to her

as well as he could. He supported himself on his hands by the ring-ropes, but presently he was compelled to go down on his knee again.

Then Jennifer woke up.

"Careful, my dear," said Philip, still a little dazed. "Don't come too close. All over sweat. Not exertion. Fear."

"Oh, do you think I care about that?"

Jennifer dodged between the ropes, put her arms round his waist, and tried to lift him up. But it was impossible; she had not the strength.

"Tell you something," he muttered in that low, groping voice. "In all ages, everything changes. Manners, customs, speech, views on life, even morals—all change. But fear is the same. Only fear is the same."

"Gently, darling!"

"Tell you something else, Jenny," he insisted. "I'll never fight again. Never go in a ring again. Swear it. Not fear; think not, anyway. But I know why."

"Lord Glenarvon!" called the Prince of Wales from above him.

Philip looked up through swimming eyes.

"I do not think, Lord Glenarvon, you know how well you have done. If there is any—"

"Tell you something, sir!" Philip said earnestly. "Never curse the crowd. They're right; you're wrong. You try to be both a Fancy Dan and a heavy puncher, and you can't. Let the applause go to the Big Puncher; he deserves it. You don't."

"Lord Glenarvon, I cannot understand a word you are saying. Nevertheless, I tell you this; if they should try to arrest you now—"

The Prince paused, startled, and lifted up his several chins.

The front doors of the church flew open, banging against the walls and rebounding. In the aperture stood a neat, withered little man in a three-cornered hat, his right hand on a tall cane with a gold knob.

Past him, on either side, poured the Runners. The chains of their handcuffs jingled against scarlet waistcoats; their white gaiters were like those of an army. They lined up along both walls, on either side of the little man with the cane, again like an army, with pistols drawn. There were many more outside.

The man with the cane, clearly a dignitary, stepped forward.

"Gentlemen," he called in a harsh, high voice, "which of you is named Philip Clavering, Earl of Glenarvon?"

Philip's wits cleared as though a bucket of water had been flung in his face. With a violent effort he stood up and turned round, Jennifer supporting him.

"I am," he called back. "And you?"

"My name is Cotterill, my lord. Sir John Cotterill, chief magistrate at Bow Street Police Office. I hold authority to take you, both by magistrate's order and verdict of crowner's quest. The charge is murder. My lord, you would be ill-advised to resist."

"Now would he, by God!" thundered the Prince of Wales.

His voice seemed to strike Sir John Cotterill like a blow in the face. The chief magistrate's lips tightened so hard that not even the line showed.

"I have been informed, sir," he retorted dryly, "of your high place. It does not absolve you from the law you are sworn to uphold. Besides, we are fifty men to your six. Have you an answer for that?"

"Yes!" said the Prince, and tears of pure fury glimmered in his eyes.

He nodded towards Philip.

"That man," he said, "has been tricked and cheated by all save a few. Whether he is innocent I know not and at the moment I care not. But fairly he has met his enemies, and fairly he has beaten them all. And now, when he is wounded and alone, shall he be pulled down by a pack of yapping curs? No! I think not."

"Take care, sir!"

The Prince merely looked at him, without troubling to reply. He made a gesture to the four men who had stood up behind him.

Each man, almost at the same time, threw the wings of his cloak back over his shoulders. There was a running *click-click* as the hammers of six pistols and two muskets snapped back to fire position.

"Again I warn you!" screeched the chief magistrate, faltering a little. "If we must do our duty, we will. You yourself may escape harm, but this will not come well to the ears of your royal father! What would you do?"

"I will make it known to you," answered the Prince.

He picked up the silver candlestick from the pulpit. With as much stateliness as though he were leading a ball at Carlton House, he moved across the platform, went down the two little steps, and went over to the side of the prize-ring.

"Lord Glenarvon," he said courteously, "if you can contrive to walk, with your faithful lady supporting you, will you both be good enough to come here and stand behind me?"

Philip, with Jenny's arm round his waist, walked pretty steadily. Horror struck him as he nearly pitched face down in climbing through the ropes on the far side of the ring. But again, crushing away pain and forgetting it, he stood up with Jennifer beside him. Just ahead was the huge back of the Prince's green coat.

The Prince glanced behind him.

"Fred! Sherry!" he said. "Walk on the left side of these two, and guard them. Hanger! Lade! Walk on the right side!"

Casually, even carelessly, the guards took their places. The little procession moved out, round the other side of the ring, and stopped. There it faced Sir John Cotterill and his Runners from a distance of about twenty-odd feet.

"For the last time—!" began Cotterill, and stopped.

"Sir," said the Prince, just as courteously as before, "take no account of what you call my high place. But I am going forth from here, and my friends go with me. I am not armed, nor is Lord Glenarvon. Therefore we are only four to your fifty. But were we four against your hundred, sir; upon my word, we should do the same. Now stop us, if you dare."

As he shouldered forward, massively, the Star of the Garter aflash against his green coat, his cocked hat jammed over one eye, his eyes moving so imperiously from left to right that there were one or two who faltered.

A heavy growl, like mastiffs on the leash, ran along the line of the Runners. Somewhere, on the left, a pistol-hand whipped up. In the same instant the Duke of York and smiling Mr. Sheridan, wheeling only slightly, covered him with four bright pistol-muzzles.

On the right, cursing, a man ran out towards them. He looked at Sir John Lade; he hesitated, with drooping eyes and uncertain mouth. Then he moved slowly back.

The Prince was now within three steps of Sir John Cotterill.

"In the name of the King—!" cried the chief magistrate. "Stand aside!"

For half a second the tension held; then it cracked. The chief magistrate wavered and fell back. His gold-headed cane dropped from his hand and rolled on the floor. The others, furious and raging, followed his example. Even the Runners outside the doors scrambled back to clear a path.

If it had not been for Philip's hurts, Jennifer's heart would have been heaven-high. She wished, how she wished, she could take his hurts for herself! But she was proud to have been there, proudest of all, when Major Hanger winked at her from the right side, and the Duke of York winked at her from the left.

And ahead of them all, drunken, untrustworthy, selfish though he might be, marched one who was still the First Gentleman of Europe.

xix

"Nothing Extenuate,
or Set Down Aught in Malice."

"My dearest!" murmured Lady Jersey, and lightly twanged the strings of the harp.

"Hey, my love?" asked the Prince of Wales in an absent-minded way. In turn *he* ran the bow across the strings of the immense bass-viol propped up between his knees.

"You are pensive, George. Are your thoughts so far gone from me?"

"Hey?"

It was a scene pastoral and even idyllic. The music-room at Carlton House, built on the same level as the street, therefore was one floor above the gardens on which its windows faced—the smooth lawns, the statues, the trees.

The music-room was papered in grey and silver, its curtains silver-grey and looped, a long mirror over the fireplace between the two windows. Its thick carpet was entwined with burning colours. If you pressed your cheek to the panes of the right-hand window, you could have seen as far west as Buckingham House, where the old King lived when they were not concealing his mental state at Windsor. If you did the same with the left-hand window, but for the smoky huddle of buildings between, you might have seen as far as King Charles the First's statue at Charing Cross.

His Royal Highness, in a very large if overdecorated chair, sat by the left-hand window and set the bow muttering across the strings as he stared into space. Lady Jersey, slim, languishing, dark of hair and eye, watched him closely as she sat by the harp, in a very thin flowered-muslin gown against the heat.

Towards five o'clock, for an April afternoon, it had now become unbelievably hot and dark. There was no puff of wind; not a tree stirred; only a pressure against the nerves. Perhaps this affected the conduct of them both.

"Oh, if it were not for this awful heat!" Lady Jersey burst out. "I declare I am all but melting! If only the storm would burst!"

Whereupon she became languid again.

"George, my dove! A bright, new, pretty penny for your thoughts?"

The Prince grunted.

"Oh, nothing," he answered, thoughtfully peering at her sideways. "Only a song."

"A song?"

"It's not good music, no. But it's a pretty little thing in its way." Again he peered at her, thoughtfully. "I've always liked it, you know. Listen!"

His Royal Highness was a first-class performer. He settled himself and let drive.

Now a bass-viol is perhaps not the best instrument, solo, for a light and sentimental love-song. It croaks like a bullfrog, and has few tender moments. Yet, as the sonorous notes thudded round the hot grey-and-silver room, some impression of gaiety danced with them.

Lady Jersey thought she did not know the song, and was not much interested. Then three lines of it flashed through her mind; she sat up straight.

> I'd crowns resign
> To call thee mine,
>> Sweet lass of Richmond Hill.

And, as he played this, his mouth was open and his eyes were fixed with passionate sentimentality on a corner of the ceiling.

The lass of Richmond Hill could mean only—

Lady Jersey suppressed a scream.

She knew, of course, that she must soon be discarded for some other fancy. In her heart she did not really care. She was much in demand among the favoured of this earth; he would not long lack a successor. What infuriated her was the mention of this particular woman, whom she had believed discarded forever. Quite simply Lady Jersey could not understand what a man could see in her, and, to speak truth, her perplexity has been shared by many of us since then.

"George!"

"Oh, rot my guts, what is it *now?*"

"You are not thinking—thinking of that odious Fitzherbert woman?"

"And why not?" asked the Prince, defiantly flinging round his several chins.

"And you with a wife!" cried Lady Jersey. "Married to Princess Caroline of Brunswick!"

"Well, damme, I married Maria first."

"Oh, God save us!"

"And what, madam, have you to say against Maria?"

Lady Jersey panted before she spoke.

"Where is her wit? Where her charm? Her teeth are *dreadful.* She is not even good-looking! She would lord it over us all, and parade her disgusting virtue like the Ark of the Covenant. And now, I hear, she is become monstrously fat."

"We-el!" said the Prince, tolerantly tapping the bow against wood. "I myself, as you observe, am not precisely a sylph. Besides I like a woman you can lay hold of."

"George! What vulgarity!"

"All men, in their hearts, are vulgar fellows. Have you never discovered that, madam, among your own hundred and fifty-four lovers?"

Lady Jersey, choked and bereft of speech, could only stare at him.

But her feelings must find some outlet. She reached forth and ripped her fingers across the strings of the harp, with an appalling *clash-jangle* which rebounded from the walls. The Prince, stung, retorted with a hideous noise on the bass-viol. Lady Jersey tore at the harp-strings again. The Prince, getting down to work, made the bass-viol sound like a herd of buffalo imprisoned in a small room.

Then, unexpectedly, he became grim.

Hoisting himself out of his chair with some effort, he propped bass-viol and bow against the wall by the window. He faced her fully, his fists on his hips.

"Now attend to me, madam. I would speak seriously."

Lady Jersey tossed her head.

"For two nights," said the Prince, "I have suffered from a bad conscience. Two nights ago, at a dinner here in your presence, a gentleman—a gentleman, I may say, whom I have since come highly to esteem—rebuked me and reminded me of my duty towards Maria. He spoke sharply; no matter; I deserved it. Glenarvon was right. I have used the woman ill, and I'll make it up to her."

(Philip, who was now upstairs in the "hot-bathe" room, where Jennifer was arguing bitterly with the surgeon attending him and Mr. Sheridan had been persuaded to accept a small sip of iced punch—Philip would have been astounded at the meaning read into his words by the Prince of Wales.)

Lady Jersey spoke with mocking tenderness.

"And the true reason for all this, George—"

"Yes, madam?"

"Is that you merely wish to go back to your fat woman?"

This was true, so true that His Royal Highness turned nasty as he often could.

"Well, Goddamme," he roared, "and what if I do?"

Lady Jersey lowered her head.

"There are some women—may I venture to include you, madam—who cannot stop talking. In some fashion they are wound up overnight, and good for all next day. Chatter, chatter, chatter; clack, clack, clack. And I am weary of it!"

He stalked up and down the room, instinctively avoiding bumping into the pianoforte in one corner. Six violins hung in a row along another wall with strangely sinister effect, like hanged men.

Lady Jersey was now weeping bitterly.

"Hum!" said the Prince, fussed. He hesitated, stopped, and turned back to her.

"My dear," he continued, with persuasive charm, "I have been guilty of bad manners. I ask your pardon. It is hardly necessary to say I meant not one word of what I said to you, and I pray you to forget it."

"Forget?" Lady Jersey cried dramatically. "How can I *ever* forget?"

"Oh, hell!" said His Royal Highness. He pressed a hand over his eyes. "Let me tell you again, my dear, that I have suffered great stress this day. Nor has the weather favoured me. And in a very few minutes, in this room, there will begin a trial for murder."

"A trial for murder?" exclaimed Lady Jersey, so astonished that she forgot to weep and raised her head.

"Precisely that. You have heard, I suppose, that Glenarvon is accused of killing a servant in mistake for his wife?"

"Yes!" breathed Lady Jersey. Deeply fascinated, she dried her eyes.

"Well! He has begged to plead his cause before me, as judge; I have granted the favour. And I flatter myself," announced His Royal Highness, rearing up and thrusting one

hand inside the breast of his coat, "that I shall be not unworthy of it. He will be here at any moment. You, if you
like, may remain as one of the jury with Mr. Sheridan."

Up to this time, hating Philip for what the Prince main-
tained he said, she would have made a very bad jurywoman
for him. Now she was speculating.

"George! Had you ever before heard report of an intrigue
between Colonel Thornton and Chloris Glenarvon?"

"No, stab me if I ever did!"

"Nor had I. She's a clever woman," muttered Lady Jersey,
her eyes narrowing. "Lack-a-day! She's *very* clever. I only
wish *I* could— No matter! But—"

So, having forgotten to hate Philip, she hated Chloris instead.

The Prince pointed to a thick stack of papers on the pianoforte, each sheet carefully written in a fine clerkly hand.

"Why, damme, in the depositions there only a few of the
servants knew it! But then servants are acquainted with
everything. Lady Oldham knew, I allow you; but then,
again, that old harridan is the only woman in London who
knows everything."

"I *like* Glenarvon," suddenly declared Lady Jersey. "I am
not overfond of his light o'love, but at least," Lady Jersey
lifted slim shoulders, "she is not fat."

"Madam!"

"Fat women," Lady Jersey said darkly. "When are they to
be here?"

That was when a footman opened the door. Philip, still
wearing his leather jacket and red neckcloth, with the calves
of his legs clearly bandaged under the breeches, came in
stiffly with the aid of two walking-sticks. Beside him was
Jennifer, holding his arm. Mr. Sheridan, still wearing his
cloak because he liked its swagger, moved just behind them
with a silver goblet in his hand.

Philip bowed. At the same instant, outside the windows

a streak of lightning shot down the dark sky—without thunder, with no noise at all. It made all of them blink. Abruptly it gave Philip some reminder of something, but he could not think of what; he trembled badly, and did not know why.

But he saw the same feeling reflected in Jennifer's eyes as she looked at him. Could this be the beginning of what she called the "terror"? No! Stop! He needed all his wits for another matter.

The atmosphere, despite the heat, had become coldly formal.

"You need not stand, my lord." The Prince spoke with immense self-importance. "That is my chair, by the window. I will turn it slightly; find a chair and sit down facing me."

Picking up the large heap of papers from the pianoforte, George Augustus marched back to his chair as though in red robes. Turning the chair a little way round, he sat down with a heavy thud.

Philip's glance flashed round the music-room. It took in Lady Jersey at the great harp, and the bass-viol by the Prince's side, and the pianoforte, and the six violins along the wall, and the small portrait of Caroline of Brunswick, now Princess of Wales. He did not know that the old King had insisted on the portrait hanging there, and that the King's son dared not take it down.

"Sir," he began, "I—"

He hesitated, because Jennifer had rolled a padded chair behind him facing the Prince from about ten feet away. She herself, after curtseying to their host with a very nervous smile, had taken the piano-stool and sat down close to Philip's chair. He sank back with relief, to ease the pain in his legs.

Lady Jersey's large, dark, languishing eyes were fixed on him. He bowed.

"Lord Glenarvon," the Prince said sternly, "I will give you

a fair trial. I cannot promise more. Should I believe you guilty, you must fend for yourself. Is that understood?"

"Entirely, sir."

"As for you, Miss Baird," continued George Augustus, mitigating rebuke with a smile, "already, at my own dinnertable, you have disobeyed my command. I trust it will not happen again. And, as an interested party, you will not speak during these proceedings."

"It will be most horribly difficult, sir," Jenny said meekly.

"Ay, well, I daresay. The jury, merely as a matter of form, will consist of Lady Jersey and Mr. Sheri—"

For the first time he caught sight of this gentleman, who was lounging cloaked against the pianoforte, with the goblet in his hand. The Prince's majesty fell away, and he spoke in a different tone.

"I say! Sherry!"

"Yes, sir?"

"You avowed to me, Sherry, that only water should dilute your gullet until you were firmly wed to Miss Ogle. What's in that goblet? What d'ye drink?"

Mr. Sheridan was deprecating.

"Oh, one or two won't hurt me. Besides," he added frankly, "I had need of 'em. That business in the chapel affrighted the very devil out of me, and I don't mind admitting it."

"Indeed?"

"I don't, for a fact! I continued to smile, else the teeth would have rattled together in my chops. I'd ha' bolted—egad, I would!—if you others hadn't been so cool it shamed me."

"To say the truth," muttered His Royal Highness, lowering his eyes, "I own I am surprised at myself. If that old ba—hem! If that honourable gentleman, my father, had given me an Army command against the French, as I begged him and he wouldn't to spite me, I might have—" This stabbed too close to the heart; the Prince became all puffed up with grandeur again.

"And there was York," proclaimed Mr. Sheridan, "as cool as you please, riding home to Oatlands and clacking away about some new dogs. Lade went home to his Letty, too; he said she was teaching him a new game at cards. 'And devil-ish interesting it is too,' says he, 'except that Letty always wins the money. *I* think she's double-dealin'. If she is, I'll tan her pretty little behind.' I ask your pardon, sir! What do I drink? Iced punch."

"Iced punch!" said His Royal Highness, sitting up as though galvanized. "Dear Lady Jersey! Will you be good enough to pull the bell beside you? I thank you."

Instantly the door opened. Portly Branley, the footman-in-chief, entered resplendent in scarlet-and-gold livery. He carried a large silver tray, ringed round with five silver goblets; in the centre was a massive silver bowl containing what was, palpably, about a gallon of iced punch.

"Oh, stab me!" said the Prince, aghast at such promptness.

"I ventured to think, Your Royal Highness," observed Branley, with a slight obsequious smile, "that Your Royal Highness might desire it at this hour."

He set down the tray on a small table at the Prince's right elbow. Deftly filling five goblets with a ladle, he handed them round. All accepted a goblet, Mr. Sheridan remarking that one or two wouldn't hurt him.

Oh, God! Philip thought desperately. *This won't be easy if the judge and the jury all get cockeyed drunk.*

"Speak up, darling!" whispered Jennifer. "Hurry!"

"And now, Lord Glenarvon, to business!" said the Prince, immensely refreshed as he set down an empty goblet, and Branley silently melted away. "I would inform you, Mr. Sheridan, that this is in one sense a court of law, and that any ill-timed jest would be out of place." He glared at Mr.

Sheridan, who looked guilty. "And now, Lord Glenarvon, where would you wish to begin?"

Another flash of lightning shot down the dark sky. Jennifer put her hand on Philip's arm, and he felt her shiver. But he gritted his teeth, and again smiled.

"By your leave, sir, I wish to begin at shortly past one o'clock in the morning, at Widestairs, on the twenty-first of April, when—"

"Stay a moment, sir!" softly interrupted His Royal Highness, and tapped the heap of papers in his lap. "I desire answers to certain questions touching matters which occurred before then."

"As you wish."

"It is here stated by Lady Oldham that in Oldham House, at six-thirty of the clock or thereabouts, a footman named Smithers heard you say you would like to wring your wife's neck. No, stop! That's hearsay evidence. You need not answer."

Philip smiled. "Yet I will answer, should you wish it."

"Well?"

"Has Your Royal Highness himself, with one lady or another, never expressed or at least felt a wish to wring her neck? Without the least intent of doing so?"

The Prince's gaze involuntarily slid up to the portrait of Caroline of Brunswick. Hastily it moved down, and across the bright-coloured carpet towards Lady Jersey.

"Lord Glenarvon!" he said, puffing out his chest. "I have already told you that this matter is hearsay evidence, and must be discarded. But to Lady Oldham, a little later, you said your intentions towards Miss Baird were strictly honourable. When asked how this could be, since already you had a wife, you bared your teeth and said it could be arranged. What did you mean by that?"

"Sir, I meant only divorce by Act of Parliament."

"Divorce? Pray, Lord Glenarvon, when did you first learn

of the—er—relationship between your wife and Colonel
Thornton?"

"About two o'clock in the morning, at Widestairs, when I
learned it from the girl Molly."

Up went the Prince's eyebrows.

"Then how came it," he asked, "that you spoke of divorce
to Lady Oldham many hours before you knew you had
cause for it?"

It was an easy question to answer, and truthfully. Yet
Philip, looking across at those steady grey eyes, felt a twinge
of dread.

And this is the man, he thought, *whom the lampoonists
show as popinjay and jack-fool!*

"Sir," he replied aloud, "I was resolved to have Miss Baird
for my wife. My present wife, notoriously, is fond of money.
I believed that by some private arrangement between us, en-
tailing most of my goods if need be, that Chloris and I
might—"

"In short, you would have brought about a divorce by a
bubble and a cheat?"

"I would, sir."

"Hum! At least you are frank. Another question! When
you and Lady Glenarvon were here at dinner, the relations
between you seemed incredibly cordial, on her side, at least.
Yet I observed how she discarded and disowned you when
you went out to fight the Bristol Smasher. In actuality, what
were your relations with your wife?"

"Sir, they were not good. At least—" Philip hesitated.

"At least—?" snapped the Prince.

"Chloris seemed to be—a little fascinated, curious, what
shall I say?—when she saw this so-called 'change' in me."

"Ah, yes!" There was a sharp rattle as the Prince ladled
out another goblet of punch for himself. "This 'change'!" He
tapped the papers. "It is here in all the depositions, and
indeed I remarked it myself. How did it come about?"

Now Philip must skate over the one lie in his whole story.
He laughed.

"It was not in truth a change, sir. I had been aware that
most thought me student and milksop. And this, as any man
might, I was resolved to alter."

"Ay, well?"

"I affected a bad heart I did not possess. For many years,
in secret, I have been tutored in the sport of boxing, though
I knew I must evolve a new-style guard and a new-style attack ere I could defeat the best of them. When I thought
the time ripe," lied Philip, "I sought out Jackson and floored
him in his own boxing-school. The time for 'change' had
come."

Unexpectedly Lady Jersey dashed her fingers across the
strings of the harp, making them all jump.

"Then that was it!" breathed Lady Jersey, who already
had been slipping across and helping herself to punch. There
were tears in her eyes.

The Prince glared at her, but did not speak to her.

"Yes," he said, "I begin to perceive the design. Lady
Glenarvon, as you say, was—hem!—fascinated by—"

"Your Royal Highness!" Jennifer burst out. "We all know
what That Woman wanted and still wants. Needs must we
discuss it further?"

"Damme, madam, I *will* have silence here!" roared the
Prince, so agitated that he again helped himself to the bowl.
So did Mr. Sheridan, remarking that another one wouldn't
do him any harm.

"Then Lady Glenarvon," His Royal Highness demanded of
Philip, "has no true fondness for you?"

"None whatever, sir."

"Good. You satisfy me so far. Now stand upon your own
defence! Tell your story in your own way! Establish your
innocence, if it may be!"

Philip braced himself in the thick heat.

"Then, sir, I would begin at something past one in the morning of the twenty-first of April. Upon leaving Carlton House—for which I crave your pardon at so unmannerly a leave-taking—I drove to Widestairs with Miss Baird, her womanservant Mrs. Poppett, and my manservant Hopwith. Chloris followed, with Lady Oldham and Colonel Thornton, in another coach some time afterwards. They drove Colonel Thornton to his home, and returned to Widestairs. I met the whole group on the landing as they were preparing to retire to bed.

"There," he added, "when the others had dispersed, I was left alone with Chloris."

At last he had caught his audience. All of them sat motionless, while Mr. Sheridan lounged by the pianoforte.

"I told her," Philip went on, "that there were certain matters which must be discussed and decided between us. And they must be so decided that night."

There was a rustling of papers in the Prince's lap.

"You and she, it is deposed, kissed several times?"

"No! Yes! Well—yes."

Jennifer began angrily to say something, but checked herself.

"Ah," murmured the Prince. "Then you had intent to—"

"No, sir! That was what all believed, including Chloris herself. But, if there be any honest deposition in all that mass of paper, you must know what it was I said. I referred, of course, to the matter of divorce.

"Chloris refused to admit me to her rooms, which by ordinary were kept locked at night. She said I might enter these rooms on any night but this. Whereat she laughed and ran into the dressing-room, locking—to be exact, from what I heard, bolting—the door on the inside."

The sky had grown so black that it seemed a wonder nobody called for wax-lights. The heat was grown so intense that the storm must burst at any time. Those five figures sat or stood in a deep dusk.

Jennifer, her head down, was clenching her fists tightly.

"Next morning," snapped Philip, "that door to the dressing-room was found unlocked. Yet, should you study it, there is no mystery about this. Molly, Chloris's maid, had been despatched to attend Lady Oldham in the Blue Room. She returned; Chloris would have admitted her at her knock, and it was left unlocked afterwards. But I did not know this."

"Well? Continue!"

"I returned to my bedroom," said Philip. "I called for tobacco and brandy, which were fetched by Hopwith. Afterwards, perhaps to ennerve me against one of Chloris's scenes and play-acting, I drank a tumbler of brandy. For I was most grimly resolved the matter should be sifted that night.

"Presently I took up a poker from among the fire-irons, as your depositions will show. I walked through my dressing-room to Chloris's, finding the *inner* door to her dressing-room bolted. A voice, which I still believed to be Chloris's, refused to open the door. I said, if she did not, I would break it down. I smashed one panel with the poker. The voice cried some such words as, 'Leave off! I'll unbolt it!'

"This was done. Then—"

Every person, in that dense gloom, appeared to be holding his or her breath.

"Then?" the Prince demanded huskily.

"I heard someone scurry off to the bedroom beyond. When I entered, the dressing-room was lighted but empty."

"*Lighted*, you say?"

"Yes, sir. As was also the bedroom beyond, with two very large wall-candles. Nay, more, I can prove it!"

"How?"

"By the testimony of two witnesses. One Morecambe, a

groom in my service, and his wife. Morecambe sat up all night with toothache, and his wife with him. They sat at their window, which directly faces the windows of Chloris's bedroom from fifty feet's distance."

"Ay, there is a sketch drawn here somewhere. But—witnesses?"

More sharp rattlings from the punch-bowl ladle, the Prince being joined by Lady Jersey and Mr. Sheridan. But the latter two, shadows on the dusk, hurried back to where they had been before.

"Witnesses?" roared the Prince. "I have read these depositions, man. I have even studied them. Where is mention of these two?"

"Do you wonder, sir," Philip asked dryly, "that I have held them secret until now? Had they been known and found, they would have been clapped into a gate-house prison. I— I long ago took the liberty, sir, of commanding one of Your Royal Highness's carriages, and bidding it be sent to Lambeth to fetch my witnesses here, together with Hopwith, who has them in charge. I wished you to judge for yourself. You will forgive the liberty?"

"It was indeed a great liberty," loftily declared His Royal Highness, whose speech showed a very slight sign of becoming thick. "However, I forgive it. You found the dressing-room, you say, lighted but empty. And then?"

"I went into the bedroom." Philip swallowed. "As you know, it was the girl Molly. Her hair was dressed like Chloris's; she wore one of Chloris's night-shifts; her face was heavily raddled with paint. She burst into tears because she thought I had intent to beat her. I—I—"

"Yes. Pray don't shrink now, Lord Glenarvon!"

"It is strange," muttered Philip, as the scene rushed back so vividly to him. Then he spoke out. "I washed the paint off her face. I pray you, don't ask me why; I can't myself say. It would appear that Molly had some fondness for me, perhaps—well, because of some idle kind word of mine in the past. She told me Chloris was with Colonel Thornton then, and made plain the whole affair."

"Ah! And what effect had this upon you?"

"I felt—I could do murder."

"Take care, my lord!"

"But only towards Colonel Thornton, I swear it! Now I urge Your Royal Highness, I urge all of you here, to mark what occurred afterwards!"

Philip, his own untasted goblet in his hand, was bending forward tensely as far as pain would allow. Jennifer, whose empty goblet had long ago rolled away on the carpet, slid the fingers of her right hand into his tense left hand.

He'll do it! she thought, frightened now by the dusk and the ghostly dark figures here. *He will! He'll clear himself somehow! But—*

"To hide my discomposure," Philip said clearly, "I took up a bottle of wine on a small table under the window not far from the bed. There was one glass beside it. I poured a glass for myself; it had an ugly bad taste; I drank little before I threw the rest on the floor. None the less, remembering civility, I poured out a full glass for Molly. She drank it all. Mark that, sir: she drank it all. One moment!"

Fiercely Philip held up his hand for silence.

"A dozen and a dozen," he said, "can testify that wine bottle was on the table for twenty-four hours. It is now in the pocket of Mr. Sheridan's cloak; for the time, let it stay there."

Rattle bang went the punch-ladle, and iced punch spilled wide.

"It is mentioned in the depositions, my lord," replied an immensely lofty voice from the Prince. "But what have we to do with a curs't wine bottle?"

"Permit me to show you, sir. At not long past two o'clock I left Molly—"

"As for the wench, you did not—hey?"

"No, sir. I went to my bedroom. I sat down to think, and on a sudden I was struck with such drowsiness that my head fell forward. I recall that I staggered to bed and rolled into it, without even troubling to cast off my dressing-robe or blow out the candle or open a window. Even then it occurred to me I might have been drugged."

"*Drugged?*"

"Exactly that. Next morning I had such a gigantic headache I could scarcely rid myself of it all day. No drug could have been in the brandy; I had drunk that over an hour before the sleep struck me. It must have been in the wine with that peculiar taste. As I then knew, the wine had been heavily doused with powdered opium."

Mr. Sheridan swore. The harp-string gave a moaning twang. His Royal Highness sat motionless. And Philip, putting down his goblet, gripped the heads of the walking sticks as though to rise up.

"If the wine had this effect on me," he asked, "what must have been its effect on Molly? She had swallowed three times as much as I. It is certain she would have just time enough to bolt the staircase door, locking out my wife from dislike, and extinguish both candles, before she stumbled to bed in a heavily drugged sleep.

"Now let me go further! Let me anticipate what you will be told by those who saw it. The windows of that bedroom had long been dark. Yet, at shortly before three o'clock, both candles were again lighted. That is fact; there are two who can swear to it. Three o'clock is agreed upon by all as the time of the murder. At shortly before three, then, the lights were kindled. Molly herself, they say, partly drew one curtain, peered out, turned as though to speak to someone, and let the curtain fall again."

Philip paused, trying to distinguish faces in the gloom.

"Well," he said, "in one thing alone my witnesses were mistaken. Bid your surgeons perform a post-mortem examination on Molly! Such examinations have been done for hundreds of years, but your knowledge of medicine is now sufficient to—forgive me! a slip of the tongue! Your surgeons will find she swallowed an immense amount of powdered opium. And the consequence of this? I will tell you. No woman on earth could have been out of bed, and walking about the room, an hour after swallowing all that drug."

"Ecod, man," exclaimed the Prince, "but do you say your witnesses tell lies? Are you making cause against yourself?"

"No!" said Philip. "There is only one person who could have been at that window. There is only one woman who, in height and shape and style of hair-dressing, could possibly have been mistaken for Molly."

He gripped the two canes. He rose to his feet, and drew the breath deeply into his lungs.

"Molly's murderer, sir, was my own wife—Chloris."

XX

The Truth

It was His Royal Highness who first burst out.

"Lights!" he bellowed. "For God's sake, lights! Are we to sit here in the dark, like a parcel of fools listening to a ghost story? Lights!"

Then, for the first time, the thick air stirred. A rising breeze swept across the gardens, making the trees rustle and fluttering the silver-grey curtains at half-open windows. Distantly, there was a rattle of thunder.

It was unnecessary to ring the bell for lights. A footman, lurking outside for just that call, entered briskly with a long waxen spill already kindled. After deep obeisance to the Prince of Wales, he lighted a great number of wall-candles, in pairs behind grey-and-silver glass shades. After carefully closing the windows, he went away like a genie.

As the whole room sprang into light, Philip had a clear look at the faces of Lady Jersey, of Mr. Sheridan, and of His Royal Highness. And his heart sank.

All three were pretty fresh in liquor. Each it affected in his or her own way.

Lady Jersey, who always tended to be lachrymose, contemplated him with languishing sympathy through the strings of the harp. Mr. Sheridan, his goblet half-lifted to his lips, whistled softly and nodded. These two, clearly, were on Philip's side.

But the Prince—

He sat up straight in his chair, with a look of outrage on his face.

"Lord Glenarvon!" he said, in the stately and ponderous tone he always used when *he* was drunk. "This is monstrous! To accuse your own wife—"

"It would *be* monstrous, sir. That is, if Chloris had not cold-bloodedly strangled Molly because the girl threatened to expose Chloris's affair with Colonel Thornton. And if, merely in passing, she had not attempted to get me hanged for the crime. Chloris and Thornton might then the sooner enjoy my money."

"What?"

"Hear me, sir!" pleaded Philip, who still stood up and intended to remain there. "Hear me only a little more. Stay! If you shall find my witnesses credible, do you believe what I have said so far?"

His Royal Highness, under-lip upthrust, moist of eye but mighty of bearing, glanced down at the papers and hesitated.

"To be sure," he muttered, "I won't gainsay I believed you up to— But that!"

"Sir!" said Philip. "This afternoon, in the church or chapel or whatever you care to call it, did you not hear Colonel Thornton blurt out that he would have no money to attend hundred-guinea prize-fights until *I* was taken and hanged?"

"He did!" suddenly exclaimed Mr. Sheridan. "Split my breeches, but Thornton did say it! I remember, because I wondered."

From the flick of memory in the Prince's eyes, from the gnawing at his lip in speculation, it was clear he remembered, too.

"Further!" said Philip. "Would you think a woman perhaps a little callous, a little cold of heart, if she sat down and made airy talk beside the body of the maid she had strangled?"

Now Philip risked a look down at Jennifer. Jennifer, completely staggered, looked back up at him with an expression blank from shock. Her hands were shaking; she could not have risen to her feet had she tried. But he was contrasting her face with another woman's face, and he was thinking, with a full heart, of how much he loved Jenny.

By all the gods, if only he could drive through the case against him and bring them both through it alive!

At the back of Carlton House rushed a high, heavy wind. Despite closed windows they could hear trees whipping in the park. A broad flash of lightning was followed by another rattle of thunder.

"What would you think, sir," Philip addressed the Prince of Wales, "of any woman who could do that? Late last night, when I crept out secretly to fetch the wine bottle in her bedroom at Widestairs, I met first Lady Oldham and then my wife. My wife sat down on the bed beside Molly's body, and she laughed. Ask Lady Oldham.

"Sir, that was when I—I all but spoke out and told her I knew, knew she had strangled Molly, after careful preparation and in cold blood. But she is clever; I think she guessed I knew. Whether or no she caught sight of the wine bottle under my cloak, I can't say. But I am sure she guessed.

"I was still a wanted man; there were three constables sleeping in the house. To quell her suspicions, I was obliged to lie and tell her I was sure *she* had no hand in this murder. And yet, near the end of our talk, there was near a blaze-out. My mood changed, and I challenged her.

"I said I would be off, and challenged her to ring the bell which would set the constables on me. I walked slowly downstairs; they could have snared me with ease. But she did not ring the bell. She dared not, lest I spoke what I knew."

Philip took a fumbling step or two forward on both canes.

"In all those depositions you have," he said, "doubtless

they have measured the height at which the red bell-rope was cut. I can tell you the height, without measuring. It is just within reach of Chloris's hand. Her hand was on the bell-rope when I left her. Who, then, cut that bell-rope for murder? Whose hand left the dressing-room door unlocked?"

The Prince kept his chins raised.

"Lady Glenarvon," he said, "is a beautiful woman. I will not, as a rule, have one word said in this house against a beautiful woman! Yet I own," he added, squinting, "I thought her conduct unusual when she smiled and left her husband to the Bristol Smasher. Certes, there was nothing she could have done—"

"She could have done," said Mr. Sheridan, "what Miss Baird did."

His nose aflame, his choleric temper up, the Member for Stafford walloped down his goblet on top of the pianoforte so that the strings jangled inside.

"My dear," he cried, turning to Jenny, "'twas in the main that action of yours, to stand by your man in defiance of the Prince of Wales himself, made me determine to shield you both when you came arunning. I say it; I mean it!"

"But that was nothing!" cried Jennifer, her cheeks burning. "I—I knew Phil—Philip could beat him." Her intense gaze moved round. "But if at long last, Your Royal Highness, I might interrupt?"

"Madam," and George Augustus folded his arms in gloomy grandeur, "doubtless it were best you did. Everyone else does. Pray let your discourse be as long and incoherent as one of my revered father's."

"But I never meant—!" blurted the horrified Jennifer.

"No matter, madam. You are forgiven. Continue."

"And may I speak too?" cried Lady Jersey, twanging the strings of the harp. "Chloris Glenarvon! Toby Thornton!" She made a grimace. "Does she truly *love* him?"

"That," said Jennifer, "was what I desired to answer."

"Then tell us, my dear. Do!" begged Lady Jersey.

"I—I knew not one word of the explanation to this crime," faltered Jennifer, "until Philip spoke just now. All the same, since I do know, I can tell you much of *her*."

Even the Prince, who had closed his eyes when Lady Jersey spoke, looked at her when she said this.

"Chloris Glenarvon," Jennifer said fiercely, "is incapable of loving anyone except herself, in the ordinary way we know it. But, in her own fashion, she does love that awful braggart of a Thornton. Please don't laugh when I say this, but in one way he's her child, to be protected. In another way she deeply and truly admired him—his scarlet coat, his superior airs, the superb figure he makes until somebody hits him as Philip did.

"Three times," she went on in a rush, "Philip made him appear foolish. Did she cease to love her colonel? No! She only hated Philip the more, and cherished her middle-aged lover. Oh, can't any of you *understand* that?"

"I can," Lady Jersey murmured very thoughtfully.

"Ladies!" said the Prince, holding up the bundle of papers. "This may be all very well as drawing-room gossip. But Lady Glenarvon cannot have done this murder! We know, by the testimony, that at three in the morning she was with—"

Abruptly His Royal Highness paused. He looked at the papers. His eyes, rather wild now, rolled towards Philip.

"Yes, sir," the latter said dryly. "She was, or was supposed to be, with Colonel Thornton himself. Shall I go on?"

"Yes! Yes! Yes!"

"My present wife," Philip said with some violence, "is somewhat horribly respectable. Her whole safety and comfort in life, or so she imagined, lay in her pose before the world as perfectly virtuous wife and faithful servant to a half-invalid—myself. With this pose she deceived the whole of the so-called *beau monde*—"

"Egad, she did!" cried Mr. Sheridan.

"—until Molly, who for some cause had a kindness for me, turned tiger and threatened to expose her. I learned this, sir, from a man named Hopwith, whom you will meet very soon. After some rambling and evasive remarks last night, touching Molly's feelings, Hopwith added, 'And even said she would tell—' He turned away the subject instantly. Yet, by consideration of what I already knew, the meaning was clear.

"My virtuous wife sincerely believed that only Molly knew of her intrigue with Thornton. She had been too clever, too careful. Even I, the worm, might turn if Molly spoke. I think, though I cannot prove, she plotted Molly's murder from that time onwards. Yet she hesitated; was it worth the risk? Molly might be bribed, or I too cowardly to take notice. In either case, I should be dead of a bad heart in a short time.

"Whereupon, on the night of April 20, my virtuous wife received a deathsome shock. My heart was quite sound, as I told her; I had already demonstrated as much at Oldham House. Though she was fascinated by this 'change' in me and could not resist, shall we say, exploring it, still I *was* a different man. By the Lord, I was! If Molly said one word, and it came to my ears, her cushioned life might be rent in pieces. She must see to Molly, and see to her that very night.

"Colonel Thornton, of course, would have no hand in actual murder. His gentlemanly feelings shuddered, though he would offer no objection to spending my money freely after I had been hanged. Otherwise he shrank from it."

And Jennifer spoke in a low voice, hardly above a whisper.

" 'Infirm of purpose!' " she said. " 'Give *me* the daggers!' "

A queer, cold stir went through the room. But perhaps it

was caused only by a dazzle of lightning at the windows, and a heavier shock of thunder.

"No, Jenny. Those words were spoken after Duncan's murder. But in spirit it is the same thing reversed. At the very end, it is the man who crumbles and the woman who fights to the death—as Chloris will.

"The whole calm work she carried out herself. First she hurried away from Widestairs, leaving a bottle of drugged wine—Madeira, which she herself admitted Molly could never resist. At The Oaks, Colonel Thornton's home, this pretty pair deliberately set up a right royal—your pardon, sir!—a most fearsome row, so that the servants should hear. When my dear wife made haste back to Widestairs, Thornton may have continued shouting at empty air. It would be his taste to enjoy insulting even that."

"Stay a moment!" boomed the Prince's throaty voice. "I remind you, Lord Glenarvon, the upper door of the staircase was bolted on the inside."

"This, believe me," Philip said wryly, "was no matter of a room all locked up inside. Had Your Royal Highness been permitted one glimpse at that door and its frame, your acumen would have seen the truth at once. Both door and frame are so loosely fitting that a knife can easily be sent through the crack to catch the knob of the bolt and draw it.

"Chloris certainly had a knife. She cut the bell-rope, and bell-ropes are not cut with scissors. More! Many times before, by carelessness and accident, she must have been locked out; I make no doubt she had the knife in her reticule.

"And so she steals up to the dark bedroom, hearing her victim breathe in drugged sleep, for the work that must be done."

"Stop!" cried Lady Jersey. The harp-strings trembled to her shudder. "If we would speak scandal, it is delicious; but this—!"

"I *must* continue, Lady Jersey, or you will not see how all things fall into place. My good wife lights both candles, to make sure of her work. She draws one curtain and peeps out, to make sure she is not spied upon. Because all the stable windows are dark, she thinks none is watching.

"She is in no danger of setting the bell ringing by cutting its rope. It needs a hard pull to make such bells ring at all. I—"

Philip hesitated, swallowed, and went on.

"I imagined, when first I saw Molly's body, that no woman's strength could so brutally have strangled her; in especial without struggle or outcry. The secret is now plain: Molly could not resist. And my dear wife, kneeling on the bed, is by that time in a frenzy of hatred. She is venting all her spite against Molly as she twists the red cord round her neck, and—"

"Stop, I say!"

"Your pardon, Lady Jersey. We have all but done with horrors. There *is* a mighty struggle and outcry just at death's point. In cases of strangling, there always is. It does not rouse the house. Chloris puts out both lights. She leaves the door bolted on the inside by reversing the former process: standing outside a closed door, and using the knife through the crack to catch the knob of the bolt and draw it into the socket.

"But I wonder what Chloris thought, as her face bent over Molly's? I wonder what she thought as she made haste back to The Oaks for what you, sir, in legal circles call an alibi. I wonder how she slept, and what walked in her dreams? No! That won't do. Ever since, I think, her dreams have been quite placid."

Philip, beginning to wobble on his two walking-sticks, still gritted his teeth against pain and made some sort of bow to the Prince of Wales.

"That is my cause, sir. Since my witnesses will be here at any moment to prove my statements about lights, you might care to examine the bottle of drugged wine. Mr. Sheridan, may I have it?"

Fumbling inside his cloak, Mr. Sheridan produced the bottle and handed it over. Philip advanced and gravely handed it to his host.

"Try it, sir. Smell it and taste it. But pray don't taste too much of it."

Turning round, he hobbled back to his own chair. Jennifer, radiant, was holding out her hands to him.

"Sit down, Phil!" she was crying. "Please, please sit down! Darling, there's no need at all for this!"

Still he would not sit down. In a singing of joy it was triumph, triumph, triumph after all the obstacles had been—

"*Glenarvon!*"

And at that shout he turned round.

The Prince was sitting up straight, the wine bottle in his hands. Philip never forgot him there, in a plum-coloured velvet coat against a canary-yellow waistcoat, with white stockings and breeches, and shoes covered by the shoe-buckles he himself invented. His brown wig was a little askew. Out of a red face, puffier and more bloated from iced punch, looked out eyes grown wild and wicked.

"What damned cheat would you put on us?" he asked, more quietly. "There's no powdered opium in this wine."

"Sir?"

"I well know the taste of powdered opium. The wine is Madeira, true; but there's no drug in it. Try for yourself!"

In sudden panic Philip hobbled back and took the bottle. He had hardly raised it to his mouth before the truth flashed over him.

"Horder!" he cried out.

"What's that?"

"Samuel Horder, Esquire! Then that's why he offered no objection or comment when I took the wine with me from the secret room! He deliberately suppressed my two letters;

he substituted another wine bottle, with wine at the same level, to ruin me and destroy my evidence. The wine bottle was mentioned in the letter to the Lord Chief Justice, so he knew. Horder! Horder! Horder!"

Without warning the storm broke. Against the two windows, rain drove with a splash and sting; it thickened and rattled, deepening to a dim roar round Carlton House.

Forward strode Mr. Sheridan, not without a slight stagger, and drew himself up before their host.

"Sir!" he began, in Parliamentary fashion. "I'll swear that's it! Your Royal Highness saw how Sam Horder detested our friend here. Damme, Glenarvon, I warned you! He changed those wine bottles while Glenarvon was asleep in the morning, my oath upon it!"

"Well, Lord Glenarvon?" demanded the Prince. "Have you any proof of what you allege against Mr. Horder?"

For that instant, at least, Philip did not even hear the words.

He felt a cold touch, and he knew what it was. At last it was the approach of what Jenny called "the terror," rushing and rushing to catch up with them. When it did overtake them—

"Lord Glenarvon! Must I repeat my question? Have you any proof of what you allege against Mr. Horder?"

Philip backed away.

"None, sir, I fear," he said huskily. "Horder will have smashed the true wine bottle long ago."

The door at their backs did not merely open. It flew open, banged against the wall, and rebounded. With an angry and embarrassed expression, in strode no less a personage than His Royal Highness the Duke of York. There were hardly a few drops of rain on his cocked hat or his military cloak.

"I say, George—!" he blurted out. Seeing the others, he stopped and looked disconcerted.

"What the devil are *you* doing here?" enquired his brother, not overpleased. "I thought you were riding back to Oatlands?"

"So I was," glowered the Duke. "Had to come back. Cost me a hundred pounds today! A hundred pounds, d'ye hear? But—well! Damn good fight. Had to come back. Got some news." He nodded towards Philip without looking at him. "About him."

"What news?"

"I was ridin' across Black Friars' Bridge, d'ye see, on my way out to Surrey. Over the bridge, from the Lambeth side, comes a devilish great dray piled sky-high with big malt-barrels that looked as if each of 'em weighed a ton. Up beside it races an open carriage of yours, George; know it a mile away. No footmen up, but a driver and three people in the back. That curs't dray! The off fore wheel broke. About half the barrels fell down slap on that open carriage."

Jennifer rose slowly to her feet. Feeling the rush of the terror, feeling it even more than Philip did, she knew what the Duke would say before he spoke.

"Naturally," he growled, "I hopped off m'horse and lent a hand at shifting the barrels. No good. Three of 'em were goners already—the driver, and a big old man, and a little old woman. *I* pulled out a rum little old cove who lived just long enough to—

"Anyway! Devil take me," said the Duke, glancing at his uniform under the cloak, "if he didn't think I was a footman in livery, and plucked at me. Rum little cove named Hopsomething. Said he was a servant of Glenarvon; said he was fetching some witnesses here to prove something, and asked me to give Glenarvon a message. Then he—well!"

"What was the message?" Jennifer cried out.

"Rum old cove," said the Duke, still glowering at his brother. "Just said, 'Tell him I did my best.'"

Philip, groping, backed against his own chair and sat

down. The walking-sticks slipped from his hands and fell on the carpet.

"Phil!" Jennifer said desperately, her face beside his. "Don't lose heart! Even if your witnesses are gone—"

"I was thinking of Hopwith," said Philip. "Poor old Hopwith."

And he put his head in his hands.

The Duke of York stamped his boots, ruffled his cloak, muttered something indistinct, and said he must be off. The door slammed behind him.

Afterwards, except for the sting and drive of the rain against windows, there was a long silence. Presently Philip heard his name being called sharply by the Prince, and he looked up.

The Prince, with much assistance from Mr. Sheridan, was on his feet. He stood with fists on hips, thick legs planted wide apart, as Philip had seen him behind the dinner-table. But in his bulging eyes there was more of pity than of wrath.

"My lord! Do you fully comprehend this situation?"

"Yes. Hopwith's dead."

"No, no! Your own position!"

"Oh. That. Well—"

"Even if I believed you, which—which upon my soul I do, despite all, how can I save you now? If I summoned to Carlton House the highest law-lords of this realm, what could I offer them as evidence? The wine bottle is gone. The witnesses are dead. There is only your word for it. And even my word would not suffice to gain your freedom."

Sharply Philip pulled himself together. Taking up the walking-sticks again, he propped himself up.

"Your Royal Highness," he said earnestly, "I thank you for a most fair and civil hearing. Also for all the favour you have done me; no man could have done more. But I understand what you say. I must be on the run again."

"You can't run!" wailed Jennifer. "You can't even walk!"

"Then I must make shift as best I can."

Once more, in the same tone, he addressed the Prince.

"Sir, it galls me to trespass more. But the matter touches Miss Baird here. She must not go with me further, as I in my madness allowed her to do yesterday. There is no warrant for her; but there will be, should this matter be noised further. If for a time she could be taken in by, say, Lady Jersey—"

"To be sure I will!" exclaimed Lady Jersey, bouncing up amid alcoholic tears. "I will do this easily; entrust me!"

"And do you think," asked Jennifer, "I'd leave you now?"

"Jenny, you must. I have never in my life ordered you to do anything, but I order this and I mean it!"

"I won't! I won't! I—"

"Hold your tongue!" snarled Philip, so savagely that she flinched. His tone altered. "And now, Your Royal Highness and my good friend Sheridan—"

"Stop!" said the Prince, gnawing at his under-lip.

He glared out of a thunder-cloud. His innate selfishness, his loathing of any trouble or vexation, warred with his instinctive sympathies. At last he made up his mind.

"Man, don't be daft!" he growled. "I—I give you leave to bide here until you can be smuggled away. Never, upon my word," he added a little enviously, "have I seen a man who made himself so popular with servants as you did when you were here. The deuce knows why, but *they* won't blab. You may not bide here long. Still—"

Abruptly the Prince raised his eyes. This time the door opened so quietly that only the flicker of movement had caught. In the doorway, seeming hollow-cheeked above his blue chin, stood Major Hanger.

"Sir," he said calmly, "we're done. We're done brown and toasted black."

"Done? How?"

"His Majesty the King. They fetched him back from Windsor two days since, and he's heard of this business. He's sent a royal warrant for the arrest of this gentleman *and* this lady."

And the Prince of Wales, who earlier that afternoon had faced a mob of furious Bow Street Runners without even blinking, turned a pasty colour.

"The warrant's full of Bedlamite charges, especially against the lady," said Major Hanger. "Still, it *is* a royal warrant. His messenger's escorted by a troop of the Horse Guards Blue; they're under the front portico now. I've held 'em off so far, but I can't hold 'em off much longer."

The Prince, choking, gasped to get his breath.

"To be sure," murmured Major Hanger, from motives of pure Irish devilment, "we could whistle in the Grenadier Guards, lock the doors, and cock a snook at 'em. Bedad, sir! I'd like to see the cavalry that could take a fortified position."

"For God's sake, Hanger! Are you completely bereft of your wits? The Guards fire on the Blues? And have all call me traitor who rebelled against my own father? Oh, Lord help me! Help me!"

The Prince raised ring-covered hands, pressed them against his face, and dropped them.

. "I told you, Lord Glenarvon, that there was one person from whom I couldn't protect you. The old devil's done it again, just to spite me! I greatly fear I must give you both up."

"Sir!" said Mr. Sheridan.

"I can't help it, Sherry! I have no choice! I— No, damme, wait! I'll give you both a running chance. Hanger! They're at the front portico, you say?"

"Bedad but they are, sir! And in a temper, too."

"You two!" said the Prince, pointing between Philip and Jennifer. "Run out of here! Run down the main staircase to the ground floor, as though you would go to the dining-room. But run out of a back window, across the gardens towards the Mall. Run!"

"He can't run!" Jennifer protested.

"I can try!" said Philip.

"Run! Run! Run!"

Amid rain the windows went white with lightning. To Jennifer, now, the room and the faces and the musical instruments and the flickering candles behind silver-and-grey glass—all these, to her, seemed moving round in a slow dance.

The dream must be on her again. For, as that lightning leaped up, it seemed to her that the Prince's bulky body was transparent; she could see lightning through him.

"You're ghosts!" she cried. "You're all ghosts! You've been dead for—"

"RUN! RUN! RUN!"

Yes, the terrifying dream had come on her again. For she was running hard beside Philip, who could not run at all. They were out into the foyer, with the wax-lights all moving and melting like footmen's faces.

Down they ran the long, broad staircase to the ground floor. For some reason it no longer seemed carpeted, but of stone. As Philip flung up one of the long windows to the gardens, Jennifer's wits whirled again; it seemed to her he had cast aside his walking-sticks. But "they," the terror waiting at the front portico, must not overtake Philip.

Rain, thick and driving, sluiced down her hair and face as they raced into open air. Dodging the white looming of a statue, they splashed out across Carlton House Gardens. Jennifer sensed that someone, someone to arrest Philip, was running down the stairs after them.

The pace increased, sawing at the breath in her lungs. She faltered. An enormous crash of thunder split across the sky; Jennifer closed her eyes, and with Philip's hand on her arm, stood still.

In her ears pierced a heavy metallic grind and squeal, a rush and slither across some paved surface.

And she opened her eyes.

EPILOGUE:

"... And Battles Long Ago."

"Wot the bloody 'ell," screamed the driver of the big motor-lorry, leaning so far out of the off-side cab-window that he seemed to have about a yard of neck, "are you two at? Run out bang into the Mall, would yer, against the rush-hour traffic?"

There was a pause, even in thought, except for the hooting and squalling of motor-cars piled up behind the lorry.

The great world swung in circles. But Jennifer's mind could not yet grasp it as time slipped into place. Rain still stung into her face. Vaguely she knew Philip's hand was pulling her back, over a slippery paved surface, and up on a curb of some kind.

Vaguely she heard Philip address the driver of the lorry.

"I crave your pardon, sir," he said, and bowed. " 'Twas a most unseemly thing to be done." Here he stopped abruptly. "I mean—"

The driver of the lorry stared back, with eyes growing rounder and rounder.

"Oh, crikey!" he breathed.

Slamming the lorry into gear with another grind and squeal, he roared away. The other cars flowed past, hooting.

Someone was pursuing them from Carlton House! Someone was—

Jennifer, soaked in rain, glanced back over her shoulder.

They were standing on the curb of the Mall. Some distance behind her, as in a dream of the modern London she had known, she saw the Duke of York's Steps. At the top of the steps, where Carlton House should have been, was only Waterloo Place, bare except for the tall Crimean column towering up into the mist.

Beyond this, more cars hooted in Lower Regent Street. Somewhere Jennifer could see an electric sign flashing, and coloured neon lights blurred to smokiness by rain.

"Hi! Sir! Wait a minute!"

Someone, a tall man in a belted raincoat and soft hat, was in actual truth hurrying down the Duke of York's Steps. Remembrance of her future life, or at least almost full remembrance, crept back into Jennifer's brain. They both knew who the man was.

Divisional Detective-Inspector Somers slowed down his pace when he saw them stop. He descended the stairs with an injured look on his face.

"It's no good running, Jenny," she heard Philip say. "It's no good at all, in this age or any other. They always catch up. But what—what—?"

Passers-by in the Mall, had their most passionate desire not been to show no curiosity at anything happening in any street, might have been curious at the behaviour of a slender girl with grey eyes and rain-limp hair in a long bob. She unbuttoned her mackintosh, and gazed slowly down over her own clothes. These clothes were only an ordinary yellow pullover, a brown tweed skirt, nylons, and high-heeled shoes.

The man with her, on the other hand, seemed concerned about the state of his legs. He was tentatively lifting each knee, exploring the calves of his legs, and seemed astonished to find no injury there.

This peculiar behaviour also struck the eye of Divisional Detective Somers as he sauntered up in the pouring rain.

"Look here, sir," he said with some concern. "What's the matter with you?"

Philip pressed his hand against his forehead.

"Jenny and I," he answered in an odd tone, "were wandering. Just wandering. In the rain."

"Well, some people seem to enjoy that," said Inspector Somers. "I don't, personally. Still—!"

"I saw you," said Philip, "jump off that—that bus in Regent Street, and hail me. So I bolted. Jenny bolted. I don't know why, but we did." All bitterness flared into his face. "All right, give me the usual warning and let's go! I don't suppose you need to use handcuffs."

Again the face of Inspector Somers, a solid middle-aged man with a wart beside the nose, looked injured.

"Handcuffs," he repeated, as though he had never heard the word. Then he frowned. "Excuse me, sir, but I still can't make up my mind whether to call you Phil Maddern or Lord Glenarvon. The Deputy Commander says you're entitled to both names."

"Not Lord Glenarvon, if you don't mind! I heard enough of that in the eighteenth century!"

"In the what?"

"He only means," Jennifer intervened quickly, "that the pressure of all his ancestors in the eighteenth century is awkward for someone who isn't very well off in this one."

"Never mind what I mean!" snapped Philip. "I didn't kill my wife. But I can't prove it; my last shred of evidence is gone. You mightn't believe it, Inspector, but I've fought hard and I'm tired. Let's get this arrest over with."

Inspector Somers studied him.

"Now is that any way to talk, Lord—Mr. Maddern?" he asked sharply. "When I was trying to bring you good news? And tell you you've won the game hands down?"

In the Mall, a taxi hooted as though derisively.

Philip, the rain trickling down through his hair and into his eyes, felt his insides become shaky.

"But I haven't won it! I've lost it! That oily crook, the one who promised to hide me if I'd do exhibition fights for him with my head shaved and under a false name, only I wouldn't, pinched the wine bottle. It was full of crushed-up barbituate capsules, the stuff my wife used to drug her maid before she crept back and killed her. But the crook smashed it. The last thing I heard, before I wandered out of my house, was that my two witnesses from the tenement had been killed in a traffic-accident."

Inspector Somers eyed a nearby tree.

"We-el!" he said, with hearty offhandedness. "It wouldn't have done to tell you, sir, now would it? Until we were sure? But do you think we didn't get statements from those witnesses before they died? As for your old fence, the Yard raided him on a different matter two days ago. Between ourselves, I think he'll do a long stretch. But they found your wine bottle."

"They found—?"

"That's it. Old What's-his-name was too proud of his work to smash it. It's loaded with barbituates, more than enough to match what was found in the girl's stomach at the post-mortem."

Here Inspector Somers looked round.

"By the way, Lord—Mr. Maddern. It's raining pretty hard, you know. Hadn't we better find shelter of some kind?"

"No!" said Philip. "I've had too many offers of shelter, first from Richard Brinsley Sheridan, then from Sam Horder, and finally from the Prince of Wales. We stay where we are!"

"Just as you like," replied Inspector Somers, with all the philosophy of the British policeman. "We'll stay here, if you prefer." His eye strayed towards Jennifer. "By the way, miss," he added, although he knew perfectly well, "aren't you Miss Jennifer Baird, now playing Lydia Languish in *The Rivals* at the Haymarket Theatre?"

"Odd's life, but I am!" blurted Jennifer, and instantly corrected herself. "That is—yes. Oh, dear, I wonder what Mr. Sheridan would say if he knew! Phil! You were never acquainted with any of these great people, were you, unless an ancestor of yours knew them? And Hopwith was never in *our* story; he couldn't have died like that, could he?"

Inspector Somers eyed them both very hard.

"Just between ourselves, sir," he said, bending forward and speaking confidentially, "you and your young lady haven't been dropping in at a pub or two, have you? Or maybe three or four?"

"By the time I make it," replied Philip, thrusting out a shaky wrist, "it's not quite six o'clock and most of 'em aren't open yet. We may not be quite sober, Inspector. But it's got nothing to do with liquor."

"Right you are, sir! Quite understand."

Inspector Somers beamed. Then his face grew heavy and sombre, rather hesitant.

"I don't know whether I'm glad or sorry to have to tell you this, sir," he said. "But your wife is dead."

"Dead?"

"You were a bit off the mark about her, you know," remarked Inspector Somers, looking at the pavement. "She was tough, very tough; I admit that. But not as tough as you thought she was.

"You see, she and her elderly boy-friend were playing the West End. When she hooked you, she thought she'd hooked money. When they found that wasn't true, they had to get rid of you—quietly, by desertion or something. But that wasn't easy. Her maid had fallen hard for you, and her maid knew a lot of ugly things about her past life that might dish her. So she gets the idea of strangling the maid, and framing you for it, while the boy-friend sits at home and plays patience. There's pretty good evidence about those electric lights and her Yale-lock key to the staircase door.

"But your wife knew you'd got ten times the brains she

could ever hope to have. She guessed you knew she'd framed you, and you'd driven her into a corner at last. So she poisoned herself last night. With the same kind of barbiturate capsules.

"And I don't think she hated you as much as you imagined. She left a written confession, in her own handwriting, that clears up everything we didn't know. Incidentally, she says you weren't so bad, and she was sorry she wasn't capable of being a proper wife to you."

Inspector Somers pulled down the brim of his sodden hat.

The others stood motionless.

"And the—the elderly boy-friend?" Philip asked through stiff jaws.

"We-el! We only catch 'em. We don't try 'em. Still, you can guess what's likely to happen to him, as accessory both before and after the fact. That's all, sir. Needn't trouble you any more, except for the magistrates' court and the trial."

Inspector Somers turned away, back a pace towards the Duke of York's Steps. Then he swung back, with a warmth of humanity Philip could never have believed.

"Bring the middleweight title back to England, my lord!" he said. "Show 'em the old blood's still there! Then marry your young lady, retire on your winnings, and write all the history you like."

And he was off, up the stairs into the rain and mist.

"Phil!" Jennifer began passionately.

"It's all right, my dear."

"About what?"

"I meant what I said. I'll never fight again. You can't be a Fancy Dan—"

"What's a Fancy Dan?"

"A fairly light and very fast boxer whose joy and delight is to make the Big Fellow miss. You can't do that, and have the heavy artillery, too. It won't work."

"Oh, Phil, that wasn't what I meant! Does this mean that —that yesterday afternoon, and yesterday evening, and part of the night, too—that they never happened at all?"

"Never mind, my dear. If you'll have me, we can marry immediately, and be hanged to what people say." He frowned. "I have the degrees to teach history and English, if I can find a post." Again he frowned, shamefacedly. "But I was never a good enough businessman to find a post."

"Oh, darling," cried the radiant Jennifer, "you leave all business matters to me. But there's only one thing I'm aching and dying to learn. Did it all really happen to teach us some kind of lesson? Or did we only dream it?"

Bong quivered the heavy note of Big Ben, on the hour of six. It reminded Philip of the clock at Widestairs. Past flowed the evening rush of people going home, with shiny umbrellas and folded newspapers; the hoot and cry of taxis; a life not so picturesque as they had seen, but now inexpressibly dear.

Philip shook his head.

"I don't know," he said. "I don't know."